Psychological
Beautiful
Angel
34 Days
Strategy
Captor
Game Players
Malignant

Supernatural
Winterscroft

Kat and Mouse Series
Murder Undeniable

Praise For Anita Waller

"a masterclass in suspense. This is Waller at her best" **Betsy Reavley – bestselling author of Murder at the Book Club and The Optician's Wife**

"a whirlwind of a read and a poignant one" **– Nicki's Book Blog**

"if you are after a book that deals with family, relationships and friendship that takes dark turns and twists that will hook you from the very beginning then you really do need to read this" **– Yvonne Me and My Books**

"Thanks for a great read Anita Waller! When is the next one out??" **Rebecca Burton – If Only I Could Read Faster**

"This book has lots of gasp out loud moments and plenty that will make you a little weepy too (it did for me anyway)." **Lorna Cassidy – On The Shelf Reviews**

"This is an engrossing read that I pretty much inhaled." **Philomena Callan – Cheekypee Reads And Reviews**

"Waller has an amazing skill to grab you and keep you interested until the very last page." **Eclectic Ramblings of Author Heather Osborne**

"WOW! ANITA HAS DONE IT AGAIN. What a bloody brilliant, outstanding, captivating story." **Gemma Myers – Between The Pages Book Club**

"This is a very gritty read...Add into the mix, the ruthlessness of the gangsters and you've got a cracking crime thriller." **Claire Knight – A Knight's Reads**

"It has twists and turns, shocks and honestly at times I had no idea what the end would be!" **Donna Maguire – Donnas Book Blog**

"A plot to keep you turning from beginning to end. I really enjoyed this . A captivating read ." **Nicki Murphy – Nicki's Book Blog**

"... a really well written, gripping book with plenty of twists for me!" **Donna Maguire – Donnas Book Blog**

"...building up to a tense, drama packed read. I was literally biting my nails by the end." **Lorna Cassidy – On The Shelf Reviews**

"The author really keeps you on the edge of your seat – the twists made me gasp and she sets the atmosphere absolutely perfectly." **Melisa Broadbent – Broadbean's Books**

"If you are looking for a crime thriller that is somewhat unnerving as it is every mothers worst nightmare, a fast paced page turner that keeps you guessing. Then I definitely recommend Captor!" **Dash Fan Book Reviews**

"Captor will have you gripped from the beginning and won't let you go until you have finished. It is a suspense filled crime thriller that will keep you guessing throughout." **Gemma Myers – Between The Pages Book Club**

For Cerys, for being my constant.
My helpful assistant.
My love.
My granddaughter par excellence!

Many men would take the death-sentence
without a whimper, to escape the life-sentence
which fate carries in her other hand.

T E Lawrence (1888-1935)
The Mint, pt 1 ch 4

If you would be known, and not know, vegetate in a village;
if you would know, and not be known, live in a city.

Charles Caleb Colton
Lacon (1820) vol 1, no.334

1

Doris wasn't convinced. 'Did the doctor actually say those words "your blood pressure is a little high"? And he didn't say you had to stop working, put your feet up and rest?'

'He did not,' Kat confirmed, 'because he didn't mean your blood pressure is a little high, you need to do something about it. He just meant my blood pressure was a little high.'

'Really?' Doris peered over her glasses, staring at Kat as if she was a little girl at school. 'Well, Katerina Rowe, I'm pretty sure he meant you have to take care of yourself, and that involves you staying at home with your feet up.'

'I've still got two weeks to go. I'm not doing any of the physical work, but I can still produce reports, and work on that contract we've taken on for background checks.' Kat felt, and knew, that she was grasping at anything to save going home to that empty house.

Doris sighed. 'Okay. Here's what's going to happen. We're changing roles. You can be on reception, and I'm moving into your office. It's temporary, and it's only till you come back after the baby's born.'

'On reception?' Kat looked aghast at the small grey-haired woman laying down the law. In her sixties, Doris tended to do that a lot, saying she was the senior boss. 'I can't do that! You told me off for messing up the diary.'

'Kat, I didn't tell you off. I merely pointed out that if someone wanted an appointment for the seventh of the month, it was a bit daft putting them in for the fourteenth.'

'It's a new diary,' Kat said sullenly, tucking her long blonde hair back behind her ears. 'I can't help it if the page turned over while I was picking my pen up off the floor.'

Doris grinned. 'Kat, go home. Please. You have no appointments from now on, so go home and take it easy. Go and knit some bootees.'

'I can't. I've tried, and then went out and bought some. Me and knitting needles don't seem to belong in the same world.' Kat looked crestfallen, and Doris tried desperately not to laugh at her.

The door at the back of the room opened. 'Kat, get your coat. I'm taking you home. You're sacked.' Mouse looked at Kat, her face set as sternly as she could make it, considering the laughter trying to bubble out of her nan. She had screwed her long dark curls up into a ponytail on top of her head, and it added height to her already impressive almost six feet. She stood at the side of Kat, towering over her.

'You can't sack me,' Kat explained. 'I own half the business. And I'm pregnant. You're not allowed to sack pregnant people, ladies.'

'You're temporarily sacked.'

'But it's lonely in that big house. I've nobody to talk to.'

'Then it's time for us to move in.'

Kat's face brightened. 'Thank goodness for that. I've missed you since you moved in here.'

Doris had temporarily moved in with Mouse in her new flat, while she was looking for a property in the area, but it had been said from the very start that when Kat was getting near her due date they would move back in with her; if she went into labour during the night, they would be on hand.

Doris realised how lonely Kat must be feeling; an absentee husband who had spent most of his life murdering people, dealing drugs and money laundering, and then an absentee Mouse and Nan moving out of Kat's home must have left a huge void.

'Kat,' Doris said gently, 'why didn't you say? I could have stayed with you instead of Mouse. I thought you would welcome the peace and quiet of being in your home on your own.'

'No, it's rubbish. Tibby's vocabulary is limited to miaow, I can't master casting on the stitches, and I can't seem to settle to reading or watching tv, so I mooch around like a lost soul.'

'Make the most of it,' was Doris's dry response. 'In a couple of weeks you'll be pleading for time out. Luckily your baby comes with ready-made babysitters. Now, if you don't want to sit on reception and twiddle your thumbs, go home. We'll move back in with you tonight, so you won't be lonely anymore.'

'Okay, I give in. I'll go and clear out the airing cupboard. Maybe make a couple of apple pies.'

Doris and Mouse looked at each and spoke simultaneously. 'Nesting.'

***

Mouse watched Kat head towards her car and lever herself into the driving seat. It was clearly a struggle to fasten the belt around the bump. Thank goodness a pregnancy only lasted nine months, she mused, because if it lasted a minute longer Kat wouldn't get into the car, let alone the seat.

Mouse thought back to the slim stunning Kat of her first acquaintance. They had met when Kat visited her in hospital, complete with the white collar around her neck showing her faith. The bullet and the gun used to try to kill her hadn't worked, and Kat and Leon, the bastard of a husband, had found her, almost dead, in an alley. But Kat hadn't given up on her, not for a minute, and had welcomed Nan into her family as warmly as she had welcomed her. Now it was their time to support their friend. They would move back in with her immediately.

***

Kat walked through into the hall, and Tibby wrapped himself around her legs.

'Hey, baby, I've only been gone a couple of hours. You missed me?'

The cat miaowed.

'You did then?'

Tibby purred then abandoned Kat for his food dish in the kitchen.

She smiled, and began the mountainous climb upstairs, her stomach reaching the top well before she did. Being eight and a half months pregnant meant never being too far from a bathroom.

She washed her hands, then frowned at the towel on the floor. 'Come on, Kat Rowe PI, work out how come that's on the floor. It's not Tibby, the bathroom door was closed.'

She held on to her stomach and picked up the offending article; it was damp. She thought back to the morning, to gathering up laundry to take downstairs. A clean towel had been hung on the towel rail, and she had dragged the laundry basket downstairs, one step bumped at a time. The damp towel on the bathroom floor was the clean one she had hung that morning. And it should be neither damp nor on the floor.

A shiver ran through her body, and she went into the bedroom. The curtains were closed, despite having been opened before she went to work. She backed out carefully, and walked slowly downstairs. She wanted no accidents at this delicate stage of her pregnancy.

She dialled the shop and Doris answered. 'Can you come now?' Kat whispered.

'You've started?' Doris asked.

'No, it's nothing to do with the baby. I'll be outside in the car.'

There was a pause, then Doris responded. 'Lock the car doors.' Her tone was firm, and brooked no argument.

Kat disconnected, picked up her bag and jacket and went out of the door. She moved as fast as she could across to the car, and climbed in, immediately clicking on the lock.

***

Five minutes later, Mouse's new Range Rover pulled onto the drive with a screech of tyres, and she jumped out. She ran across to Kat's car, and Kat unlocked her door.

'Somebody's been in the house,' she said. 'There's only five people have keys; Mum, you, Nan, me. And Leon...'

'Could it be your mum? What am I talking about? They're in Spain until tomorrow, aren't they? You think it's Leon?'

Kat nodded. 'I was always picking up towels after he'd dropped them on the floor. There's a damp towel on the bathroom floor, one that was hung fresh this morning. The curtains are closed in the bedroom. He's been here, Mouse, I know he has.'

Doris had remained in the car, awaiting instructions, so Mouse called her over. 'Sit in here with Kat, will you, Nan? She'll explain what's happened.'

Mouse crossed towards the front door and inserted her key. It opened easily and she stepped inside, wedging it ajar with an owl doorstop. If she needed an escape, she wanted the door open.

She walked swiftly through the downstairs rooms; empty of anything human. Moving back to the bottom of the stairs, she stood and listened. There were no discernible sounds.

Slowly climbing, she headed towards the many doors along the landing. Only one was open. The rest were closed.

Mouse worked methodically through the rooms and finally reached Kat's bedroom. The closed curtains created a dim light, and Mouse moved across to open them and let in the sunshine. Whoever had been in this house definitely wasn't still there. She tried to recall what Kat had said, following Leon's departure. Both Mouse and Doris had suggested having a big bonfire of everything Leon had left behind, and they could burn an effigy of him made by using one of his designer suits, but Kat had laughed and said everything was already packed into a suitcase and stored in his wardrobe.

Mouse walked across to Leon's wardrobe and opened it. It was empty.

***

The three women sat at the kitchen table, all of them feeling shocked. Nothing had been heard of the murderous Leon Rowe since the night Nan had blown his hand apart.

'I'm scared,' Kat said. 'I didn't want him knowing about this baby, but what if he's been watching for me leaving the house? This bump is huge. It's obvious I've not just put on weight.'

'It makes no difference whether he's seen you or not, Kat,' Mouse said gently. 'When I went upstairs the nursery door was open. He knows a baby is coming into the house, and he knows how long it is since he left. He's not daft. To Leon, two and two will make four. I know you resisted it but you have to change the locks, and they need doing today. Then you have to ring DI Marsden. If you don't, it makes all of us complicit, and we need to be squeaky clean.'

'Am I ever going to be free of this man?' Kat looked very pale. 'I'll ring George Mears from church, locks are his line of business. He'll sort everything out for me.' She picked up her phone and very quickly arranged that George would call around within the next hour.

Mouse spoke at length with Marsden, who promised to send a forensics team out to check for fingerprints and ascertain that it was Leon Rowe who had been Kat's visitor.

By ten that evening, all their immediate concerns had been addressed, with DI Marsden promising identification by early next morning.

***

'Kat, before you go to bed, change your alarm code. I really can't believe he's been so brazen as to come back here, but he's a dangerous man. We need to make it as difficult as possible, he can't have free access to this house.' Mouse had already taken the decision to sleep downstairs, and that thought had brought the alarm code to the forefront of her mind.

'I will. What shall we have? Yours and Doris's birthdays? Leon doesn't know them, so if we don't put anything linked to me he can't even begin to guess.'

'Okay, use 0628. We have to remember it, no writing it down,' Mouse warned. 'But don't set it tonight, I'll be sleeping down here. I'll be your alarm for the next few hours. It must always be set when we sleep upstairs, we mustn't take any chances with him entering at ground floor level.'

***

By midnight all was quiet. Mouse was on the sofa, reading in darkness, thankful her eReader had a backlight. She heard the gravel crunch, and threw back the duvet. She moved silently towards the window and peered around the edge of the curtains.

She breathed a sigh of relief. DI Marsden had ordered the local police to make random checks throughout the night, and she recognised the uniform, if not the man. She also realised if the police visits carried on through the dark hours, she would have to get up and check every time she heard the crunch of the gravel, just in case…

It proved to be a long and restless night, but thankfully free of unwelcome visitors.

2

Despite Kat agreeing to stop working until after the birth, all three of them arrived at the shop together.

Kat explained that she didn't feel competent enough to be left on her own with the Internet and without Doris, so it would be better for her if she could accompany her two ladies at all times. In reality she was scared of being left at home alone. Her pregnancy made her vulnerable. She promised she would take her hospital bag and her notes everywhere she went, so she would always be prepared for any situation arising from the huge bump that preceded her every move.

'We need a meeting in my office,' Mouse said. 'All three of us. I haven't had chance to discuss a new case we've picked up because of yesterday, so we need to talk about it now. Kat, I just want you as an observer, because you're way beyond tackling anything physical. Other than giving birth,' she added with a grin.

'This bump doesn't stop me typing.'

'Yeah, right. You can't get near your desk. But unless your brain's turned to mush, you're our best thinker. We need you for your logic, Kat, not your running abilities.'

Kat held up a thumb in agreement. 'So tell us what's needed. I presume it's Mrs Carpenter, the lady who came in yesterday.'

'It is. She's called Judith but prefers Judy. She lives in Hope, her husband died about a year ago and she wants to trace his birth mother. It seems he was adopted as a tiny baby, and towards the end of his life she says he regretted not having tried to find her. He died from cancer, nothing genetic, but she has decided she'd like to go where he couldn't, and find this lady. We have nothing to go on, no starting points, and she's already given us a hefty deposit.

I've copied her contract for the three of us, as well as the notes I took as I was speaking to her.'

Doris and Kat groaned. 'Do these notes come translated?' Doris asked.

'Nope. If you can't fathom anything, just ask, and I'll have a go at working out what it says. I never said I could write legibly, did I.'

She handed out the scribbled sheets and they picked them up.

'Good Lord,' came from Kat.

'Bloody hell, Mouse,' came from Doris.

'You're so picky, both of you. Which bit can't you decipher?'

'All of it. But don't worry, we'll send it to Bletchley.' Doris grinned at her granddaughter.

'Look, basically what it's saying is that her husband, Thomas Edward Carpenter, died when he was forty, twelve months ago. She called him Tom. He had always understood that his adoptive parents kept the Christian names given to him by his birth mother, along with a tiny silver cross and chain. She no longer has that, but she thinks Tom may have given it to his aunt as a keepsake. Both Tom's parents have died, although his mother had a younger sister, Alice Small, who is still alive. This is the lady who possibly has the cross and chain. Alice doesn't know Judy is trying to trace Tom's birth mother. Tom's adoptive dad was James Carpenter, his adoptive mother was Margot Carpenter, nee Foster. I'm assuming this means Alice was a Foster, too. The Carpenters, until their deaths, lived in Baslow.'

'And that's it? That's all we have to go on?' Kat's eyes were still scanning Mouse's handwritten sheet, hoping that somewhere in the scrawl there were other snippets of information.

'That's it,' Mouse confirmed. 'We have his adoption certificate, of course, but because he died before trying to trace her, Judy said he hadn't applied for his birth certificate or his adoption pack. I actually think our starting point might be with Tom's aunt, Alice Small. Kat, do you want to take on that part? Ring Judy and get as much information as possible. She's expecting our call. She didn't have addresses or anything with her yesterday.'

'Will do,' Kat responded, feeling happy she wasn't being shelved just yet.

***

Doris and Kat were each dealing with their individual jobs, with Mouse out doing fieldwork following a client's daughter, when DI Marsden walked into the shop.

'Mrs Lester,' she said. 'You alone?'

'No,' Doris laughed. 'We can't leave Kat now. Mouse is out on a job, and Kat is in her own office, working on a new piece of business. Do you want her?'

Kat opened her office door. 'I'm here. You have news?' She had just finished speaking with Judy Carpenter, and making legible notes of addresses and dates.

'Only what you're expecting, I fear. It was your husband who was in the house. You've heard nothing from him?'

Kat shook her head. 'No, but I suspect I might. It seems he saw the nursery, so he'll know I'm pregnant. He'll make it his business to find out if I'm nearly due and then he'll know the baby belongs to him. That will cause problems.'

'I don't doubt,' Marsden said. 'What will you do?'

'Tell him to fuck off,' Kat said angrily. 'What do you think I'll do? He can't resurface, you'll arrest him.'

'Don't swear, Kat,' Doris said mildly. 'It doesn't become you.'

***

Tessa Marsden tried to hide her smile. Doris Lester was a force to be reckoned with, and she kept a close eye on her two girls. 'I'm more than a little concerned for your safety, Kat. He's not going to forgive any of you. He no longer has a wife, no longer has an income, a home… His life is the complete opposite of what it was a year ago. And now there's the baby. I think that's going to be a massive problem inside Rowe's head. That's the biggie, isn't it? A child he's unable to acknowledge, and he knows that once we track him down and arrest him, you'll be able to serve divorce papers, putting the baby even further away from him.'

'Don't worry, DI Marsden. We've got Kat's back.' Doris spoke with emphasis.

'I don't doubt it, Mrs Lester, but I want to have someone out at your home, Kat, installing a panic button. Until we arrest Rowe, I want you to feel a little more secure. You will only be two minutes away from help arriving. They'll be there at three this afternoon, so make sure you're there to let them in, will you. They'll put one in the bedroom and one in the kitchen. Do you need one in the lounge as well?'

'Yes, she does,' Doris answered.

Kat looked at the fiery pensioner and smiled. 'Whatever Nan says is fine with me,' she said to Marsden. 'She's always right. Maybe I should have one in the loo, I spend most of my time in there. I think this baby sleeps on my bladder. You don't think Leon will come here, to the shop?'

'No, this is too public. He'll want you on familiar territory, the home he shared with you.'

'Then as soon as Mouse gets back we'll finish here, and work from home for the rest of the day. Thank you for doing this for Kat, DI Marsden. He's an evil bastard, is Leon Rowe,' Doris spat.

'Hey,' Kat said. 'Don't swear, Mrs Lester, it doesn't suit you.'

Marsden turned to leave, then paused in the doorway. 'It goes without saying, I hope, that if you do see Rowe you'll not try to handle it yourselves. We need to know. He's an evil murderer, Kat, he wants putting away, whether he's a new daddy or not.'

'Don't worry,' Kat laughed. 'I want him out of our lives. You'll be the first person we call.'

***

Leon Rowe watched as Mouse entered the shop, then stared more closely as Kat and Doris followed Mouse out some two minutes later, and into the Range Rover. His view from the attic of his old pharmacy, directly opposite The Connection Detective Agency, gave him a perfect picture of Kat and the massive stomach concealing a child that was almost ready to be born. The nursery had created the question, the size of Kat's stomach had shown him the answer.

The baby was his.

***

The installation engineer for the panic buttons was quite delicious, Mouse decided. And then she realised he was the first man she had looked at in that way since seeing Anthony Jackson killed a year earlier. Watching a head being blown apart tended to put away thoughts of relationships and sex.

She signed the engineer's paperwork, and escorted him to the front door. 'Thank you,' she said, wondering if he would appreciate a quick kiss on the cheek, but deciding against being a brazen hussy. 'Let's hope they never get used.'

'Very few do,' he responded. 'But don't hesitate about using them. The lads would rather come out to a false call, than you not recognise there's danger and end up dead.'

She thanked him again, closed the door and leaned against it. End up dead? Would Leon Rowe really go that far with the woman who was supposedly the love of his life?

She knew the answer. He would.

Mouse returned to the kitchen to see Kat leaning forward over the sink, rubbing her back.

'Do I need towels and boiling water?' she grinned.

'It's backache. He or she is a proper lump, you know. And heavy with it. It's going to seem a long two weeks.'

Mouse gave her a hug and Kat winced. 'Sorry, did I hurt you?'

'No, I just had a twinge. A bit stronger than the last twinge.'

'Oh my God, you're having contractions?'

'No, it's backache.'

Doris eventually intervened. 'Kat, stand up straight, stop leaning over the sink.'

Kat slowly pushed away from the sink and as she became more upright she stared in horror at the pool of water appearing on the floor beneath her feet.

'I'm so sorry,' she gasped. 'It's only five minutes since I last peed.'

Doris shook her head. 'These ante-natal classes you attended, what can you remember about labour starting?'

'Contractions?'

'Before you get to that.'

'Waters breaking…'

'And backache?' Doris smiled.

'Shit.' Kat visibly paled.

'Not yet, that comes later.' Doris laughed. 'And stop swearing, young lady, it's not becoming of a woman of the cloth.'

Mouse was rigid. 'You mean…?'

'Kat's in early labour. Go get a couple of towels, Mouse, and put them on a chair. That will soak up any more fluid, and then we'll get Kat's bag and ring the hospital. There's no rush, I hope.'

Mouse ran upstairs, and returned with the towels, then lowered Kat onto the seat. She was biting her lip.

'Another one?'

Kat nodded. 'I've been having them on and off all day, but put it down to the stress of yesterday, finding out Leon had been here.'

'And you said nothing?' Doris looked concerned.

'I thought it was these Braxton Hicks things they talk about. It didn't occur to me it could be the real thing, it's too early.'

'Ring the hospital, Mouse. Tell them we're bringing her in now. Her waters have broken, and the contractions seem to be about two minutes apart.'

Mouse picked up the phone, and Doris stroked Kat's hand.

'Don't worry, lovely, you'll be fine, and we'll have our new baby very soon. Is your bag ready?'

Kat nodded again. 'In the hall, ready to go.'

***

Leon missed seeing the car as it hurtled through the village centre, Doris driving, Kat and Mouse on the back seat, with Kat on a mound of towels and emitting the occasional moan as another contraction washed over her.

Seeing Kat so heavily pregnant had changed all his plans; his intention had been to enter the house when he saw all three women at work in Connection, get the substantial amount of money, the gun and ammunition he had stashed away under the floorboards in the summer house, pick up the last of his clothes and disappear.

And then he saw the nursery.

His temporary camp in the pharmacy attic wasn't practical in any sort of long term; he was living off the out of date items still left as stock in the shop, but he had envisioned that situation as being for a couple of days at the most, then he would disappear for ever.

He knew the baby was his. Disappearing was no longer a choice, not until he had met his child and made decisions about the child's future.

***

Several things happened during a two-hour time frame that afternoon; an aeroplane landed at Manchester airport returning two unknowing brand new grandparents, Enid and Victor Silvers, back to home soil, Leon and Kat Rowe became first time parents, Doris Lester and Mouse Walters held Kat as she delivered her baby, and Martha May Rowe, tiny at six and a half pounds, entered all their lives and was immediately loved.

3

Enid and Victor stared down at the tiny sleeping baby.

'Well,' Enid whispered, 'I thought this day would never come. She's perfect.'

Her husband put his arm around her shoulders. 'I hope you'll still think that when you start your child-minding duties in a few weeks.'

'Of course I will. I've waited so long for this. I'm happy to help out, as you know. You are on board with that, aren't you?'

Victor smiled down at his Martha. 'Oh aye,' he said, 'aye, I am.'

***

Kat was unsure what to do about telling Alan and Sue in Canada. They had every right to know they had a granddaughter, but if they were in any sort of contact with Leon…

'What shall I do, Nan?'

'I don't know, sweetie. It's a hard one. But if Leon is keeping an eye on you, and we know he is, eventually he's going to see you pushing a pram instead of looking like a whale, and he'll know he's a daddy. I think you have to tell them.'

'I think I knew that anyway.' Kat's tone was rueful. 'I'll ring them and get it over with, but ask them if they are in touch with Leon, not to say anything. It's all I can do. It will be up to them whether they respect my wishes or not.'

She looked at the phone as though it was something from another planet that would kill her if she touched it. She sighed deeply and picked up the receiver.

'Sue, it's Kat.'

***

Mouse had left everyone cooing over the baby. She put in the satnav co-ordinates for the house in Bradwell she needed to visit, and drove out of Eyam, enjoying the sunshine that still didn't have much heat to it but always managed to lift Derbyshire to a whole new level.

She didn't miss living in the industrial city of Sheffield at all, couldn't imagine living anywhere else but her beautiful new flat. She owed a lot of her peace of mind to her nan, but felt a sense of dread that Leon Rowe was clearly back on the scene. Her biggest concern was that he had seen the nursery, and knowing he was no idiot, she guessed he had put two and two together.

The baby's arrival added to all their worries, and she knew that Kat would be filling her parents in at the moment, explaining what had happened while they were soaking up the sunshine on the recent holiday.

She drove over the bridge marking the entrance to Bradwell village, and listened to her satnav's disembodied voice.

The house she was seeking proved to be very near to the sixteenth century inn, Ye Old Bowling Green, and she smiled. Every place a winner in Derbyshire.

She sat for a moment and looked at the house. A pretty stone-built cottage with a tiny front garden bursting with springtime flowers, it looked loved and lived in. She took a deep breath before getting out of the car; back to work, forget newborn babies and problems arising from that.

Alice Small opened the door; her smile looked slightly forced.

'Mrs Small?' Mouse held her ID card in front of her. 'I'm Beth Walters. Thank you for agreeing to see me.'

'Come in, Miss Walters.' Alice held the door open.

The house was so like how Mouse imagined a cottage to be, it brought an instant smile to her face. 'Oh, this is lovely. And please call me Beth.'

'Thank you. It's taken me a couple of years to get it how it always was in my imagination, but I think I'm there now. Please, come through to the lounge.'

Alice indicated that Mouse should sit in the armchair, and Alice sat on the small sofa.

'Now, how can I help with this crazy idea?'

'You don't agree with it?'

'Tom's dead, so it's not him wanting to find his birth mother, it's her. Judith.'

Mouse took out her iPad. 'Do you mind if I make notes?'

'Of course not, but I'm not sure if I know anything worth making notes about.'

'I'm sure you will, probably without realising you do know something. Let's start with Tom's parents. I understand his mum, Margot, was your sister.'

This time the smile that lit up Alice's face was genuine. 'She was. She was ten years younger than me, would have been seventy this year. Same age as James. They both died nine years ago, in the same year. It very nearly broke Tom. He adored them, and I think it's why he didn't try to find his birth mother, not at that time anyway. He and Judy had discussed tracing her, and he had said one day he would do it.'

'What do you mean? Did he try? And you're eighty?' Mouse's face reflected her shock. She hoped she looked as good when she reached four-score.

There was a long hesitation. Slowly, Alice spoke. 'He applied for his birth certificate and his adoption pack. He did it as soon as he found out he had cancer, way before he knew it was terminal. He came here one day with a folder and asked if I would save it for him, he didn't want Judy to see it before he had something concrete to tell her.' Alice smiled. 'And yes, I am eighty. I keep myself fit.'

'Why didn't he want Judy to know?'

'The marriage was going sour. I know they would have split up, but that terminal diagnosis changed everything. He more or less decided to put up and shut up. It saved having to divide everything, saved having to sell their beautiful house in Hope, she just had everything when he died. After they told him there was no long term future, he only lived four months or so.'

'And you still have that folder?'

Alice nodded. 'I do, along with his tiny silver cross and chain his birth mother gave him. He gave it to me when he knew he was dying.'

Mouse sat, digital pencil in hand, hardly daring to breathe. Would Alice say she couldn't see the paperwork? She briefly wrote on her iPad, words that made no sense but served to diffuse the tension inside her.

'Would it be possible to see the file?' Mouse held her breath.

Again there was a long pause, as if Alice was going over thoughts she must have been having ever since Mouse had rung to make the appointment.

Suddenly she spoke. 'I know Katerina Rowe, your business partner. And because I know her, I'm going to let you see it. You can't take it away, but I assume that fancy gadget can take photos?'

'It can. And I'm sure you'll be pleased to know Kat had a little girl yesterday, Martha May. They're both home now.'

'Oh, that's wonderful. I have a little gift for her that you can take when you leave. She's led many services at our church, a lovely lady, far too good for that thug she accidentally married. They caught him yet?'

'Not as far as we know.' Mouse smiled.

Alice stood. 'Would you like a cup of tea?'

'That would be lovely, thank you.'

Alice went out of the room, and Mouse heard the cold water run. The sunlight had moved around slightly and was coming through the leaded windows, lighting up the interior. Alice had used a subdued chintz, perfectly in keeping with the furniture. The inglenook fireplace was welcoming, and as Mouse watched a log crumbled and dropped. She desperately wanted to place another log on the fire, never having had the opportunity before, and giggled to herself at the thought. Pyromania, that was the word for it.

Alice returned to the lounge bearing a bread board with buttered scones, and Mouse stared at it. 'Is that a mouse carved into it?'

'It is. It's a Robert Thompson. He carved a mouse into all his work, and I'm lucky enough to own one.'

'It's my name, I've been called Mouse all my life. Apparently I looked like a little mouse when I was born, and the name stuck. My nan and Kat always call me Mouse, and I expect I'll be Aunty Mouse to Martha.'

'You are clearly loved then. Tom was a very much loved and wanted child. James and Margot couldn't have children, adoption was their only option. He was just six weeks old when he came to live with them.'

Mouse waited, sensing there was more to be said.

'Margot died from a heart attack, but James had already been diagnosed with lung cancer before she went. He lived an extra six months. It devastated Tom, but I always felt Judy didn't really support him. They seemed to live separate lives, and after Tom died I honestly didn't expect to hear from her again. Why is she doing this, Beth? Do you know? She didn't care two hoots when he was alive, and now she's fulfilling his last wish. If it was.'

'That's exactly what she said when we agreed to take the job, that it was Tom's wish she track his mother down. Did you know his birth mother? I know in the sixties they used to arrange private adoptions.'

'No, and even though I know her name, it doesn't ring any bells with me. Her address is on Tom's birth certificate, but she doesn't live there now. Her birth certificate is in there, too. Tom obviously intended finding her, because he would have applied for a copy of that, it wouldn't have come as part and parcel of the adoption pack.'

Alice stood and walked to the small sideboard that fitted perfectly into the alcove. She took out the folder, and passed it to Mouse.

'You can photograph whatever you need, but I would prefer to hang on to the originals. It's all I have of Tom. Judy never asked me if I would like anything to remember him by, and I was too stubborn to ask. Inside the folder is a copy of a photograph of

Tom, taken a couple of years ago. You can take that with you. You may need it when you find his birth mother.'

'Of course I won't remove the originals and thank you so much for the photo,' Mouse said. She took the folder and pulled out the documents tucked neatly inside.

'I'll get our cups of tea,' Alice said. 'And please help yourself to a scone. You'll need to build up your strength with a new baby to be an aunty to.'

***

She returned with the drinks. 'Tom was very good to me,' she confided. 'A friend of mine died, a friend who lived here, and I had always loved this little cottage. I had enough money to buy it outright because it was very run down, needed lots doing to it. I was living in a rented property, so it made sense to buy this, and do the repairs as time went on, but Tom paid for everything that needed doing, and six months after I bought it, I had this.' She waved her arm around. 'Since then I've added the little extras, and I love it here. And of course I was only five minutes away from Tom and Judy's house.' A look of sadness crossed Alice's face. 'I miss him so much.'

***

Mouse didn't pause to read any of the documents; that would be a job for later. She laid them one by one on the coffee table, and photographed each piece with the iPad.

She snapped everything, even the little envelope addressed *To my darling son, Thomas Edward.* Inside the envelope had been a letter written by the birth mother, but Mouse knew if she read it she would end up crying. Best to leave it until later, when she was with people who understood her occasional tears. She placed the photo of the remarkably handsome man in her document case.

The scone was on a par with one of Nan's scones, and after finishing her tea Mouse stood to take her leave.

'Thank you so much for all of this, Mrs Small.'

'It's Alice,' the elderly lady said with a smile. 'And if you need anything else, don't hesitate to ring me. I felt very antagonistic towards you when you arrived, thought you would be on Judy's side, but you've been impartial, and extremely pleasant.' She handed Mouse a carrier bag. 'This is the little gift I've made for baby Martha, and please congratulate Katerina for me.'

Mouse took the bag. 'I most certainly will. If you think of anything else, no matter how insignificant, please ring me. I've left my card on your coffee table. Just so you know, I won't be telling Judy I've seen you. We don't make a point of telling our clients how we get information. They only pay us to get it.'

Alice nodded. 'Thank you. I understand what you're saying.'

***

Alice remained in the doorway until the big car disappeared around the bend. The afternoon had gone much better than she expected; she hadn't wanted any of this to happen, but Judy had taken it out of her hands. Damn the woman. She should have been the one to die, not her husband.

4

Mouse glanced at her watch, and made the decision to call into the shop and print out the pictures from her iPad. If baby Martha gave them a quarter of an hour break at some point during the evening, they could all look at them and discuss the next move.

She pulled up outside Connection, raised the shutter and let herself in through the front door, stopping the alarm before it woke the neighbourhood. Locking the door behind her, she downloaded and printed all of the pictures, knowing Kat found it easier to view a piece of paper rather than a computer screen. The thought made Mouse smile, as it had done so often since she had met the church deacon. Dinosaur Kat.

Mouse put the pictures into three cardboard files, and reset the alarm before going outside to lock up and lower the shutters. She turned to go to the car and shivered. 'Get off my grave,' she grumbled. She looked around, aware of the ever-present Leon threat and almost wishing he was standing by her side; her shoulder no longer pained her and her fitness was at Wonder Woman level. One day he would pay for injuring Kat... one day.

Mouse could see no one. In fact the centre of the village was remarkably quiet. She climbed into the car, and drove home, eager to tell her co-workers everything she had learned.

***

Leon watched her drive away, wondering where Kat and Doris were. They usually formed a coven of witches; it was rare to see Beth Walters on her own. He hated not having cohorts he could use to watch the three women, but with his henchman Brian locked up for life, and the entire business disbanded, he had no one he could trust to do anything.

Leon's home in Spain was ready and waiting, he had collected everything he needed from his old home; he just needed to see this baby when it was born. A mixed-race child would prove its parentage, and he could then take steps accordingly. A white child, and he could walk away.

***

Mouse opened the front door quietly and stepped into the hall. Silence. She looked into the lounge and then walked through to the kitchen. Deserted. Still keeping noise to a minimum, she headed upstairs. She tapped softly on her nan's door, and opened it. Doris was asleep on the bed. Mouse smiled, and backed out.

Kat's bedroom door was open, and she was also asleep, her hand tucked in between the bars of Martha's crib, holding her daughter's tiny fingers. Martha's delicate coffee-coloured skin was a stark contrast to Kat's.

Mouse slipped her phone out of her jeans pocket and took a picture. It was stunningly beautiful.

She headed back downstairs and placed the files on the table. Time enough to look at them when her two sleeping beauties woke. She pulled her laptop towards her, and began to search.

***

Kat wrapped a towel around her wet hair, checked on her sleeping child as she went past the bedroom, and headed downstairs. She smiled as she saw Mouse. 'I needed that sleep. And I feel better for having a shower. I'd feel really good with a cup of tea inside me,' she said with a grin.

'Your wish is my command,' Mouse responded.

'Oooh, that would be nice.' The voice of Doris travelled as a whisper down the stairs.

***

They sat around the kitchen table engrossed in the files Mouse had prepared, each having individual thoughts and making notes on the documents.

Kat sighed. 'What a brave woman. I can't imagine having to give Martha away, and yet she was forced by narrow-minded parents to give Tom up. She had already bonded very strongly because she called him Tommy, although she used both his forenames on the envelope. I'm really pleased Margot and James respected her wishes and kept his name, it was obviously important to her. It makes me wonder why, in view of the letter she wrote to Tom. Did she have a boyfriend, maybe?'

Without lifting her head, Mouse spoke. 'Will you put Leon's name on Martha's birth certificate?'

'I have six weeks before I need to do anything,' Kat replied. 'It seems that I can't put his name on unless he's there, and that's not going to happen, is it.'

'I do hope Pamela Farrar is alive, when we eventually track her down,' Doris said. 'Love for your children is unconditional, and she will want to know what happened to Tom. She was sixteen when she had him, so she'll only be around sixty now. There's every possibility she's still alive, all we need to do is find her. Simple!'

Mouse laughed. 'Okay, clever clogs. I'm finding no trace of her through any of the normal channels, and I don't think this one is going to be as easy as we're all assuming it will be. And what do you know of Robert Thompson?'

'He carves mice.' Kat spoke first.

'Mice are his trademark.' Doris followed.

Mouse frowned. 'How come I didn't know about him then? It's my name.'

Doris laughed. 'You need to watch more antiques programmes on television. Then you'd know about him.'

'Well, Alice Small has a bread board of his. It was lovely.'

'A discerning lady, then. Look him up online, you'll be amazed at his stuff. It's beautiful. And expensive.'

There was a knock at the kitchen door and a tall bearded man opened it and grinned at them. His salt and pepper hair showed him to be in his fifties, a big man with many lines on his face showing his proclivity to laugh a lot.

'Afternoon, ladies,' Danny McLoughlin said. 'As promised, Kat, I'm here to give your lawn its first cut.'

Kat smiled. 'Things have changed, Danny.' She patted her stomach. 'We have a brand new baby in the house, so it would be better if you used the mower when she wasn't sleeping. Come in, I'll sort out a rota with you. Thank you so much for this, the garden's starting to look a bit of a mess.'

'No worries,' he said, and stepped inside. 'I'll get you in the diary. I suggest once every two weeks for the grass cutting and general tidy up – shall we say two hours maximum? We'll negotiate any bigger jobs that might crop up.'

'Perfect,' Kat said. 'Can you start tomorrow? I'll make sure I put the baby in the lounge to sleep, you won't disturb her then.'

Danny took out his diary. 'Okay, I can do tomorrow afternoon. Is that good for you?'

'It is. Thinking about it, I'll maybe take Martha to my mum's for the afternoon, so it won't affect us. Doris and Beth will be working, I imagine, so won't be here. Best bring a drink with you, though. This house is on lockdown at the moment, and I can't hand new keys out on pain of death.'

'No problem, Kat. I usually take a flask with me anyway. Anything I need to be aware of?' A frown briefly crossed his face. The whole village knew of Leon Rowe's activities, and had applauded when Brian King was sent down for the rest of his life.

'Leon's been back. We have panic buttons and locks that Houdini couldn't fathom. We also have random police cars driving up and down, keeping an eye on us. Nothing to worry about, although if Leon is still in the area, I imagine they'll worry him.'

Danny nodded. 'Let's hope he comes when I've got a spade in my hand.' The deacon was a very popular lady in the area, and everybody had been upset by what she had been forced to go through. Rowe disappearing had caused uncertainty and more than a little fear in Eyam, but that had slowly settled down when he hadn't resurfaced.

Now it seemed he had.

Danny closed his diary with two appointments made, and headed for the door. 'Take care, Kat.'

'Don't worry, I will.'

***

The letter had a little heart drawn on the top. Kat read it for the second time with tears running down her face; her hormones were all over the place, aching for what the young sixteen-year-old had been forced to go through.

My darling boy, my Tommy,

I will always love you, and the pain I am feeling now is killing me. I cannot keep you, my parents cannot bear the shame. I haven't told them who your father is, even though they have asked so many times, because I don't know. I was attacked and beaten until I was unconscious, as I walked home from work.

I woke up in the hospital, and had to answer lots of questions but I couldn't tell the police anything. I didn't know the man who beat me. Four months later I found out I was pregnant.

I was sent to a mother and baby unit in Chesterfield before I started to show too much, and my parents told everybody I had gone to a cousin's on the south coast to recuperate after the attack.

I had you, my darling son, and we were together for six weeks, then they took you one day.

I didn't get the chance to say goodbye, and they made me write you a letter the next day before sending me home to my parents. They never saw you.

But I did, and I pray you will go to a good home, where they will love you as much as I do.

My love, my life, my precious child, my Tommy.

Always know it was not my wish that you be adopted. You are mine and always will be.
Mummy
Xxxx

***

Beth put her arm around Kat's shoulders and held her tightly. 'Hey, come on. Maybe you shouldn't be involved in this case, it's a little close to home at the moment, isn't it?'

'It's heartbreaking.'

'They were such narrow-minded times,' Doris joined in. 'I remember them well.'

'Lots of babies were adopted then?' Mouse spoke with concern.

'Definitely, although things were starting to change in the seventies, when Tommy was born. I suspect Pamela's parents couldn't handle it because she had been raped. Maybe it would have been different for her if this was a child born of a love relationship and not a brutal one. If babies were conceived in the seventies, the parents of the baby tended to marry. It began to change in the eighties and nineties; marriage lost its popularity, women became more independent and brought babies up on their own, but of course the era that was really to blame for everything was the sixties.' Doris sat back with a smile on her face.

'They were good then, the sixties?' Mouse asked. 'You enjoyed them?'

'Mouse, I lived them. Free love, drugs, you name it, it went on. The country had put World War Two behind it, and the post-war babies became teenagers. We thought we ruled the world. No, we knew we ruled the world. Wonderful, amazing years. We didn't have freedom from parental authority, so we took it. It was the best time of my life, and remember we didn't have technology, we had music, glorious music that can't be matched today.'

Kat laughed. 'Stop it, Nan, you're making me jealous. Would you go back to those times, give up your technological expertise, your phone, your iPad?'

'In a heartbeat. I met my Harry in 1964 when I was just fourteen, and we married five years later. We danced the sixties away. The Beatles, the Stones, all the Liverpool groups, Rod Stewart, unbelievable music. And it's all still played today.'

'It wasn't all about music though, surely?' Mouse asked.

''Course it was. It's what we had. By the mid seventies we were starting to grow up, having families, colour televisions, it was a period of massive change. Which is why it's so strange that Pamela was forced into giving up her baby. Times were becoming much more liberal, but clearly not liberal enough for this young woman's parents.'

Kat stood. 'I hear a baby.' She headed upstairs, and they could hear her talking to Martha, via the baby monitor. She returned, cradling the baby in her arms.

'Guess it's feeding time. I'll make her a bottle and then she can sleep in her pram.'

***

Half an hour later they were all rereading everything in the files. Pamela Farrar's birth certificate showed that she had been born on the fifth of January 1960 in Grindleford, and as Doris filled them in more and more about life in the sixties and seventies, it became clear that although the bigger towns and cities embraced the new freedoms afforded by the end of the war, the small villages retained their insular complexities. People began to move out to the cities where factories needed workers to rebuild the destruction caused by the war, leaving a hard core of villagers to manage their lives, reluctant to let the old ideas go.

And it seemed that Pamela Farrar had paid the price for the old-fashioned values of her parents.

Thomas Edward Farrar was born on the twenty-third of April 1976 in Chesterfield, and subsequently adopted on the seventh of June 1976 at Renishaw Magistrates Court. Margot and James Carpenter of Baslow, Derbyshire, were the adoptive parents, and until a couple of days prior, that was the end of the trail as far as the Connection Detective Agency was concerned.

They finished reading everything, then sat back and looked at each other.

'So,' Kat began, 'the adoption pack told us very little. No father, but we know why anyway, and the last known place of residence for Pamela was Grindleford. We have an address there, but I'm presuming you've already checked this out online, Mouse?'

'Yes, a Mr and Mrs Palmer live there now. However, next door at twelve Haddon Row is an elderly lady by the name of Joyce Graham who has lived there all her life. She's eighty, so I don't want to just turn up on her doorstep. I think we need to ring her and make an appointment. I'm sure she'll know the family. She may have some snippets she can pass on to us.'

Doris made a note. 'I'll ring her if that becomes necessary. At eighty, I don't really want to trouble her. Anything else we've gleaned from this first foray into it?'

'I think Alice Small loved Tom very much, but didn't rate Judy at all.' Mouse held her hand to her lips. 'Oops, bear with me a minute.' She stood and headed outside. They heard the slam of the car door, and she returned carrying a white carrier bag. She handed it to Kat.

'This is from Alice. She apparently knows you, you take the service at her church occasionally, and she thinks you're lovely. It's something for Martha.'

Kat took the bag, and pulled out a pink-wrapped parcel. She carefully opened it to reveal an exquisite crocheted white coat and hat. 'Oh my word. I must ring her. This is stunning, and I'm going to dress Martha in it when I take her to Mum's tomorrow.'

Mouse put the paperwork back into the individual folders, and called a halt to work for the day.

'I may go on the computer later,' she said, 'but officially we're closed. Kat, get your feet up, get some rest. And let's make sure all these doors are multi-locked and alarms primed.'

'I'll find us something to eat,' Doris said. 'Us working girls need to keep our strength up. But, Kat, please try to remember you're on maternity leave.'

5

'Okay, I'm off now,' Kat said. 'It was good the midwife visit being early today, so I'm heading to Mum's for lunch. You two can stop babysitting me for a couple of hours, and go to work.'

She strapped Martha into her baby seat. 'I think I've got everything, but it's like packing to go on holiday. I'll be back around five, so you don't need to be on tenterhooks thinking I'm on my own.'

Mouse looked up. 'Text me when you get to your mum's house. No pissing about, Kat. If you don't text we'll come over and find you. Leon can track you on the road just as easily as he can invade your space here.'

'I know. If I've not texted in fifteen minutes, you text me. I'm still a bit woolly headed, I might forget.'

***

She didn't forget, and ten minutes after the reassurance that she was alive and well and drinking tea, Mouse and Doris drove down through the village to the office. On their journey they had passed Danny McLoughlin heading in the opposite direction towards Kat's house, his hand waving at them through his open car window.

'It'll be good to get out and sit in the garden again,' Doris said. 'I'm always so relieved when winter's over and we get flowers once more.'

'He did a cracking job of tidying the garden to get it through the cold months,' Mouse said. 'I'm glad Kat's asked him to come back. I don't mind pottering, but I'm not into cutting lawns and stuff.'

She parked outside the shop, and pulled on the handbrake. 'You go in, Nan. I just need to go to the cash machine. There's no money in my purse, I feel as though I've been mugged.'

Mouse waited until Doris opened the shutter and door, then crossed the road towards the small village supermarket, and its ATM.

The sun was in her eyes and at first she didn't notice the woman slumped on the floor by the side of the machine, the little boy next to her trying to soothe her, unsuccessfully. She was crying harshly, and trying to control it, equally unsuccessfully.

Mouse dropped her purse back into her bag and ran to the woman. 'Hey, come on. Are you hurt?'

She shook her head, clearly unable to speak for the moment.

'Then let me help you up.' Mouse's arms went around her, and the woman struggled to her feet.

Tissues appeared from Mouse's bag as if by magic, and she handed them to the woman, who was trying desperately to stifle the sobs. Her little boy was staring up at his mum, a scared look fixed on his face.

'Has someone attacked you?' Mouse probed gently.

'No, they took my money.'

'Look, Mrs…?'

'Roy. Keeley Roy. And this is my son, Henry.'

'Okay, Keeley, my name's Beth Walters, and I co-own Connection over there.' She pointed to the shop. 'Will you and Henry come across with me, let me get you a drink, and tell me what happened?'

She hesitated for a moment and then nodded. 'Henry hold my hand. We're going to cross the road.'

'Let me just get some money,' Mouse said, 'and we'll get over there.'

She quickly made her withdrawal and they walked over to where Doris had already switched on the kettle and coffeemaker. She had been watching the scene play out, conscious that Leon Rowe could be anywhere, and for as long as that was the case, her granddaughter needed to be in her sights. The scar from the last bullet Mouse had taken was still very clearly visible, and Doris was frightened to death there might be a second one on its way. Leon Rowe was a cold-blooded killer.

As the three approached the shop, she opened the door.

'Nan, this is Keeley and Henry. We've come for a drink. Keeley's had a bit of a shock.'

'Kettle and coffeemaker already underway,' Doris said. 'Milk or cordial, Henry?'

'Milk, please,' the little boy said with a shy smile, clearly overawed by being in a building he'd never been in before.

'Nice manners. A credit to you, Keeley. Would you like tea or coffee?'

'Tea, please, milk no sugar.' She took a great heaving sigh, finally losing the emotion that had followed the realisation of the robbery.

'Okay. You go in Beth's office, and Henry and I will get to know each other in here. We can draw some pictures. I'll take care of him,' she said to the haggard-looking young woman. 'Go and talk to Beth.'

***

It wasn't only Doris who had scrutinised the developing scene from beginning to end. Leon had seen Beth's large car pull up, and watched both her and Doris climb out. No Kat.

It seemed that Kat could have been left at home to rest; maybe she had even stopped work now until the birth, which couldn't be far away.

He stared intensely as he saw Beth help up the woman, and briefly wondered why she was on the floor in the first place. His eyes must have been so firmly fixed on Connection that he hadn't seen what had happened prior to Doris and Beth's arrival.

The two women and the little boy crossed the road and went into the shop that had been the object of Leon's surveillance, and his decision was made. He was going to head up the back hidden path, following the brook, and enter his old home by the garden. If he stayed behind the summer house... He didn't want Kat to see him, he just wanted to see her, to confirm that his eyes hadn't deceived him when he saw her rounded shape.

On such a beautiful afternoon she was bound to be pottering around the garden; he would look and come away. He was prepared to play the long game until he could decide what to do about the child.

He pulled his hood up and forward so that most of his face was hidden. Letting himself out of the side door, supposedly sealed and padlocked by the police but with a padlock that was so easy to break, Leon closed the door and slipped the huge lock back on, making it look as though it was still secured.

***

The early May sunshine was warm, but hadn't yet begun to warm the soil, and digging around the roses in the rose bed was proving to be hard work. Danny stood upright, and wiped the sweat from his brow. He stabbed the fork into the previously dug earth, and headed up to sit on the patio for two minutes.

He sat down and pulled his flask towards him. It was silent, not even a bird seemed to be singing. He poured out his coffee and tentatively sipped at it. He enjoyed working in this garden; it wasn't hard work as it had always been well maintained, but since Kat had announced her pregnancy, he had been doing the work for her.

This was his first visit of the new gardening season, and already it was looking lovely with spring flowers in evidence. He took out a cigarette, and sat quietly, almost dozing in the unexpected warmth of the sun.

And then there was a noise. He looked down towards the summer house, and Tibby sauntered out, then wandered up onto the lawned area before lying smoothly down in the warmth of the sun.

He smiled; he liked cats, and this one was extra friendly, always twining himself around his feet, eager to be with him.

He stood and moved back towards the rose bed. Another half hour and he would be done. He saw the figure, hood obscuring its face, almost at the same time as the figure saw him. Whoever that bugger was, he'd no place being behind Kat's summer house, and he was going to make sure he knew it.

'Oy! Dickhead! What do you think you're doing? Go on, get out of it, on your way.'

The figure turned at his shout, paused for a moment as if in thought, and then scrambled back down towards the brook path, intent on getting away. A tall climbing rose snagged on his hood, and it fell from his face, such an instantly recognisable face in Eyam. Posters were all over the place still, stuck on every available hoarding, keeping the man in the forefront of everybody's mind.

'Rowe!'

***

Leon heard the growled name, and moved fast; the dozy old gardener wouldn't have the speed to catch him, but being spotted by him could only lead to trouble. Police trouble.

The crash of wellingtons hitting various rocks and bushes as Danny slipped and slithered down the difficult terrain told Leon that this particular dozy old gardener was intent on reaching him.

Leon stopped.

He turned, slipped his right hand into his pocket and took out the silenced gun.

Danny gave a huge roar. 'Oh no you don't, you evil bastard!' He threw himself at the black-clad figure of Leon Rowe.

Leon fired twice. The first shot dropped Danny to his knees. The second splattered his brains around the path and in the water.

All was silent again.

Leon ran.

6

Doris settled Henry at her counter with some paper and a pencil, and carried a tray of drinks through to Mouse's office. Mouse smiled and thanked her, and Doris headed back out to the little boy who seemed much too quiet.

'I'm sure Mummy won't be long. What shall we draw?'

'Ducks.'

'O... kay. We can draw ducks, I'm sure.'

She picked up a second pencil and bent her head.

***

'So, now we've got a drink and you're a little calmer, tell me what happened.'

There was a huge sigh. 'Henry and I are going on holiday. I've been paying for a year for it, paying monthly because we don't have a lot of money. His father died and so we have no financial help, but finally it's here. We're going on Saturday... or we were. I don't know what's going to happen now. I've paid for a caravan at the coast, nothing special, but he'll love the beach. I had saved £300 for spending money, and we'd made a big thing about coming down to the cash machine to get it out.' She paused for a moment, and Mouse remained silent.

'I put my card in the machine, put in my pin number and pressed for £300, then felt Henry move. He's quite lively, a bit of a handful, and I turned to grab him but he was heading for the road. I ran after him and he fell off the edge of the pavement and landed face down on the road. I picked him up, sorted him out, and went back to get my money. It had gone.'

'But the machine would have reclaimed it, wouldn't it? I'm pretty sure if you don't get it within a certain amount of time, it whips it back.'

'I thought that, so I waited a few minutes. I tried again and it said insufficient funds. I suspect somebody went to the supermarket, walked past the machine and helped themselves. I felt overwhelmed with worry, burst out crying and sat on the floor. That's when you turned up.'

Mouse nodded. 'Okay, first things first.' She pushed the telephone across the desk towards Keeley. 'Ring your bank and ask them if the machine took back the money. It may be something simple like it takes time to re-credit your account.'

'Erm… I can't really do this. I have no money to pay you for your time.'

'Just ring the bank, Keeley.'

'I will, but I'll do it on my own phone, the number's in that.'

'You always this stubborn?' Mouse asked.

'Probably,' Keeley said. 'I've had to be.'

She pressed the call button, and it took some minutes of other keys being pressed before she reached a person.

The answer was short and sweet, although not to Keeley's ears. She looked up at Mouse after disconnecting.

'The money has come out of my account.'

'Okay. Let's not panic. There must be CCTV at that cash machine, either a camera installed by the bank over the machine, or one installed by the supermarket. We'll go over and talk to the manager, see if he can help.'

Mouse pushed her chair back and picked up her bag. 'Come on, let's go and see what we can find out.'

Henry was quite happy to be left with Doris for a few minutes, and Mouse and Keeley left the shop, hurrying across the road towards the supermarket.

The manager was unhelpful, stating several times that the cash machine wasn't their problem, that it was a bank problem.

'I know that,' Mouse said. 'But think on this, Mr Newton. If you won't help us, we'll have no option but to call the police. A crime has been committed. The shop will have to close while they investigate and dust for fingerprints, and it won't be just for an hour. You might as well send your staff home and tell them to come back the day after tomorrow, because I'll raise so many issues it will stretch out that long. Now, what's your decision?'

***

He stared at the pretty girl he'd been seeing for months going in and out of Connection, and knew he'd met his match.

He straightened up, tugged on his suit jacket and said, 'Follow me.'

He took them through a double swing door made of rubber, and led them to his office.

He sat in his chair, and Mouse pointed to the other chair, indicating that Keeley should sit down. Mouse then perched her bum on the desk, leaned across to the man and said, 'Anytime you're ready, Norman. Show us what you have.'

Despite her worries and concerns, Keeley looked as if she was trying desperately hard not to laugh. The poor man looked terrified.

He swung the monitor around so they could see it, and then proceeded to rewind the picture it was showing to an earlier time. He looked up in query, almost afraid to speak.

'Half an hour should do it,' Mouse said.

The rewind stopped, and the two women watched the screen.

It eventually showed Keeley and Henry walking up to the cash machine, and Keeley placing Henry in front of her, facing the keypad. She keyed in her pin number and Henry reached up and added an extra digit. The machine clearly said it was an incorrect number because the card was returned. She moved Henry to one side, and reinserted the card. This time her pin number was accepted and she completed the request for £300. The machine ejected her card and she took it at the same time as Henry ran away from her side and towards the road. Clutching the returned card, she ran after him and caught up to him as he fell into the road.

They saw her comfort him, and then saw a figure in light coloured jogging bottoms and a sleeveless running vest with the number nine printed on it, jog into view. He bent and took the money still in the cash machine dispenser, and increased his running speed as he ran off with the money.

'Do you know him?' Mouse asked Norman Newton.

He didn't answer immediately, his eyes were glued to the screen, a look of horror on his face.

'Mr Newton? Do you know him?' she repeated.

He turned to face Keeley. 'How much did you have taken, Mrs...?'

'Roy, my name is Keeley Roy. And I had withdrawn £300. We've already told you this.'

He stood and moved into a smaller office attached to the room they were in. They saw him open the safe, and he returned holding a bundle of money.

'Please take this,' he said, and handed over money bound by an elastic band. 'I do know him, and I'll deal with him.'

Mouse stood. 'Whoa. If you know him, then this is definitely a police matter. Who is he?'

Newton sighed. 'He's my son. And trust me, he'll live to regret doing this. The money will be paid back into that safe in full by tonight.'

'You promise you'll deal with him?' Keeley looked up at the man who was clearly distressed.

'I do, and I also promise he'll make a full apology to both of you for causing such heartache. Please leave me your address, he will be visiting you, alongside me.'

Keeley hesitated for a moment, then pulled a small scrap of paper towards her. She scribbled down her address and stood.

'Come on, Beth. Let's leave Mr Newton to sort this. Thank you for replacing my money,' she said.

***

They were back in Connection before Mouse spoke again.

'You sure about this?'

Keeley nodded. 'I am. I have a son, and one day somebody may have to forgive something he's done. I certainly don't think Newton's son is going to get away with anything, do you?'

Mouse laughed. 'I wouldn't want to be in his shoes, that's for sure. Did he give you the full amount?'

Keeley took out the money she had dropped into her bag, and began to count it. She stopped at three hundred, still holding extra in her left hand. She carried on and finally looked up. 'He's given me five hundred. Five hundred, Beth! There'll be no shortage of ice creams on this holiday.'

'If that's the case,' Mouse joked, 'I almost wish I was coming with you. Can you do me a favour and just fill out one of our contract forms? There's no charge to you, of course, I haven't really done anything, but I'm taking a course and we have to talk about a couple of real cases. I think this will be excellent for it. Don't worry, I won't use your name, but if I have to provide proof I actually did the work, then I'll need the contract.'

'Happy to oblige,' Keeley said, and took the official-looking form. 'It's been an eventful trip out for us and Hoppy.'

'Hoppy?'

'He's a toy rabbit. He belongs to Henry's class, and they take it in turns to look after him for the week. We have to take him out and photograph him in different places. The idea was to bring him to Eyam, and snap him in the churchyard, by the plague cottages, that sort of thing, and to combine it with the trip to get our money. If I'd stayed local, none of this would have happened.'

She shook her head almost in disbelief, and bent to sign the contract.

'Thank you so much, Beth,' Keeley said, as she pushed the contract back across the desk towards Mouse.

***

Five minutes later, peace was restored, and both Doris and Mouse waved off their unexpected visitors.

'That was easy to solve,' Mouse said. 'Let's hope finding Pamela Farrar is just as easy. We got any water in the fridge? I'm really thirsty.'

'There's a couple of bottles. Help yourself. I'll file this contract, and then we'll have a chat about where we go next with the case that actually makes us money,' Doris said with a laugh.

She picked up the contract, photocopied it, and walked towards the filing cabinet. She took out a folder marked contracts, and inserted it alphabetically. The photocopy was placed into a newly opened file and it was only as she was closing it that she noticed the address.

'Mouse, did Keeley say where she lived?'

'No, I know it's not Eyam, because they came here for a treat, but she didn't say anything other than if she'd stayed local, none of this would have happened.'

'Local is Hope. Her address is two, Journey Street, Hope.'

'How odd that we've two cases both from the same village,' Mouse said, trying desperately to open the sports top of the bottle of water, and not really listening to her nan.

'Tom and Judy's address is one, Journey Street.'

Mouse put the bottle on her desk.

'What?'

'They live next door to each other. The other side of the road has no houses on it, it's open land, hence the consecutive house numbers. What did she say about Henry? His daddy was dead?'

'You don't think…?'

Doris shrugged. 'You said Alice Small spoke about the marriage being on the point of collapse when he was diagnosed with cancer.

I know it's a longshot, but if that young man is Tom's son, it opens up inheritance issues. And I tell you something else, when I saw Henry, it was like seeing someone I already knew. Look at the photograph we have of Tom Carpenter.'

'We need to tell Kat. She's our thinker.'

Doris nodded. 'Let's go home.'

***

The dog sniffed at the body lying half on the path and half in the stream. The blood had attracted him, and he walked around the man several times. He nudged him with his nose, but there was still no reaction. In the end the dog gave up and walked away.

The squirrel high up in the tree watched the dog until it was far enough away to prove no threat, and then it scampered down the trunk and sat for a while on a root. He waited patiently.

***

Mouse and Doris drove home, arriving at the same time as Kat. They helped her in with assorted bags and the baby, then sat for a moment around the kitchen table, watching the sleeping Martha in her car seat.

'She's been so good,' Kat said. 'I've had precious little to do with her; Mum and Dad are besotted.'

'That's good,' Mouse said. 'It will give you peace of mind when you're ready for work again. We've had a strange afternoon. And when it was all over, it got stranger.'

She laid out the contracts on the table, and Kat scrutinised them. 'They're next-door neighbours. Who's Keeley Roy?'

Mouse and Doris explained the circumstances of the afternoon and the final result, telling Kat they had only noticed the addresses once Keeley and Henry had set off for home.

Kat digested their words. 'You think this little boy is Tom's child?'

'We need to do some careful checking, but it kinda finished off the odd circumstances. I'm not sure how we find out, without asking Keeley, and maybe she won't want to tell us. Why is the lawnmower in the middle of the lawn?'

'What?' Kat spun around and stared out of the kitchen window. She stood and walked to the door, unlocked it and went outside. 'Mouse!'

'Nan, watch Martha, will you?'

Mouse followed Kat outside. On the patio table was a small plastic box and a flask – Danny's refreshments. In the middle of the lawn was the lawnmower, and a garden fork was dumped in the middle of the roses.

'Something's wrong,' Kat said. 'Danny wouldn't leave anything like this. You should have heard him tell me off for leaving earth on a trowel last year. I'm worried. I'm going down to the stream. What if he's fallen and needs help…' She walked over to the back of the garden, towards the trickling stream.

She climbed down the incline carefully until she was standing on the well-worn path. Mouse followed her.

7

They spotted the body at the same time.

'No…' Kat breathed, anguish in the one word.

Mouse grabbed her from behind. 'Don't move,' she whispered. 'Think this through first. Why would Danny be down here? Why are the tools left out? What made him leave them to clamber down onto this path? Did he spot somebody here who shouldn't have been? Leon? We can't tackle this, Kat. I won't let you go down there. Let's run back to the house, get that panic button working.'

Kat hesitated, every instinct telling her to go to Danny, but knew, even from that distance, that it was too late for her gentle friend.

Her head slumped and she nodded. 'Quickly, Mouse. We need someone here quickly, just in case…'

***

Nan was standing at the kitchen window when she saw her girls hurtling up from the path into the garden, and knew something bad was happening. Their faces told the story, without having to use words.

She opened the door, and watched as Kat hit the panic button.

***

It was almost exactly a minute later when they heard the first sirens telling them that help was on its way. Mouse was at the front door as the first car pulled onto the drive, and she took the two officers straight through to the kitchen.

She took over the telling of the story when it became obvious that Kat was faltering. The taller of the two officers moved to the back door first.

'I'll take a look,' he said.

'I'm with you,' his colleague responded and they headed across the garden, lowering themselves carefully down onto the path.

They reached the man, and Dave Irwin and Ray Charlton looked at each other. Dave bent down and checked for a pulse, knowing he was only doing it because it was regulations. 'He's gone,' Dave confirmed. 'And it is Danny McLoughlin. I've known him years. Play darts with him at times.'

He spoke into his radio, organising an ambulance and CSI unit and requesting a call from DI Marsden.

***

Within the hour a cordon had been thrown around Eyam, although privately Tessa Marsden thought it was a waste of time. The second Leon Rowe had shot Danny McLoughlin, he would have already been leaving the area. She had no doubt Rowe was to blame for the murderous act; the bullet would indubitably have come from a gun known to them.

Marsden sat at the table with Kat, Mouse and Doris, and opened her notebook. 'I'll need you to make an official statement later, but talk me through this afternoon.'

'There's not much to talk through,' Mouse said. 'Kat and Martha left a couple of minutes earlier than us, just before twelve I guess.'

'Kat?'

Kat nodded. 'That's right. I knew Danny was coming to mow the lawn, so I took Martha out of the way because of the noise. It's a fair size lawn and takes a while to cut. The two of us went to Mum and Dad's place.' As if in confirmation, Martha snuffled in her sleep, and Marsden smiled.

'She's certainly a beautiful baby, Kat. Do you think Leon knew she had been born?'

'I wouldn't have thought so. I suspect he came here to check close up that I was still heavily pregnant, and Danny must have seen him. I've been thinking about this, and it actually leads me to believe Leon saw Mouse and Nan arrive at the shop. I apologise if I'm teaching you to suck eggs, DI Marsden, but have you checked his closed down pharmacy lately? It's directly opposite the shop, and if he's hiding out there, he could have seen them arrive for work, and then come up here to spy on me. He could have been watching us for weeks, months even.'

'It's sealed off, has been since we closed him down.'

'Sealed off with that?'

Tessa felt embarrassed as she answered. 'A padlock. And boards at the windows.'

'A padlock?' Doris stared at the police officer. 'You've put our lives at risk by using a padlock?'

Tessa picked up her radio. 'I want a firearms unit to Eyam. Meet me in the village square. This is urgent.'

She stood. 'I'll be back later to finish this conversation. I'm leaving two officers here with you, and use the buttons if you need to.'

***

Marsden parked outside the supermarket and looked at the pharmacy, once a thriving village chemist's shop. Its pharmacist was locked up for two years, the shortest of the sentences handed out to the members of Leon Rowe's empire who were behind bars for many combined years. Brian King would never come out, and Marsden was beginning to think Leon Rowe would never go in. The man had a charmed life.

All the shops in the square were on lockdown, with police officers inside with the customers. It was a briefly ironic thought that she hoped Leon Rowe hadn't decided to buy himself a loaf of bread as the doors were locked, keeping him on the inside.

She glanced across at Connection, pleased to have been kept informed of every stage of its development and equally pleased that it seemed to be growing in stature for the three women she had come to know and respect.

The view in her mirror changed as a car pulled up behind her. Dave Irwin held up a hand in acknowledgement, and she returned the gesture.

A minute later they were joined by the large firearms unit vehicle. She wound down her window and held out her warrant card.

The lead officer from the van used the cover of the two cars to approach her, and asked if there had been any sightings.

'No. That pharmacy is the focus of this exercise. The entry door is down the alley at the side of the shop. It's obviously the back door, where deliveries are taken in. It has been sealed and a padlocked bar is in place.'

'Thank you, ma'am. Stay in your cars, please.'

He headed back to his vehicle, and silently his marksmen appeared on the pavement. She counted six, all heavily armed. She knew she would never get used to the sight of guns on British streets.

They crept along the front of the boarded up shop, and five of them disappeared down the alleyway. One was positioned outside the front of the shop, his gun at the ready.

She listened carefully. Silence. There should have been the noise involved with smashing open a heavy duty padlock, but there was nothing and instinctively she knew it meant that Leon Rowe had been inside the shop, possibly hiding there for some time.

She wasn't aware of how long she waited; the men reappeared and one headed towards her.

'Sergeant Franks would like you to go in, ma'am.'

'Thank you.' She turned and indicated to Dave Irwin to accompany her.

They walked to the shop together. 'Looks like he's not here now, but I'll lay odds on that he was,' Dave said.

'I suspect you're right, Dave. They certainly didn't have to smash off that padlock.'

It was extremely dark inside, tiny chinks of light came through the boards, but she switched on her torch as they followed Sergeant Franks up the stairs.

'This is the first floor,' he said. 'Still got some items stored in here, and some boxes of foodstuffs are opened, so I reckon he's been using them to save having to go out for food. He's definitely been staying here.' He led them to a further set of steps, ones that had appeared from the loft hatch in the ceiling. 'I'll go up first, ma'am, it's awkward getting out at the top.'

Once they had been helped through, Tessa and Dave moved further into the attic room. There was a sleeping bag with a blanket thrown over it, and a further blanket rolled up and used as a pillow. Several candles stood on saucers, all burnt down to some degree.

'We've thoroughly checked everywhere, ma'am, and he's gone. I don't believe he came back here after the shooting, if it was him who shot your victim, because the loft ladder you've just climbed up was folded away. If he was running, he wouldn't have taken the time to do that. It's an awkward procedure; it doesn't quite fit correctly, which is why it was difficult for you to get off it when we came up here.'

She nodded. 'He would have taken his sleeping bag if he'd come back here. It's going to be pretty cold at night without it.' She stared around at the spartan conditions in the loft. It was a large space, and daylight showed through where a couple of slate pieces were missing. The small window in the roof looked directly onto the village square, and she realised it was perfectly positioned for him following the movements of the three women who had brought the wrath of the gods down on his head.

'How are the mighty fallen,' Tessa mused aloud, thinking of the beautiful home he had lost, and where his wife and daughter lived.

'Thank you, Sergeant Franks, for your help. Stand your men down for now and return to base. I'm sure when we do find Leon Rowe, we'll probably need you again. I'll get forensics up here, let them prove it's Leon Rowe's hideaway, and then I'm going on television. I want this man found, and I don't want him walking into one of the many camping and hiking shops we have in the Peak District, to replace his sleeping bag. I shall be asking all of them to look out for him buying any camping equipment at all; he's got to sleep somewhere.'

Franks nodded. 'Thank you, ma'am. I'll leave it with you. Be careful going back down those stairs.'

***

Marsden watched as they emptied the loft space of everything that was in it, and she quietly asked for results as speedily as possible. She needed proof legally that Rowe had been the occupant; in her heart she needed no proof. She knew it was him.

Crime scene tape was once again wrapped around the building, the side door was re-padlocked, with promises of a sheet of metal covering the entire aperture being installed as soon as it was no longer going to be needed by forensics.

Ray Charlton was standing outside the front of the shop, and all three of them walked back to their respective cars.

'You two go back to the station, write up your reports and get off home. Tell everybody it's a seven o'clock briefing tomorrow. I want everybody there for half past six on pain of death. We have to find this man.'

'You're going home, boss?'

She shook her head. 'No, I'm going to try to get a two-minute slot on the late news that's local for the Peak District and the Sheffield area. I need to alert shops. He's going to need equipment replaced. Not on my watch, Leon Rowe, not on my watch. I'll head back up and fill Kat Rowe in on what's happened, but first I have to go see Danny McLoughlin's family.'

***

'Mrs McLoughlin?' Tessa showed her warrant card. 'My name is Tessa Marsden, and this is PC Hannah Granger.'

49

Hannah had been with Kat, Mouse and Doris since they had arrived en masse at Kat's house earlier, and would have preferred staying there to having to go to tell somebody their husband was dead. Kat, in her role as deacon of St Lawrence's, wanted to accompany her, but Hannah had suggested it might be better to wait a day, let the news sink in with his family first.

She had no idea which was the best one, but Kat looked ill. A two-day-old baby, and she was feeling she had to go back to work – not a good plan, Hannah decided.

'Oh! Yes? You want something?' Bibi McLoughlin stared at the two women in front of her, a bewildered expression on her face.

'May we come in, please, Mrs McLoughlin?' Tessa's voice was gentle.

'Mais oui. Please, follow me. But what is this about?' Her French accent was strong, although she spoke perfect English.

She led them into a small lounge with pale grey walls and bright yellow curtains and cushions, a welcoming room that impressed both police officers.

'Please... take a seat. What is wrong?'

They waited until the three of them were sitting on the chairs indicated by Bibi, and then Tessa spoke.

'I'm sorry, Mrs McLoughlin, but we have some bad news for you. Your husband, Danny, died this afternoon.'

Bibi looked at Marsden first, then Hannah. 'What? He is working. At Kat's house. Then he was going to do a quote in Bakewell. He can't be dead.' Her eyes opened wide, and Hannah could see she was struggling to accept what they were saying.

'Can I get you something, Mrs McLoughlin? Cup of tea? Glass of water?'

Bibi shook her head. 'No, I'm fine. You must have the wrong person. My Danny is at work.'

'I'm sorry, Mrs McLoughlin, but we are sure it is your husband. He was at work at Mrs Rowe's property. We believe he saw an intruder and gave chase. The intruder shot him.'

Bibi's silence stretched on and on, until finally she spoke. 'Maybe a glass of water…'

Hannah stood and went to find the kitchen. She returned to see Marsden holding Bibi's hand, and the woman shaking uncontrollably.

'How will I live without him?' she whispered.

Nobody answered her. Nobody could.

Bibi let go of Tessa's hand and took the glass of water.

'Merci,' she said, and sipped at it.

'Do you have anyone we can contact? You shouldn't be on your own.' *Platitudes, all platitudes,* Tessa thought. *This woman is struggling.*

'Our daughter, Petra Hunter. She lives in Grindleford. It will only take her ten minutes to get here. Please… be gentle when you tell her. She adores her father.'

***

Petra and Iain Hunter took over, comforting Bibi, promising they wouldn't leave her, allowing Tessa and Hannah to head back to Kat's house.

Two officers were stationed at the front, and two in the back garden. Photographs had been taken of the lawnmower, garden fork, and Danny's flask and sandwich box; the tools had been fingerprinted and put away, and the flask and sandwich box bagged in evidence bags.

Marsden and Hannah went into the house through the garden door. Kat was feeding Martha, and the other two women were on their laptops. Both closed them as the police officers entered the room.

Kat lifted her head. 'You didn't find him?'

'We confirmed he had been hiding in the loft of the pharmacy, but he's gone now. He can't have gone back there; his sleeping bag and blankets were still on the floor. I think he would have taken them, he has to sleep somewhere and it's still damn cold at night.'

'Was there a large brown suitcase?'

'No.' Marsden shook her head.

'Then he has somewhere else set up. When he broke in here,' Kat said, 'he took a suitcase full of his stuff from the wardrobe. He has a back-up hiding place, DI Marsden. I know the way my husband thinks, particularly about me. He only stayed at the pharmacy once he realised I was pregnant.'

8

Marsden, back in her office, called in reinforcements. She led the briefing, filling everybody in on the events of the day, and added that nothing was more important than catching Leon Rowe.

Full protection had been afforded to Kat Rowe, Beth Walters and Doris Lester, and Marsden was confident that it would be sufficient to keep them safe.

'Where do we start, boss?' Tessa heard the question from three different places.

'We start with every piece of available CCTV in that village, and every house on every road out of the village must have a visit. Ray, can I leave you to organise a map and allocate officers to the visits, please? Leon Rowe is very recognisable; his dark, dark skin is obvious, and I would imagine everyone in Eyam knows him, through the pharmacy. I want full reports of every visit you undertake by tomorrow, then go out again and carry on. Somebody must have a clue where this man is, he's too well known to just disappear.'

Marsden left the briefing room, and sank into her own leather chair behind her own desk, in her own office. Exhausted. Her mind was full of Leon Rowe. Where had the bastard fled to this time? She briefly closed her eyes and tried to envisage him, running across the Derbyshire landscape, heading for sanctuary before anyone saw the black face and connected him with the missing man.

***

Five minutes later she was outside the station, a bank of cameras and microphones in front of her, talking to the people who were at considerable risk. 'Do not approach this man; we believe he has already killed today and is in possession of a gun. If you see him, we need to know immediately. And now I have a special message for the owners and staff of camping and hiking gear shops in the entire region. He no longer has the survival gear he had, we have that. It may be that he tries to buy more. Please study his photograph. If he comes into your shop, don't challenge him, he is dangerous. We need it reporting as soon as you can get to a phone.'

As she spoke the words she knew that every black male who walked into any sort of shop in Derbyshire would be reported. But there just may be that one…

She thanked the public and stepped away from the microphone.

***

Leon Rowe watched the broadcast on his mobile phone and smiled. *Smart arse,* he thought. He recognised the picture that had been displayed; Kat had taken it in the days when they were happy, loved each other, hated being apart.

Leon still hated being apart. Brian King's greed had led to Leon's present predicament; wanting more than he was prepared to offer from the business. Brian's sentence had pleased Leon. He had proved not to be the loyal friend Leon had always thought he had, and the stupid man had talked.

Leon smiled to himself as he thought of the others that Brian had taken down with him, all equally incarcerated and gunning for the ginger-haired idiot. If Brian lasted another year, he would be lucky.

Leon's phone was losing power so he stood and plugged it into the charger, His bolthole looked nothing from the outside and had served him well for a few months while he made his plans to leave the country, and recuperate from the loss of his left hand brought about by Doris, the gun-toting granny. Obviously her admiration for him had died a death that day.

The old petrol station was well set up for his everyday needs and had been bought for the specific reason it was now being used. The large front doors hadn't been opened for years, and he needed to get them to open… just in case. The small back door – very small, he had to duck his head to enter – was his preferred method of accessing his property. Long before he met Kat he had recognised he might need an escape one day.

An efficient generator took care of his electrical needs and the building itself was perfectly positioned away from any other properties. He could take time to work out what to do next. Until he had seen the baby, he could make no decisions.

He spent the evening cleaning his gun, regretting that it had been Danny McLoughlin who had taken a bullet. He liked Danny, one of the good guys. He guessed Danny hadn't thought the same about him.

Leon left a candle burning through the night. If anything happened he didn't want to be fumbling around in the dark, he needed to be able to see. He sank down into his sleeping bag and grinned. *It's okay, Marsden,* he thought, *I don't need a new one. Stand down your army of shop assistants.*

***

Nobody really wanted breakfast, and yet all three knew they should have something. In the end they settled on cornflakes, so their stomachs knew they had eaten.

Doris tilted the teapot, poured out the tea and they all picked up their cups at the same time. Speech wasn't coming easily.

Eventually Mouse took out her diary. 'Okay, we can't sit around here moping. If we do, bloody Rowe will have won.'

'Don't swear, dear.'

'Sorry, Nan.' The response was automatic. 'I'm going to see Keeley Roy, see if I can get anything out of her. I can't just say, "is Henry the love child of Tom Carpenter", so I'll cobble together an invoice that says it was a pro bono job, but I need her signature for our accountant.'

Doris held up her thumb. 'When in doubt, blame the accountant.'

'You three are staying here,' she said. 'Please don't go out. This is the safest place for you at the moment.'

'Martha promises she won't walk out of that door, not for all the tea in China,' Kat said solemnly.

'Kat, I'm serious. Leon killed yesterday, outside here. Nan, I'm trusting you to control Kat. Make sure she rests.'

'Don't worry, she will.'

And Kat knew she would.

***

Keeley looked surprised to see Mouse. 'Is everything okay?'

'Yes, it's all good. I need your signature on an invoice that basically says no charge, but we need it for our accounts.'

'Okay, come in.' Keeley held the door open. 'Tea?'

'That would be lovely.'

Mouse followed Keeley into the kitchen and sat at the table. 'You're okay after yesterday?'

Keeley smiled as she switched on the kettle. 'I'm fine. I can't believe I sat on the floor and cried. I'm such a wuss. I just felt… overwhelmed.'

'Natural reaction. You'd had your money stolen. It can't be easy bringing a child up on your own, and I presume you only work part time?'

'I do. It'll get easier as Henry gets older, but it's a struggle at the moment. We get by, but it's the extras in life that floor me.'

'What happened to Henry's father? Don't answer if I'm being nosy. I don't mean to be.'

'He died last year. Cancer.'

'I'm so sorry. That must have been hard for you both.'

'It was more than hard for me, but Henry didn't know he was his father. He thought he was simply our neighbour.'

The kettle clicked off and Keeley poured water into the mugs. There was silence while she made the drinks, and then she sat down at the table with Mouse.

'He was older than me, by about ten years, but we got on so well. Three years after we met at our front gates, we had Henry, but Tom didn't have the courage to leave her, his wife. She's a bit of a psychopath. I know he was scared how she would react, he thought I would be in danger, and possibly Henry. I said it didn't matter, I loved him anyway, and I was prepared to wait.'

Mouse sat quietly. This was more than she could have hoped for, and it seemed ridiculous that she had worried all the way over to Hope how she would approach the subject. She suspected Keeley didn't have many people she could talk to about the tragedy that had hit her; Mouse was happy to listen.

'He died the width of a wall away from me. I saw the doctor come, and I knew. The next day his wife came around and told me. She actually smiled. I'm sure she knew about us. But, it didn't matter, we loved one another and we had the child he longed for. Tom's mum and dad couldn't have children and they adopted him. Tom was so happy when Henry was born. It added something to our relationship, and it gave him a blood relative. Henry looks a lot more like his daddy than he does his mummy,' Keeley added, pride in her voice.

'That must compensate in some way. However, you've taken me a little bit by surprise.' Mouse hadn't anticipated Keeley being quite so forthcoming, and knew that she had to tell her that Judy Carpenter had employed them. If it came out later, it could be catastrophic.

'Tom's wife, Judy, is our client. Everything you've just told me hadn't occurred to me at all.' She offered up a silent wish that the lie would never be discovered. 'I obviously can't tell you why she is our client, but I promise I will never speak of you to her. The case she has asked us to check out doesn't impinge on your life.'

Mouse saw Keeley's face relax slightly.

'That's a relief. It's all very well me saying she suspects, but she doesn't know for definite. And I've no intentions of admitting anything to her. She's a nasty piece of work. If she found out, I would have to move. I don't want to leave my memories of what I shared with Tom behind, and those memories are all linked to this house.'

Mouse breathed a sigh of relief. She felt she had covered the bases; Keeley trusted her.

They talked of inconsequential things, including how Tom visited her by going up into his loft and down through hers. The whole row of six terraced cottages, typical Derbyshire homes, had a huge shared loft space.

Keeley's tone was wistful. 'I remember the night he told me about the cancer. We cried together. That was the last time he used the loft route to see me, he wasn't well enough. He tried to spend time with Henry, but Judy was always there, watching his every move. He only lived eighteen weeks after getting the terminal diagnosis. I loved him so much, but he didn't have time to make provision for Henry, and to be honest, I didn't even think about it until Henry needed new school shoes. Tom had bought his shoes right from the very first pair of Clark's, and I had to think twice about whether I could afford Clark's for him any longer.'

'I'm pretty sure you would be able to make a claim against Judy, but it would mean having a DNA test done.'

Keeley shook her head. 'Not an earthly. I'll manage.'

Mouse smiled. 'I knew you'd say that.' She finished her drink and stood. 'I'll head back now. Thank you for the cuppa, and have a lovely holiday.'

***

Keeley walked Mouse to the door, and watched until she had driven away. Keeley wondered what the invoice was that Beth Walters had brought her to sign. She certainly hadn't signed one; hadn't even seen one.

9

Kat laid Martha down in the crib and just for a moment, Kat stood and gazed at her perfection. All the bad things that had happened over the last year were still hovering over them, blighting their lives, but this one tiny individual had brought sunshine.

Doris came and stood beside Kat.

'Look at us,' Kat said. 'Grinning like Cheshire cats. I've been up twice in the night with her, and smiled through it all.'

'She seems to be a good baby so far, Kat. You go and have a rest while she's sleeping, we can take care of her if she wakes. I'm working on the Carpenter case, hoping some information has come in, but until it does I can multi-task and listen out for this little one. I left a programme running overnight, so it should be delivering something soon.'

Kat held up her hand in mock horror. 'I don't want to know. Just tell me the results, not how you got them.'

***

The front door opened and they heard Mouse speaking to the officer stationed on the driveway. She walked through to the lounge, crossed the room and looked down into the crib. 'Perfect,' she said. She turned to Kat and Doris. 'I have news.'

'Good. I'm hoping I do, as well,' Doris responded. 'But let's move into the kitchen, then we won't wake Martha. Kat, go and rest.'

'Are you kidding?' Kat raised her eyebrows. 'I'm going nowhere if everybody has news. I promise I'll not do anything, but I'm staying down here.'

Doris gave in, and made coffees for all four police officers tasked with keeping them safe, before joining Kat and Mouse around the kitchen table, cradling their own drinks. Both Mouse and Doris opened their laptops.

There was a sharp intake of breath and Doris punched the air. 'Tom Carpenter's birth mother, Pamela Bird, lives or lived in Buxton. I'll do the electoral check, find out if she's still alive, where she's living now, that sort of minor detail,' Doris added, a huge smile on her face. 'Then we need to tell Judy Carpenter we will make the initial contact by letter, not just go in with heavy boots on.'

'And now, of course, there's a further complication.' Mouse's face held no smile. 'Little Henry Roy is Tom Carpenter's son. He would have a very legitimate claim on his father's estate, and it's quite possible Tom's birth mother will want to be a part of her grandson's life. She loved Tom very much, we could tell that by the letter she left for him. It's too late for that relationship, but it's not too late for her to bond with his son.'

Kat sipped slowly at her coffee, her thoughts playing with the information rolling around the table. 'Why does Judy Carpenter want to know who Tom's birth mother is? There's something not right here.'

'Hey,' Mouse said with a clap of her hands. 'Our thinker is back. Talk us through what you mean, Kat. I also feel we need some brainstorming on this one, something's not sitting right, as you said.'

Kat marshalled her thoughts. 'I just can't see what Judy gains from knowing who the mother is. Judy and Tom had no children, so it's not even as though she wants a grandmother figure for anybody. I think we need more facts on Pamela Bird before we let on to Judy that we've found out anything.' Kat leaned back. 'And all that is without recourse to a laptop.'

'You're right. We'll send her an interim report telling her we're following several leads, and we'll get back to her with full results as soon as we can.'

Doris exhaled slowly. 'Wow…'

'Nan?' Kat stood and moved behind Doris to look at her screen. 'Wow is the right word. Where's that?'

'It's where Pamela Bird lives,' Doris said. 'My thoughts, for what they're worth, are that Judy Carpenter knows this. She simply doesn't know how to approach Pamela Bird without it looking as though she's in it for Pamela's money. If the initial approach comes from a reputable agency, it makes it so much more official and acceptable. I'll bet anything that when we tell her we have nothing to report yet, she just accepts it. All she has to do is wait for us to furnish her with Pamela on a plate, and she's in. There's no rush, as far as she's concerned, as long as it all looks above board. Do you two agree?'

'Unfortunately I do,' Kat said.

'Me too.' Mouse's frown said more than her words. 'Alice said that Tom wanted her to look after the stuff he had accumulated about his adoption, and it was really because he didn't want Judy involved in it. What if Judy had already seen it? I bet if we could get sight of Judy's phone, we'd find pictures of all the documents including Tom's birth certificate with his mother's name on it.'

'It's been easy finding this house, and Google Earth provided the picture,' Doris explained for Kat's benefit, pre-empting Kat's next question.

Kat dipped her head to look at the picture once more. 'If she owns this, she's loaded.'

'Give me a couple of minutes and I'll let you know,' Doris said, her fingers already flying across the keyboard.

***

There was a tap on the kitchen window and the taller of the two officers held up empty mugs. Mouse left her seat and went to the door. She took the cups and leaned against the jamb, chatting.

Kat looked at Doris and grinned. 'It's love.'

'You think?'

'She follows him with her eyes. Quite funny really.'

Doris waggled her fingers. 'Not funny at all. You have any idea how much working outside the box that girl does to get the results we need? And she's fancying a policeman?'

***

Mouse closed the door gently, then locked it before returning to the table. The two women looked at her.

'What?' she said. 'Stop looking at me.'

'What? What?' Doris tried to keep a serious face. 'He's a policeman.'

Mouse giggled. 'I know. I love a uniform. You found anything about that house?'

'I have. It just came through. Pamela Bird owns it outright. Her late husband was CEO of a manufacturing company in Derby, died eighteen months ago. I'll track down his will, see what we can find out about their family.'

'Okay. What about we tell Judy we've found the birth mother's identity, but we now have to contact her for permission to release her details as it is Judy's late husband who is the relative, and not Judy herself.' Kat spoke slowly, thinking things through as she talked.

'I think it's vital we don't tell her too much,' Doris agreed. 'Not at this stage, and certainly not if we get proof of what we're all thinking about her. Maybe we should do a bit of a side-track now and have a look at her – we're uneasy about her motives, aren't we?'

Mouse lifted her head from her screen. 'It's not only us, though, is it? Alice Small didn't have anything good to say about her. She knew the relationship between Judy and Tom had run its course.'

'Then here's what we need to do,' Kat said. 'Firstly, we need to interview Judy, explain we can't just pass the name over, but we're happy to broker the meeting between her and the birth mother. We don't need to admit at this stage that we know who she is, we're paving the way for the next stage once we do have a name. We'll see what reaction we get to that. Plan?'

Mouse and Doris bobbed their heads in unison. 'Plan.'

'And I think it's important we're there to see her face, rather than email her. If this had been straightforward, an email would have given the information we're going to tell her, which is basically nothing at all really, but I for one would like to see her reaction.' Kat paused, waiting for the inevitable *you're not ready yet*.

'Then we'll go together,' Mouse said. 'You're doing nothing without back-up until loony Leon is caught.' She turned to look out of the kitchen window. 'We'll take two of our protectors with us, and leave two here with Nan.'

Kat grinned. It didn't take a genius to work out which one Mouse would like to be their driver. She pulled her own unopened laptop towards her. 'You want me to start filling in the results sheet?' It was one of the necessary actions she had actually mastered.

'Yes, please, Kat,' Doris said. 'But bear in mind you're officially on maternity leave...'

'Martha's asleep,' Kat said.

10

Leon opened a tin of soup and poured it into a pan. He warmed it using a small gas ring, craving steak and chips washed down with an expensive bottle of Chateauneuf du Pape.

His thoughts flickered to the fourth wedding anniversary meal he had shared with Kat, seeing that night as the beginning of the end of their marriage, their love. He wondered how Kat had reacted to the news that she was pregnant. Had there, at any point, been thoughts of an abortion? Had she hated him that much?

His mind flashed to the sight of her on the bedroom floor, blood pouring from the head wound he had caused. She had reason to despise him, and as everything about his life had come out, he guessed she must be regretting ever having met him.

The soup started to bubble; he lifted the pan and poured chunks of vegetables into his plastic dish. He dipped in Ryvita, detesting the cardboard taste and sensation but knowing he had no chance at all of going outside during daylight hours to buy bread. His dessert was two digestive biscuits and a black coffee, but once the hunger pangs had been sated he felt more positive, more in control.

He needed to find out when the baby was due. That was a priority.

***

The baby in question was hungry just like her daddy had been, and eagerly took the milk Kat proffered. Doris and Mouse remained in the kitchen, allowing Kat to have a modicum of peace.

Kat finished feeding Martha and sat her upright, grinning inanely as the burp rattled out of the baby. Who would have thought that such an anti-social activity as a burp would cause her so much happiness, she mused.

She replaced Martha in her crib then carried the Moses basket up to her bedroom, placed it in the cot, switched on the monitor and said, 'Night, God bless, my little one.'

Returning to the kitchen carrying a nappy and the empty baby bottle, she was surprised by a cup of tea waiting for her.

'We heard your conversation on the baby monitor,' Mouse explained. 'And tonight I'll have Martha in my room, if you're okay with that. I'll feed and change her and you can sleep all night. How hard can it be to look after a baby?'

Kat and Doris looked at each other, and Doris shook her head, bemused. 'You'll probably find out tonight,' she said.

Kat hugged Mouse. 'You're a star. Thank you so much. I'm trying to ignore the exhaustion.'

'Will you be okay to go and see Judy tomorrow? We'll only be an hour, so if we go after Martha's feed, she should sleep till we get back, and Nan won't have any worries.'

Doris looked up. 'Can I just explain to you two numpties, I am the only one in this room with experience in babies? Bethan Walters, I've cleaned up your arse more times than I care to think about, mopped up your sick, made endless bottles for you – and I did the same for your mother. And, what's more,' she said with a finality that invited no argument, 'I bet I know twice as many nursery rhymes as the two of you put together.'

Kat turned to Mouse. 'She'll be fine,' she said, trying desperately to keep the serious expression on her face.

Mouse looked horrified. 'She called me Bethan Walters. I must be in trouble, she only calls me by my proper name when I've done something wrong.'

Doris said nothing further on the subject; she quietly sang *Humpty Dumpty*, and Kat continued with the reports she had to type. Mouse slipped out into the garden to organise the police escort for them for the following day, and came back in feeling disgruntled.

'He's not on duty tomorrow,' she said, her back to Doris and Kat as she locked and bolted the kitchen door. She missed seeing the grins on their faces.

'Told you it's love,' Kat whispered.

***

There was quiet for a time, and then Mouse closed her laptop. 'So, let's just talk a couple of things through. We've had no word about one-handed Rowe then?' The reference was to the fact that Doris had blown away his left hand with a well-placed bullet.

'None at all. Marsden hasn't been in touch,' Kat confirmed. 'He's definitely got a hideaway somewhere. He was only using the empty shop to keep an eye on me. He's gone back to his first place, and nobody's safe until they find him. I know she thought he might be having to replace his camping stuff, but I know Leon. He wouldn't leave anything to chance. Wherever he is, it'll be well set up for him. And he'll have had it years.'

'Kat, did you ever notice any strange payments coming out of your joint account? Things that you queried at the time?' Mouse's mind was in overdrive.

'I never saw any statements. Leon dealt with everything. All the household bills came out of the joint account. I had my own personal one that was really for me to spend on what I wanted, when I wanted it. He had an automatic top-up set up on it when it dropped below five grand.'

'Kat, please tell me there isn't still a joint account!'

Kat shrugged. 'I suppose there must be. I've never used it, so wouldn't know. But he'll not have access to it. When he went, I withdrew the contents, and I've not touched it since. I know the police blocked his business accounts, but nothing was ever said about me taking out that money. I used the cash for a while then put the last few thousand into my account. That all happened six months ago and nobody queried it.'

Mouse rolled her eyes. 'Kat Rowe, you scare me. I'll get the statements. Let's not make waves that could drown us by going down official channels. We'll have a look at them, if that's okay with you, Kat. This is your personal life…'

Kat laughed. 'The whole world knows my personal life, thanks to Leon.'

'Then I'll get them up on screen.' Mouse saw the panicked look on Kat's face, the same look that appeared every time screens were mentioned. 'Stop worrying, Kat, you'll simply have to scroll.'

The relief was evident in Kat's exhalation of breath.

***

Doris watched her two girls chatting, and shook her head. She had taught many people the intricacies of assorted computer activities, but she couldn't teach confidence. Each student had to find their own level of that. Kat knew so much more than she had when they first met, but her insecurity refused to let her believe it.

Doris reached her hand across the table and squeezed Kat's fingers. 'Sit next to me, Kat, you'll be fine. We'll be examining every entry; in particular, look for utilities. Gas, electric, water bills, because if he has a bolthole he'll need some kind of power.'

Mouse lifted her head and looked at them. 'I figured that, but I reckon Leon's too smart to leave that trail. A generator and camping gas take care of gas and electricity, and bottled water covers water. We're really going to have scrutinise every little entry, debit or credit. Somewhere there has to be something that tells us where he's hiding away. Don't close your minds to other things by concentrating on utilities. He may pay rent on a property, may even have bought one. And tonight we're only looking at the joint account. Did he have a personal account, Kat?'

'He did. And let's not forget he had credit cards.'

'And presumably off-shore accounts,' Doris said drily. 'Surely the police will have checked everything we're looking at?'

'They will,' Mouse said. 'But we have something they don't have. We have Kat, who has intimate knowledge of their lifestyle. And what's more, it would have been about nine months ago when Leon scarpered and they checked these accounts. I know he won't have used them since then, but nine months ago they couldn't have realised he would have a bolthole, so what they were looking for then isn't what we're looking for now. Sometimes immediacy isn't so good.'

'You're right, of course,' Doris said. 'And his joint account would be about household bills and other such simple things; direct debits, standing orders, all would have been checked out, but as I keep saying, Leon was damn clever. Hiding something in plain sight? In a joint account used for household expenditure? That's clever.'

Kat was listening to the backwards and forwards ideas coming from Doris and Mouse. Finally she spoke. 'And the police could access his accounts legally? Because I didn't give them his ID and passwords. Nobody asked for them.'

Doris and Mouse moved as one and swung around in their seats to face her.

'You have them?' Doris asked.

'Yes. He wrote every one down, even his Amazon login.'

'And the police didn't find it?' Mouse knew they had taken the house apart after Leon's vanishing act.

'I wouldn't think so. They never asked me for the combination of my safe, so I'm assuming they didn't go into it. That's where he told me to keep the list.'

'Where is your safe? I'm presuming it's not the one built into the lounge wall?' Doris spoke quietly, scared of raising her hopes that Mouse wouldn't have to take risks hacking bank accounts.

'The big one in the lounge was Leon's, to keep papers and stuff secure. Sometimes money, which I now presume was drugs money, although I didn't know that at the time.' She hesitated. 'I was the ideal partner for him, wasn't I? Silly little church deacon Katerina, his thirty-year-old virgin who knew very little of life outside Eyam.' Her tone was bitter.

Shaking her head, she forced a smile. 'My much smaller safe was for keeping my jewellery secure. When we had our bedroom altered and fitted with built-in furniture, he had the safe concealed in my dressing table. You wouldn't know it was there, and you have to know how to release the central panel. The safe is under that.'

'And Leon didn't go into it when he broke in?'

'No. He set the code when I began to use it, but I struggled to remember the right sequence of the numbers. I reset it, but never thought to tell him.'

'So we have all the information we need to access the accounts legally?' Mouse asked.

'We do,' Kat conceded. 'He wrote everything down just in case he ever had an accident – he did a lot of motorway driving. When Martha wakes, I'll take you up and show you exactly how to access it and what the combination is. The contents are for Martha, should anything happen to me.'

'Understood,' Mouse said. 'But please put that in writing. Until the murdering bastard is either dead or divorced, he's your next of kin. Write it down, sign it, we'll witness it, and leave it with your solicitor.'

'Don't swear, please, Mouse,' Doris said, looking up from her screen. 'It doesn't become you.' She was aware that the girls ignored her protestations, but she figured she might as well keep on telling them, maybe one day they would listen.

11

There hours later, Martha had enjoyed another nappy change and feed, and had been deposited in Mouse's bedroom for the night.

The three women sat on Kat's bed and looked at her dressing table.

'There's no clue that it isn't just a solid piece of furniture,' Mouse said.

The dressing table top was segmented into three separate areas; the two sides were almost oval in shape, linked by a straight central piece. The mirror was a triptych with a large central mirror surrounded by lights, and two half-size side mirrors. Underneath the attractive marbled surface were three small drawers, shaped to fit the contours of the top.

'Can you see anything that would reveal a hidden compartment?' Kat asked.

Doris and Mouse scrutinised the piece of furniture and eventually conceded defeat.

'I can understand why the police didn't find it. I can't see anything, and it would certainly bamboozle any burglar,' Doris said with a smile. 'It's genius.'

Kat stood, moving towards the dressing table. 'Watch,' she said, and angled the right-hand mirror slightly inwards. There was an almost inaudible click. 'Did you see anything move?'

'Only you moving the mirror.'

Kat put her fingers under the overlap of the dressing table top and lifted. Inside was the safe.

'Good lord,' Doris said, and moved towards the piece of furniture. 'That's brilliant. The front part is a regular drawer, the back half the safe. Is the release catch on the mirror?'

'It's actually concealed in the hinge, but all it does is make that tiny click. The top doesn't move, so a burglar wouldn't know anything had happened at all.'

Mouse joined them. 'And Leon's passcodes are all in there?'

'Yes. My combination is 0873. It's not written down anywhere so we're the only three who know it.' Kat keyed in the digits and the safe door opened. She shuffled the boxes until she saw the one with Cartier on the lid.

Nestled inside were shards of light and brilliance in the form of diamond earrings. She pulled forward the padded velvet cushion that secured the jewels in place and lifted out the piece of paper underneath.

Mouse held out her hand and Kat passed her the paper.

'Not that, numpty, the earrings,' she said with a grin. Kat handed over the box and then lifted out other boxes.

'While we've got it open you may as well look at them all.'

For a brief moment, the three women put aside all other issues and enjoyed the immense pleasure afforded by the sparkle of the stones, the gleam and weight of the gold and platinum.

'Leon certainly loved you,' Doris murmured, stroking the ruby pendant.

'Not enough to give up his lifestyle,' Kat said drily.

They carefully replaced every item in the safe, and then Kat took them through opening it.

'Kat, say no if this isn't appropriate, but the gun Leon forced us to have is fully operational even after being in the freezer. It's cleaned and ready for use. Again,' Doris added the final word with a twinkle in her eye. 'However, it's only hidden in the garage. I would feel happier with it in a safe, either the downstairs one or this one. The downstairs one has its drawbacks in that the police know about it. This smaller one is upstairs and the gun isn't to hand if Leon should happen to come calling, but the police don't know this safe is here.'

'Let's put it in this one, Nan,' Kat said. 'I know Leon knows about this safe, but he can't access anything in it. It's not even a moveable piece of furniture, so he's completely stymied by it. The funny thing is, this was all built at his insistence. I thought it was a bit over the top, but...'

'The joke's on him.' Mouse finished off the sentence.

Doris went down to the garage and retrieved the gun. She checked it was fully loaded and carried it back upstairs.

Five minutes later, the safe was locked, the dressing table put back to its original state.

Mouse hugged Kat. 'Thank you for trusting us with this. I can't even begin to imagine the value of all that stuff in the safe.'

Kat laughed. 'And most of it only worn once. I think it pleased Leon to buy it more than it pleased me to wear it. He also, of course, would have seen it as an investment.'

They headed out of Kat's bedroom and downstairs, where, after an hour of watching television, they decided enough was enough and headed back upstairs.

Kat slept soundly.

Doris read for half an hour then fell asleep, her book resting for the night on the quilt.

Martha slept, lips occasionally twitching as if trying to smile, apart from the two times she woke wanting sustenance.

Mouse hardly closed her eyes. As temporary custodian of the tiny human, it was important she stayed awake. That night convinced her she never wanted children.

***

Leon slept intermittently. His mind wouldn't close down; he needed a plan that would give him access to his wife, and so far he didn't have one.

12

'Come in, ladies.' Judy Carpenter's smile was in place, without reaching her eyes.

The officer designated to accompany Kat and Mouse remained outside, after asking Judy to ensure the door was left unlocked. He even tried it, to satisfy himself.

Kat and Mouse both accepted the offer of a drink, hoping that it would nullify any tension, make their discussions easier.

They waited until Judy had handed them their mugs of tea before speaking.

'Thank you, Judy,' Mouse said. 'We've managed to uncover some details, but felt we should come and chat to you about what happens next. Clearly we can't simply hand the information over, it wouldn't be ethical. There may be reasons why this lady doesn't want any contact with the baby she gave away, so we will make the initial approach by letter. What happens after that will depend on her reply.'

'So you have found her?' There was no smile, just the beginnings of a frown.

'We have her name. We are in the process of uncovering details of where she lives.'

Kat's eyes were glued to Judy's face, watching for any expressive changes. She saw them. The flicker of triumph. Things were going Judy Carpenter's way.

'Tom never disclosed anything about his mother to you?' Kat queried gently.

'He never knew anything.' Judy's response was a shade too quick, too sharp. 'He intended to find her, but once the cancer was diagnosed it became very debilitating, very quickly. It was the last thing on his mind to do. It's why I'm doing it now, in honour of his memory.'

'And you and Tom never had children? It could be a swaying factor in this lady's decision about whether to meet with you or not.' Kat still kept her voice solicitous, gentle.

'No. We had no children. We didn't want any.' Judy's tone was bordering on harsh.

Kat made a note on her pad. It was for show only.

They both sipped at their drink, and waited.

'How quickly will you write to her?'

'As soon as we have an address. We have to go through legal channels…' Mouse said, and Kat swallowed her mouthful of tea quickly in case she choked. She rather thought that Mouse believed a legal channel to be a large body of water between Dover and Calais filled with lawyers swimming across to France.

'I see,' Judy said. 'So… within a week or so we should know something?'

'Hopefully,' Mouse said. 'We will contact you as soon as we hear from the birth mother, whatever she says. You have to be prepared for her not wanting to meet with you. It is her right to say no, although in these enlightened times it would be unusual for her to do that.'

They finished their drinks and, as one, stood to leave. 'Thank you for the tea, Judy,' Mouse said. 'We'll be in touch soon.'

***

'It has to be about the money,' Kat said thoughtfully, peering through the rain battering the windscreen. 'What other possible reason could she have for tracking down Tom's birth mother? It's not a normal thing to do, is it? Pamela Bird, at first sight, seems to be a very wealthy woman. Maybe Judy is playing the long game, making friends with her, becoming a part of her life, inheriting eventually. It's strange, isn't it, but I believe it would simply take the appearance of little Henry Roy in Pamela's life to put a stop to Judy's hopes and dreams.'

'You're spot on, but Keeley doesn't want Judy to know about her and Tom's affair. We can't say anything. It's such a shame because that young man could be a very wealthy young man one day.'

Mouse steered the car onto the drive, and she and Kat jumped out and ran for the shelter of the porch. Their escorting officer waited until they were safely inside the front door before heading back to join his companion for the interminably boring surveillance of the area. Mouse clicked the car locks on, and they crept in. They could hear the strains of *Ten Green Bottles* as they closed the door, and headed for the lounge.

Doris was on the sofa, cradling a somewhat bemused-looking Martha; not yet able to rustle up a smile, but intent on watching the wonderful lady singing to her.

'That's never been a nursery rhyme,' Mouse laughed.

'If it was good enough for you, it's good enough for Martha,' Doris said. 'This baby will be able to add and subtract by the time she is four.'

Kat watched the two of them. 'She'll certainly be better on a computer than her mother is.'

Kat took Mouse's coat and went to put them up to dry in the utility room, before returning to her daughter. Doris seemed keen to hang on to her.

'I don't get to hold her nearly enough,' she said. 'And I certainly feel as though she's part of our family.'

'She is,' Kat said simply. 'She is.'

By the time they had given Doris the details of their conversation with Judy Carpenter, Martha had closed her eyes for her nap. Kat removed her from Doris's arms and placed her in the crib.

Kat smiled down at her daughter. 'It's almost as though she's been here for ever, now, isn't it?'

They switched on the monitor and took the receiver into the kitchen with them. Kat pulled her laptop towards her. 'I'm going to type up this report while I can still remember everything that was said. My baby brain can get a little fuzzy.'

'And I think we need to start going through these accounts of the errant Mr Rowe, Nan,' Mouse said. 'Let's see if we can't find out where he is. Our own lives are on hold until the b–'

'Mouse,' Doris said, her finger raised in the air. 'No swearing, please. Martha might hear.'

There was a humph from Mouse as she opened up her laptop. Inside her head she said, 'Bastard, bastard, bastard.'

***

DI Marsden made an appearance later in the day. She didn't stay long, having said that she was just touching base to reassure them that they were following leads of sightings.

'And you believe these sightings?' Kat asked.

'Not at all,' Tessa responded, a frown creasing her forehead. 'He's far too clever to be seen. But he'll slip up. And we'll be waiting. The fact that he's in this country and every police force in the UK is on the alert for him leaves him with nowhere to go once he moves away from wherever it is he's holed up.'

'But don't you realise what Leon is like, even after all this time?' Kat said. 'He will have been prepared for this happening. Trust me, I know him. He'll have enough food, water, warmth. Creature comforts to keep him going for a long time.'

'And he'll go stir crazy,' Marsden said drily. 'We've made him so well known that he can't move out of whatever property he's found for himself. He's on every news item, that handsome face is so out there that someone is going to recognise him before too long.'

'Let's hope so. We're just as much prisoners as he is, we can't go anywhere.'

'I know.' There was sympathy in Marsden's voice. 'But it will come to an end, and hopefully sooner rather than later. Bibi McLoughlin won't feel any sort of closure until this evil man is caught, either.'

'It should be my job to go and see Bibi, offer her comfort.' Kat's voice was very low. 'I can't even do that for her. I can't even go to my church to pray for her and everybody else touched by Leon's actions. He will expect me to do that, and he could be waiting for me. And now there's Martha to consider…'

'Have patience, Kat,' Marsden said, standing and heading towards the door. 'And trust us. Something will break soon, and it will be Leon Rowe, not us.'

13

Ben Charlton was a little late getting home from school. Knowing nobody would be in the house worrying about where he was, he opted for walking home instead of taking the bus. Living in such a remote location meant the bus dropped him off leaving him with a fifteen-minute stroll anyway, so he took advantage of the afternoon sunshine and walked the whole way. The roads and fields surrounding him as he walked were defined by the beautiful dry-stone walling so embedded in Derbyshire and its history.

His mind was partly on the English homework that he still hadn't finished, and partly on his plans to go down to the river and have an hour's fishing. He did this most days, filling in the time between his arrival home from school and his parents' staggered homecomings from their jobs.

His dad, Ray, was a detective constable working on the Eyam murders, and prone to arriving home at odd hours. His mother, however, he could calculate to the minute; she closed her library at six every day except Friday, when it was seven.

Ben unlocked the front door and walked through to the kitchen. Quickly making a cheese and tomato sauce sandwich, he wrapped it in foil and carried it through to the utility room where he kept his fishing tackle. His basket was tidy and he stored his sandwich, two cans of Coke and the maggots removed from the tiny fridge kept specially for the wriggly creatures, before hoisting it onto his back.

It took him about ten minutes to walk down to his preferred spot on the river bank. Over two years of sitting there had seen him hollow out bits of the bank until he had a secluded place where, if necessary, he could put up his small khaki bivouac.

The sun meant such an activity wasn't called for, so he made secure his chair, popped his drinks and sandwich into the side pockets of his chair and set up his rod and rod rest.

With his alarm set for six, he cast in.

Ben sat quietly, enjoying the moment, then stood and optimistically set up his second rod rest that he used specifically for hanging his keep net; most days he fished and most days he fondly imagined breaking his record of six fish in an hour.

The float wasn't moving so he pulled it out and recast, then threw a few maggots in the area of the float. He balanced his rod on the rest and settled back into his chair.

It was quiet; no sounds of children running on the path above him, no parents telling them to be careful, they could fall into the water. Life was good.

The river wasn't wide at this point, and Ben was surprised to see another angler set up on the opposite bank, about twenty-five yards upstream. He watched the older man struggle to get his seat level, but eventually he seemed settled just as Ben pulled out his first catch. It was a small tench and Ben dealt with it swiftly and efficiently, as his dad had shown him so many times, dropping it into the keep net for the next couple of hours.

He cast in again and watched idly as the man opposite caught one then dropped it straight back into the river. Ben acknowledged the catch with a lift of his hand, repeated by the stranger.

The warmth of the late afternoon sun sank into Ben, and he stared across the river and up the banking towards the derelict petrol station standing a couple of hundred yards from where he was sitting. It had been there for ever as far as Ben was concerned, a bit of an eyesore that was boarded up all the way around, and he couldn't ever remember it being a functioning garage of any kind.

It was while he was musing along the lines of if he had some money he could buy it, do it up and spend the rest of his life fishing this stretch of the river, that he saw movement.

The tiny rear door to the property moved inwards, and at first nothing happened. Ben's eyes were fixed on the building, his float forgotten in his surprise at anybody being inside the abandoned structure.

A minute later, a tall man stepped over the wooden base below the door, pulling his hood up to cover his head and partially obscuring his face as he did so. Nothing could have hidden the dark skin.

Ben froze. He thought he was out of the man's line of sight, but he wasn't sure. The angler on the opposite bank wouldn't have seen anything; his back was to the petrol station. Ben thanked his lucky stars that fishing was a mainly silent occupation and hoped that the man on the other bank wouldn't make any sound.

The tracksuited man had exited the tiny door, lit a cigarette and stood for five minutes or so, unmoving, taking in the warmth and the fresh air.

Ben had noticed his float bobbing up and down but chose to ignore it. He sat, motionless. He did not want the black man's eyes to turn towards him.

Eventually the man ducked and went back inside. Ben breathed easier. He pulled in the float, released the tiny fish back into the river along with the one in the keep net, and took out his phone.

He rang his father, knowing that he would panic as soon as he saw the name Ben on his screen. Ben had never rung his dad at work before.

'Ben?' Ray answered immediately.

'Dad… I think I know where Leon Rowe is.'

***

Ray Charlton couldn't think straight. The panic inside his chest was immeasurable as he waited for the phone call from Ben to say he was safely back at home with all the doors and windows locked.

The team had gathered in the incident room and Ray had pinpointed on the map exactly where the tumbledown building was. His phone was in his hand, and there was an expectant murmur in the room as they all waited to hear that Ben Charlton was out of harm's way. Until that happened, they could do very little. When his phone pinged, there was a collective whoosh of exhalation, of relief.

'Right, troops,' Marsden said. 'The firearms unit will be in position in thirty minutes. The main road going by the property will be closed off here,' she pointed with her stick, 'and here. I want this bloody man alive, so let's hope he doesn't do anything stupid. But one threatening move towards anybody, and they will take him out. Ben is now safe, although we understand that when Ben left the river bank, another man was nearby. Ben says this angler can't be seen from the garage, but that also means we can't see him either. We have to make this man safe before we do anything, so I will take a walk by the place where Ben was, and attempt to speak to this fisherman. Once I've told him to go home, we're clear to get Rowe out of the building.'

Several heads nodded as they listened to her words.

'Let's go. I'll go on my own, it will look less suspicious if he can see that part of the riverbank from the building. There's never a spare little dog around when you want one, is there?' she said, glancing around.

The room cleared quickly, and Tessa drove her own car without taking any officers along with her. She had no idea how much Rowe could see from the garage, and knew it had to look as though she was just a casual walker.

Her hair, always worn for work loosely coiled into a bun, was released from its restraints, and she pulled it forward to hide as much of her face as she could. She was aware that Leon Rowe had seen her on a couple of occasions; it would be disastrous if he recognised her. She hoped that the distance was great enough to make her unrecognisable.

She parked her car some way from the road block set up by the team, and walked down the path that followed the river. The detailed description of just where Ben's fishing spot was had been drilled into her by his father, and she soon found it. Without stopping, she carried on walking, praying that the other angler had given up and gone home.

He hadn't. She walked along until she was directly opposite.

'Have you caught many?' she called across to him.

He smiled at her across the expanse of water. 'Four today. Put them all back though.'

'Have you got a name?'

He looked startled. 'I do. Do you?'

'I do,' she said. 'It's Tessa. DI Tessa Marsden, Derbyshire police. And you?'

He hesitated for a moment. 'It's Malcolm, Malcolm Keane.'

'Right, Malcolm. Can you hear me? I have to speak quietly.'

He nodded. 'I can. Is there a problem?'

'Yes. I want you to act normally, pack everything away and leave the area. Which way will you be walking?'

'Which way do you want me to walk?'

'The way that I've come. When you reach the road, please make yourself known to one of my officers. I'm going to walk on for a couple more minutes, then reverse my journey. Please hurry.'

***

Malcolm nodded, immediately threw everything into his basket and dismantled his rod. Within two minutes, he had set off to walk in the direction he had seen the woman walking. He was intrigued; not scared, but he sure as hell was nosy. And he guessed it was all to do with the young lad who had been quietly fishing on the opposite bank then had suddenly packed everything away.

Malcolm's home was in the opposite direction, but he knew he had to follow the pretty lady's instructions. Somebody would sort him out when he reached the road.

***

Tessa strolled casually back towards where she had left her car and saw that Malcolm was with Hannah and being looked after. She was thankful that he hadn't argued, just seemed to pick up on the gravity of what she was saying. If he had been a younger man, the outcome could have been so different.

She sat in her car and rang Ray, firstly thanking him for the precise details he had given her for the river bank walk.

'You're welcome, boss. That chap's being looked after now, so we're good to go.'

'Not till I've put my bloody hair back up into a bun,' she growled.

***

'Leon Rowe, this is DI Marsden.' Her voice carried at many decibels across the broken concrete of the garage forecourt. 'Please come out with your hands raised, and lie down on the floor.'

She kept the megaphone at her lips and waited. The firearms officers were strategically placed outside the surrounding wall, with three officers in almost the same place that Malcolm had been in half an hour earlier. If Leon chose to run instead of following her instructions, he would either be spending the night in a cell, or on a slab in the mortuary. Tessa hoped it would be the first alternative.

She spoke again. 'Leon, come out now. Don't make us come in to get you.'

Her voice echoed across to the derelict tumbledown structure, and still there was no reaction. She turned to the navy-blue clad figure behind her and shrugged.

He spoke into his shoulder radio. 'Okay. We're moving in.' In the split second that he spoke the last word, the boarded up front door was blasted open by gunfire from the inside. Guns were immediately trained on it and Tessa held her breath.

Forcing herself to breathe slowly, she raised the megaphone to her lips. 'Leon Rowe, throw your gun out first to one side of the door so that we can see it, then exit the property with your hands raised.'

***

Leon stood just inside the door and to one side. What happened next would be on his terms, not bloody Marsden's; he would regret not knowing about his child, regret losing Kat, regret...

He stepped outside, spraying the area with bullets. One shot to the head stopped him.

14

Kat was hurting so badly. Her mother cradled her in her arms, wanting to take the pain away; she knew how deeply her daughter had loved this evil man, but most of all she knew Kat's Christian beliefs would never have let her give up completely on her husband.

And now he was gone.

***

DI Marsden had delivered the information before it appeared on News at Ten, and Kat had held it together, even thanking Marsden for letting them know. Mouse had escorted the DI to the door, then returned to find Doris physically supporting Kat as she went into meltdown.

Mouse immediately rang Enid and Victor, who had arrived wearing pyjamas. They had been settled for the night, and about to head off to bed. Now they were wondering what the hell to do with their devastated daughter, how to comfort her, to let her see there could be a future without Leon Rowe in it.

Kat eventually stopped the sobs, and following Mouse's insistence that she take a couple of paracetamol, she finally drifted off to sleep on the sofa. Enid placed a blanket over her and kissed her forehead.

'What shall we do about Martha?' Enid asked her husband. 'Shall we take her back with us?'

Victor shook his head. 'No. Martha will save her. Kat will be strong for that little one.'

'Don't worry about the baby,' Mouse said. 'I'll take the crib into my room for tonight, we'll let Kat sleep downstairs as she appears to be zoned out completely.'

Enid smiled. 'Thank you, Mouse, I'm sure you're right. But if you need us, you ring. We're only ten minutes away.'

Doris and Mouse escorted them to their car, and watched until they could no longer see their tail lights.

'Shitty night,' Mouse remarked.

'Awful,' Doris agreed, 'and merits a bit of bad language, I reckon.'

***

Mouse stared out of the bedroom window, shocked to realise that the police car that had been so visible for quite a while wasn't there.

No longer needed. The evil that had blighted their lives for so long was gone, and it was as if a dark cloud of lethal gases had evaporated, leaving everything in the world that was good in its place.

Baby Martha would one day have to be told about her father, but she would never have to be influenced by him, by the fact that he existed still.

Leon Rowe was dead.

Mouse punched the air in a silent hallelujah, knowing she could never let Kat see how she felt about his death. She guessed all the partners, wives, mothers, children of Rowe's other victims would all be punching the air over the following days and weeks.

***

Kat woke around six, and the feeling of dread was instant. It was over; the worry had gone, eliminated by a single bullet and without injury to any of the police officers present, but the day, despite the early morning sunshine, felt grey.

She wandered into the kitchen and switched on the kettle.

Five minutes later she was on the patio, clutching a mug of tea, all too aware that their police guards had disappeared. It was good not to have to be alert for every tiny movement, and her logical brain hoped that Bibi McLoughlin would experience closure of a sort for Danny's death.

It felt as though her future for a while would be all about decisions, but for now she would enjoy the peace of the morning, followed by a different sort of peace when she put Martha into her pram for the short walk down to church. She needed prayers, silence and a little solitude.

'Hey, you feeling a bit better?'

Kat turned her head and smiled at Mouse, cradling Martha in her arms.

'She's been fed, you want her?'

'Always,' Kat said, and reached to take the baby. 'We're going to church later. I need to.'

Mouse nodded. 'I know. Nan and I will head down to the office for a while, keep out of your hair while you come to terms with things. Ring us if you need us.'

'You'll tell me whatever I need to know later?'

'We will, but seriously, Kat, I think you need some time out. You've only just given birth, and maternity leave is there for a reason, you know. And then there was last night's news…'

'Martha and I can still work.'

At the stubbornness in Kat's voice, Mouse gave a brief nod.

'Okay, I give in. I'm going to take some time today to put together the letter that we need to send to Pamela Bird. I'll make sure you say yes or no to it before we post it. I'll send it recorded, and for her signature only, so that we know she's got it, and then we'll wait for her to contact us. Sound like a plan?'

'It does. We need to move with this now, because I feel there's so much more to this than when we first picked up the job. The first thing that Pamela Bird is going to ask us is are there any children. Did my son provide me with grandchildren? We have to be prepared to be honest with that, but that means breaking a confidence that Keeley trusted you to keep.'

Mouse gave a huge sigh and looked at her colleague. 'You want a bacon sandwich?'

'Yes, please.'

Mouse grinned. 'You said that, Kat, without moving your lips.' She turned around and saw her nan, already dressed for the day. 'That'll be three bacon sandwiches then, unless Martha wants one as well.'

***

By half past nine, Doris and Mouse had left for Connection, unable to rid themselves of the uneasy feeling that had been part of their lives for quite some time; knowing Leon was dead didn't seem to be helping.

It did, however, feel good to be going back into the office, and Doris immediately went to work on the report of the wayward daughter who seemingly hadn't cared that she could be easily followed, proving to her parents that she was indeed wayward.

Mouse composed the letter to Pamela Bird, asking her to contact them as they had information on the child she had put up for adoption. Mouse didn't feel comfortable writing it; there was half a chance this woman wouldn't want to know anything about Tom.

Mouse deliberately kept the letter brief, printed it off for Doris to digest, and rang Kat, reading it to her over the phone.

'That sounds good to me,' Kat said. 'Not too much, but enough hopefully for her to want to speak to us. Send it if Nan agrees. We need to get this sorted before I have to take some time to solve the problem of Leon.'

'And after I've posted it I'm going to pop over to Hope, and see if I can weasel anything out of Judy that we don't already know. She needs to be aware that the letter to the birth mother has gone. After, I'll nip up to Alice Small's house and borrow the silver cross and chain. If we do get to meet Mrs Bird, it will be the first thing we ask her. If she does say that she left one with him, I'd like to be able to show it to her. Alice did say she would make it available to us should we ever need it.'

'Good idea. I'm going to walk down to church now, let everybody admire this beautiful child I have produced, then I'll pop into the shop afterwards, catch up on whatever you managed to do. Okay?'

'You're on maternity leave…'

Mouse heard Kat laugh as she put down the receiver.

***

Kat fed and changed Martha, and laid her in her pram ready for walking down through the village. She then topped up the baby bag with nappies and a bottle of baby milk, fastened it to the pram and wheeled it towards the front door.

She opened it to be faced with Tessa Marsden, her hand travelling towards the doorbell.

Kat felt the blood drain from her face. 'God, you scared me.'

'I'm so sorry,' Marsden apologised. 'I took a chance you'd be in. I'm heading back from the crime scene, and thought I would fill you in on the bits I'm allowed to tell you.'

'Come in. You want a drink? I'll pop Martha in the lounge, and we can go through to the kitchen.'

***

Marsden walked through and clicked on the kettle. It briefly occurred to her how familiar she had become with this particular kitchen, and with the three occupants currently living here.

She turned around as Kat came through. 'Sit down,' she said. 'I'll wait on you for a change. You're doing okay after the birth?'

Kat smiled. 'So-so, but don't you dare say anything to Nan and Mouse. I'm a little bit sore, and my breasts feel like balloons because I'm bottle feeding, but I know in a week all that will have passed. Apart from those little niggles, I'm good, and loving being a mum.'

'Good. And no more worries about Leon causing problems.' Tessa watched Kat's face carefully. The smile disappeared. She handed Kat her mug of coffee, then carried her own to the table. They wrapped their hands around the drinks, as if the action gave them comfort.

'I don't know how to feel,' Kat said quietly.

Tessa held Kat's hand briefly. She fished in her briefcase and took out an evidence bag.

Kat took it from her, and looked at the piece of paper inside it.

Tell Kat I will always love her

Kat lifted her head and stared at Tessa. 'Oh my God…'

'I wanted you to see it. We're obviously signing it into the evidence we've collected from the garage, but I think he knew he wasn't going to survive. He would have never left prison, and I guess he chose suicide by cop rather than face that. He exited that building shooting, and we had no choice but to fire back. I guess he wrote that note as soon as he heard me on that megaphone. He would have known his time had run out.'

'Oh, Leon…' Kat whispered, and wiped away the tear that escaped.

They sat for a couple of minutes, sipping at their drinks, Tessa waiting for Kat to regain control, and Kat allowing her emotions to flood her.

Eventually Kat found words. 'I'm grateful for you showing me this. I know it seems odd, but it has given me some comfort.'

Tessa picked up both of the mugs and carried them to the sink. 'Thank you for the drink, Kat. There's just one more puzzling thing. We found some unlabelled antibiotics, so we're assuming he got them from his pharmacy. He had a badly infected stump where his left hand used to be.'

Kat remained calm. 'I'm pretty sure he had a left hand when he hit me with it that last night in the bedroom.'

Tessa fixed her eyes on her, then nodded. 'So you don't know what happened to blow that hand off his arm? No stray bullets from anywhere?'

'Oh, come on, you think I know how to fire a gun? Remember Leon had one or two people he had upset who definitely knew how to fire a gun.'

Tessa waited for a moment. 'That's what I put in my report. I am sorry for your loss, Kat. I did actually want to take Leon Rowe alive, but he was never going to let that happen. You need to put him out of your life, and start a new one.'

She walked towards the front door. 'Bye, Kat. Let's hope we don't have any more bodies linked to you, Nan and Mouse,' she said with a slight laugh.

'There definitely won't be,' Kat said fervently. 'Bye, Tessa, and thank you for showing me that. It's helped.' She closed the door and leaned her head against it; her sorrow washed over her. So many deaths that could be attributed to Leon, and yet she couldn't help but ache for the man she had known and loved.

15

Martha obligingly slept while Kat spent almost half an hour deep in prayer. Her colleagues at the church allowed her the time, recognising the depth of angst she must be feeling; news had very quickly spread of the manner of Leon's death.

She finally stood and walked to the front, lighting a candle for Leon. Then she turned and pushed Martha in the direction of the small church coffee shop. She lost count of the number of hugs she received, and after finishing her glass of water, she left to go into the churchyard. She went to all the graves that were there as a result of Leon's activities, and saw the newly opened one ready to receive Danny McLoughlin.

She stayed longest at Craig Adams's graveside. As far as she knew, he was Leon's first victim, and her prayers were for eternal rest for the young man. At twenty-two he had had everything to live for, and for the sake of a missing two hundred pounds his life had been snuffed out by Leon, accompanied by Brian King. Kat removed the small bunch of roses from underneath the pram and laid them gently on Craig's grave before walking away.

***

It was only a short journey back to Connection, and Doris was its only occupant. Mouse had left to visit Judy and Alice, and came bustling through the door five minutes after Kat's arrival.

She went straight to the phone, and winked at Doris and Kat.

'Hi, Judy,' she said. 'It's Beth Walters. I'm so sorry, but I've accidentally picked up your phone. It looks exactly the same as mine, so I gathered it up when I left. I've just tried to use it, and guess what! My contacts aren't in your phone,' she said with a laugh.

There was silence for a minute and then she said, 'No, I'll bring it back straight away. It's my stupid mistake, I hadn't even had my phone out in your lounge. We both have black covers on iPhones, I assumed it was mine. On the plus side, you haven't missed any calls, although if you had I could possibly have turned around while I was out and returned it to you. Don't worry, I'll be there in half an hour.'

She put down the receiver and grinned. 'Couldn't miss the opportunity,' she said to Kat and Doris. Mouse took the phone out of her bag, and opened up the photos app. She scrolled back through around twelve pictures then hit pay dirt.

'I knew it,' she breathed. 'Every document we got from Alice Small is captured on here. She saw them before Tom gave them to Alice for safe-keeping away from his wife.'

Mouse quickly sent them via Messenger to her own phone, then deleted evidence of the action on Judy's phone. 'She has no security, no passcode, no fingerprint technology on this phone,' she remarked thoughtfully. 'What about you, Kat?'

Kat looked guilty. 'I promise I'll do it right now,' she said.

Five minutes later she was on her way back to Hope, picking up a bunch of flowers on the way to say sorry for being so stupid.

***

Kat was feeding Martha when Mouse reappeared. 'She didn't suspect a thing, thanked me for returning it so quickly, and for the bunch of the flowers I took as a sweetener. I promised her we'd be in touch as soon as we heard back from the birth mother, and she nodded.'

'You've posted the letter to Mrs Bird?' Kat asked, sitting Martha upright. The baby obliged with a very loud burp.

'I have, sent it first class so hopefully she'll contact us tomorrow. I think two of us should go to see her, so I suggest Nan goes with me, and if you don't mind, Kat, you and Martha can be in the office while we're out. Now Leon's not here as a threat, we need to be manning this place all the time. I wouldn't mind betting we've lost business during the last few weeks because we haven't been here.'

'He left me a note,' Kat said quietly, still holding Martha upright.

'A note?' Surprise was written on Mouse's face.

'It said *Tell Kat I will always love her.*'

'Oh my God, Kat.' Mouse moved towards Kat and put her arms around her. 'How do you know?'

'Marsden arrived as I was heading out to go to church. She brought it to show me, but it's now logged into evidence.' She dragged in air. 'Something else she mentioned was the lack of a left hand. I told her he definitely had a left hand when he hit me with it the night he walked out. She seemed to accept that. Sometimes it's good to act the dumb blonde. And it wasn't a lie.'

The gentle tones of Doris cut into the conversation. 'And how do you feel, Kat?'

'Anger, more than anything, Nan. After Marsden left, I walked down to the church, had half an hour of prayer and me time, then went to the coffee shop in the back of the church. Martha collected lots of money because everybody wanted to press pound coins into her hand. Some sort of custom to do with newborns that you see for the first time. I kept putting them in the baby bag, no idea how much she has to open her bank account, but she could be a millionaire by the time she's two. We came out of there and walked around to Craig Adams's grave, and that's where the anger really bubbled out of me. I talked to him, prayed for him, placed some roses on his headstone and promised there would never ever be any flowers for Leon.'

Nan gave a slight nod. 'You have to sort out his funeral?'

'No idea. That's not cropped up yet. If it is down to me, and let's face it, his parents aren't here to do it, are they, it will be cremation and I'll scatter his ashes in the Wye in Craig's memory.'

'Oh, Kat,' Doris said, 'don't let him win by making you less than you are. You have beliefs, Christian beliefs. You owe yourself so much more than this, and Leon Rowe mustn't hold you back from everything you can still give to this world. If you're in chains, how can you fly?'

Kat placed a sleeping Martha back in her pram and walked across to Doris. She put her arms around her and hugged her. 'You're a wise old bird, Doris Lester. Want a cup of tea?'

***

Their evening was spent quietly, Kat reading and Doris and Mouse playing Scrabble. Nobody wanted the television to give them any more news on the Leon Rowe shootout.

At just after eight, the telephone interrupted them and Kat stood to answer it. It was Leon's parents ringing from Canada.

She spoke to both of them, all three maintaining a measured tone of voice. They had received minimal information, and it was left to Kat to tell them as much as she knew.

She had last spoken to them the day after Martha's birth, and they had been ecstatic to hear the news. Now the mood was much more sombre. Sue had difficulty holding back the tears, and asked Kat what would happen about Leon's body. She had to admit she knew nothing about procedures, and Sue said they wanted him to go to them. They would be happy to pay all costs involved, and Kat said she would follow up on their request to see if it was feasible. Or allowed.

She said goodbye to them, and thoughtfully replaced the receiver. She sat down, and the two women paused for a moment to look at her.

'Okay?' Mouse asked.

'It seems Leon will have his last resting place in Canada. If the authorities agree, of course. I don't see why they should say no. And he should be where he is loved the most, and that's with his mum and dad. There is no love in me for him now; there is regret, there are memories, there is anger, but he killed the love.'

She picked up her book. The other two looked at each other and returned to their game, and Martha snuffled in her sleep.

And peace came to the house in Eyam for the first time in a long time.

***

And Kat remembered Doris's words of wisdom from the afternoon. If you're in chains, how can you fly?

She was ready to fly.

16

Keeley unloaded the luggage from the boot of the car and followed Henry down the path to the front door. 'Glad to be home?' she asked.

'Kind of,' the little boy answered. 'I missed my friends. Can I go and see Mark?'

'Tomorrow,' she responded. 'It's too late tonight.'

'But it's still daylight,' he protested.

She laughed. 'It might still be daylight, but it's seven o'clock. Now come on, let's get you in the bath, then bed, and it will soon be morning.'

She could hear him grumbling with every stair he climbed; it was so funny that she stopped unpacking for a moment to listen to him. Tom would have enjoyed this child so much.

Keeley followed Henry upstairs, ran his bath and left him to play for a few minutes with his variety of bath toys. She moved into his bedroom and turned down his bedclothes before crossing to the window to close his curtains. Judy Carpenter was out in her back garden, dead-heading some flowers, pulling up the occasional weed, doing different things in different areas. Keeley felt the loss of Tom more deeply every time she saw Judy.

The woman had kept Tom from her. Keeley had pleaded with Tom to leave Judy when he had spoken of his diagnosis, but he had said he wouldn't burden her, his only love, with his death. She had enough to cope with, as Henry was still very small.

And so Judy was the one who had shared his last moments, and as she stared down at the woman digging up a dandelion, Keeley felt murderous; she wished Judy Carpenter was dead.

***

Pamela Bird admitted that the postman had arrived and delivered the letter, and it took her all of thirty seconds to reach the decision to ring Connection. There was a tremble in her voice; Doris couldn't tell if it was excitement, fear or nerves.

'We'd like to come out to Buxton to see you, Mrs Bird, tell you something of the circumstances, and then leave you to decide what the next move should be. Are you available this afternoon?'

***

Martha was asleep in her pram, so Kat pushed her daughter through into Mouse's office and set up the baby monitor. She figured if she needed anything from her own office, she would disturb the baby, so Mouse's room was the logical choice.

Passing the investigator's exam would give her further qualifications, and it had proved to be interesting and thought-provoking. She pulled the worksheet towards her and settled down to study. She became immersed in it, one ear tuned in to the monitor, one ear on the telephone, and her brain focussed on the highlighted problems she had to solve in less than five hundred words.

It came as something of a shock when the door opened and the shop bell pinged. No ears had been available for recognising that sound. She looked up, quickly closing the worksheet.

A middle-aged woman walked across to the reception desk, her hair slightly frizzy, and framing a face that bore definite signs of worry. She wore a long skirt, shades of blue giving it an almost ethereal appearance, and a strappy T-shirt under a short-sleeved cardigan completed the ensemble.

'Can I help?' Kat said.

'Is this yours?' the woman said, waving her arm around and encompassing the office space.

'The business? Yes it is. I'm Katerina Rowe, co-owner of Connection.'

The woman held out her hand and Kat reached over the counter and took it.

'Hi, I'm Roberta Outram. Please call me Bobby, I don't think I've ever been Roberta except on my wedding day.'

'So you're Mrs Roberta Outram? What can I do for you?'

'I'm not sure. I've come here on a bit of a whim, and now I'm not sure I should have. My husband Keith says he's sick of hearing me go on about it, and I should either tell you or the police. I'm not convinced it's a police matter, not yet anyway, so here I am.'

Kat was beginning to get the feeling this woman was going to walk out the door, talk herself out of whatever it was she had come to tell them. 'Bobby, would you like a cup of tea? Coffee?'

Her defences visibly crumbled. 'I'd love a coffee.'

'Then come around here.' Kat lifted the end section and led Bobby through to her own office. 'I'll just go and lock the front door. My two colleagues are going to be out for a couple of hours, so I'll put the closed sign up and we won't be disturbed.'

She set up the coffee machine, then walked into reception, found the *Back in an hour* sign, and locked the front door, hanging the smaller sign beneath the *Closed* one.

Bobby hadn't moved. Her hands were clasped in her lap as she sat waiting patiently for Kat, who placed the baby monitor in the middle of her desk. 'Baby in the next room but she shouldn't disturb us. The coffee will only be a minute, and then we'll talk.'

'Your baby?' Bobby asked.

'She is. Martha May, born seven days ago. Fortunately she's still at the sleeping most of the time stage.'

Kat stood and took down two cups from the cupboard. She placed a dish on the desk with small pots of milk and cream in it between the two of them. It killed another two minutes preparing the coffee ready for them to drink, and finally there was no escape for Bobby.

'I don't know if I'm doing right by coming here,' she began hesitantly.

'Then let me start by telling you that nothing leaves this office. Whatever you tell any one of the three of us is held in strictest confidence. We speak of it to no one without your permission to do so. Does that help? I'll listen to everything you have to say, and then before we talk terms, I'll tell you if we can help you. We aren't in the business of giving anyone false hopes.'

Bobby Outram gave a brief nod. 'Okay. I understand. But I don't think I'm here to hire you, I'm here to give you some information on a case you already have. First of all I need to tell you who I am, and then you'll understand why I'm being so dithery. I'm not normally like this…' Her voice faded.

Kat waited patiently.

'I am Judy Carpenter's sister.'

Kat tried to keep her face inscrutable. She wasn't wholly successful.

'You are obviously aware that Judy is our client. If there is a clash of interests…'

'No, there will be no clash of interests. I'm here to clear my conscience and, as I said, to give you some information. I don't agree with what Judy is doing; over the years she's become a nasty scheming bitch of a woman, but now I believe she could be bordering on something that could be criminally wrong.'

'And this is connected to the work we're doing for her?'

'It is. I don't want to see Connection dragged down with her, because no good can come of what she's planning.'

Kat felt that as Bobby had started talking, the rest would come easily. She opened her drawer and took out a notepad and a recorder. 'Bobby, do you mind if I record our conversation. It will be easier than writing everything down, or trying to remember everything you tell me. I promise I will delete the conversation after I've transcribed it for my colleagues.'

'No, of course I don't mind if you record it. I came here to give you facts, so however you listen to me, I don't care, as long as somebody listens.'

Kat switched on the recorder and left it on the desk. 'Okay, whenever you're ready.'

Bobby Outram took a long shuddering breath, stared at the recorder for a moment and spoke. 'As I said, Judy is my sister. I wish she wasn't. We used to be very close, but then she met Tom

Carpenter and she became…' Bobby hesitated for a moment, '…all about money. I think that's the only way to describe her. Tom was quite well off, they had a very lavish wedding and he funded IVF when they found out they needed help to have children. But all the money in the world wouldn't have been any good. Judy developed cancer of the uterus and had to have a full hysterectomy. That's when she really changed.'

Kat saw that Bobby was sipping constantly at her coffee, almost as if was giving her strength, so she stood and picked up the coffee pot, refilling Bobby's cup.

Bobby smiled. 'Thank you,' she said softly. 'She became hard. When adoption was mentioned, Tom was against it. He had been adopted and had had a wonderful life, but he felt that his birth mother had abandoned him, and he didn't want a child coming into their lives who would feel like that in future years. It was Judy who suggested he try to find her, to find out the real truth behind why she gave him up for adoption. He eventually agreed, but then he became ill, and within four or five months he was dead.'

'Judy has told us most of this,' Kat said. 'Not about her hysterectomy, we didn't know that, but the rest we had gleaned from our chats with her. She told us they had decided not to have children.'

Bobby nodded. 'I guessed as much. But did she tell you that Tom did apply for his adoption pack, his birth certificate, his mother's birth certificate? And did she tell you that she saw everything that arrived? She got very clever at opening letters and resealing them. Tom went for an interview when he applied for his adoption pack, and he didn't ask her to go with him. He didn't want her to know he was going. He said he had a hospital appointment. He told me, because he wanted to show me his birth mother's letter. It broke his heart.'

Kat waited. She sensed there was more.

'Last week she told me she had approached you for help. She had used the information on the documents and had tracked down where Tom's birth mother was living now. She had done lots of research on her and realised that she was very wealthy. She didn't want to see the woman just by turning up on her doorstep, she thought it would look as if she knew nothing about her vast wealth if the approach came from your company. It would look more... authentic. For Judy it was a case of slowly, slowly, catchee monkey. She's in this for the long haul, she told me. All she could talk about was how rich this Pamela Bird is, and she intended being in the will.'

Bobby picked up her cup and drank deeply. 'So that's why I had to come to see you. She's duping you. I can't believe she's turned out like this. When we were growing up she was brilliant as a sister. There's only a year or so between us, I'm slightly older. But she always seemed more mature, more in control. Now it seems she's more calculating.'

Kat was at a loss. Bobby was telling her what they had all guessed; this was confirmation. It threw up many questions and no solutions.

And right at that moment, Mouse and Nan were at Pamela Bird's house giving her the good news that she had a daughter-in-law; no son, but a daughter-in-law who was really looking forward to meeting her.

Bobby took out her card from her bag and passed it across to Kat. 'You can call anytime, and if I can help, I will. What Judy is doing is so damn wrong, and Pamela Bird needs to know. I've had sleepless nights worrying about this, about who to tell, and I decided it had to be you. I can't go to the police, she hasn't actually done anything wrong yet and there's no proof anyway; I can't go to Pamela Bird because I've no idea where she lives, so basically you're my one hope that something can be done about Judy. Connection is my only hope, Kat.'

17

Within seconds of getting out of the car, Pamela Bird was outside her home waiting to greet her guests. She was small, not much taller than five feet, with straight silvery hair that had clearly been well-looked after by a hairdresser with considerable skills. She wore minimal make-up, but what dominated her face were her beautiful startlingly blue eyes. Her smile reflected in them.

'Welcome,' she said. 'Just leave your car where it is, I'm not expecting anyone else today.'

Mouse stepped forward with her hand outstretched. 'Ms Bird? I'm Beth Walters and this is my colleague, Doris Lester.'

'Please... come in, and call me Pam. I've never really been a Pamela,' she laughed. 'Occasionally maybe, when my husband bothered to inspect the credit card bill.'

Mouse grinned. She already liked this woman. She could, however, sense a tension in her. The sooner they told her their findings, the better.

Doris and Mouse followed Pam into the house. From the outside it had all the spine-tingling appearance of a large Victorian villa, and so it came as no surprise to them that the interior was totally in keeping with the exterior. The hall was magnificent, with sweeping stairs leading up to the upper levels, and Pam smiled as she saw their faces.

'I'm very proud of this house. Oh, not of what its value is, but of what we put into it. We spent many years restoring it and my husband had all but finished when he was taken ill.' She held out a hand to direct them. 'Let's go into the lounge.'

It was pale blue, accented with cream. The long velvet curtains were a darker shade of blue, and everything… toned.

Mouse stared around her. 'Are you an interior designer?'

Pam laughed. 'No, I have an eye for colour. I wouldn't trust myself to do anyone else's home, but this is mine and I was more than happy to let my imagination free on it. Please – sit down and make yourselves comfortable. Grace has made us tea and coffee.'

Mouse looked at Doris as if to say, *She has a maid?* But no words were exchanged. They sat side by side on a sofa, and Pam sat opposite in an armchair. Within seconds the door opened and a tall smartly dressed woman came into the room carrying a tray with crockery, cakes and biscuits.

'I'll get the tea and coffee pots, Pam,' she said, and disappeared.

***

Seconds later she returned and placed another tray by the side of the first one on the coffee table.

'Grace, thank you. Now will you go and get yourself a cup and saucer, I'd like you to stay.'

Grace frowned. 'Are you sure?'

'Of course I'm sure.'

Grace gave a brief nod and left the room once more.

'Grace Earle is my right-hand woman,' Pam explained. 'She's invaluable. She arrived when my husband was first taken ill just over two years ago, and has stayed. I have a condition called ME, Myalgic Encephalomyelitis, or Chronic Fatigue Syndrome. It's got several names but the doctors can't agree whether it's real or not. Trust me, it's real. Some days I can't get out of bed if I'm having a particularly bad attack of it, and then other days I am as you see me today, no major pain, and normality is the order of the day. Grace takes care of the bad days.'

The door opened and Grace re-joined them. She poured drinks for all of them, handed around cake, and finally they all settled back into their respective seats.

'So,' Pam began. 'My son.'

Mouse nodded. 'I need to start from the beginning. We had a visit from a client who lost her husband a year ago. As I explained in our letter, her husband was the child you gave up for adoption. Please stop us and ask questions as we go along, you may forget them by the end.'

Pam nodded.

'It seems,' Mouse continued, 'that Tom had decided to try to track you down, but was then hit with a particularly aggressive form of cancer, and from diagnosis to him dying was only about eighteen weeks. He didn't get the chance to do much more than request his adoption pack and apply for your birth certificate. He certainly didn't have time to begin the search, he was too ill.'

Pam's beautiful blue eyes clouded over. 'His adoptive parents kept the names I gave him, then?'

'They did, and he had a wonderful childhood according to his wife and his aunt. Your selfless action in giving him up wasn't detrimental in any way. His parents have died, but his aunt is still alive, a lovely lady who I'm sure you will meet one day.' Mouse smiled. 'We were a little undecided about taking on this case, because Tom had died and it all seemed a little pointless, but then we realised, after reading the letter you wrote to him when you gave him up, that you might need closure as well.'

Doris nodded in agreement. 'There are three of us at Connection, and we all felt the same. It became more about you and less about Tom.'

'And his wife?' Grace asked.

A shrewd one, Mouse thought. *She's picked up on something being amiss.*

'She's our client, so we can't reveal details of her. She is aware we are seeing you, and obviously she would like to meet with you, but that is why we're here. We refused to give her anything until we had spoken to you, found out how you felt about it.' Mouse unzipped her document case. 'I have something for you.' She handed over the photograph of Tom, taken just before he became ill.

The blue eyes turned to grey as tears flowed down Pam's cheeks. Grace stood and moved to sit on the arm of Pam's chair, placing her arms around her friend's shoulders. They saw a man of around six feet in height, dark brown hair, and a smile that would light up any room. There was no doubt about it, she knew, that she had given birth to a handsome man.

'He's beautiful,' she said softly, stroking the picture. 'May I keep this?'

'Of course,' Mouse said. 'I had a copy done of the original, as the picture belongs to his Aunt Alice.'

Pam passed the photograph up to Grace, who stood and moved back to her own chair with it. She studied it, and said, 'He has your chin but that's all I can see. He's certainly very good-looking.'

'You didn't know his father?' Mouse probed, keeping her voice in gentle mode.

'N... no...' Pam said hesitantly. 'I have flashbacks even after all these years, and I've never been able to say it was so-and-so who attacked me, but sometimes I think...'

'You know him?'

'Oh, I don't know. If I did, it's way in the past now. Knowing the father won't give me back my son. I loved him so much, my Tom.'

Doris smiled. 'We know. We've read your letter. Do you remember leaving something else with Tom?'

'Oh, I do. A small silver cross and chain. I bought it with the only money I had.' Pam looked around her. 'How times have changed.'

Mouse reached into her document case and took out a small blue box. She handed it to Pam.

Her eyes showed shock. 'Is this...?'

Mouse nodded. 'Open it. I can't leave it with you, because again it belongs to Alice. He gave it to her when he knew he was dying, as a keepsake. It's the only thing she has of him, apart from the documents he managed to acquire in his search for you.'

Grace leaned forward. 'Alice has the documents, not his wife?'

Mouse was saved from answering by Pam opening the box, and this time it wasn't just tears, it was full-blown heartbreak and sobbing. There was no consoling her, so Doris stood and poured her a second cup of tea.

'Drink this, Pam,' she said quietly. 'It will help.'

There was a huge long drawing-in of breath, followed by a hiccup, and Pam began to recover. She lifted the teacup to her lips and sipped at it, still staring at the tiny silver cross and chain.

'So many years wasted,' she said. 'Not knowing where he was or even who he was. They could have changed his name very easily. I'm so grateful they didn't. it means my Tom has always been my Tom.' She put the piece of jewellery back into the box, and stroked the lid before handing it back to Mouse. 'Please, return this to his aunt. Alice, did you say?'

Mouse slipped the box into the document case. 'I did. She's lovely, cared deeply for Tom. It's obvious with every word she says about him.'

'And now to the big question,' Pam said. 'Did Tom have children? Do I have grandchildren?'

Mouse took a deep breath. 'Tom and Judy didn't have any children.'

Pam's face fell. 'Oh… I had no other children after Tom, but I would have loved grandchildren.'

'I need to know what you want to do, Pam, but I don't need to know today. Our client is no relation to you now, and you have every right to say no to meeting her. Take as long as you need to think this through, talk it over with Grace. Contact me when you've made your decision, and then I will know what information to pass on to our client.'

'I have a question.' Grace spoke quietly. 'Why does his Aunt Alice have the documents Tom applied for? Why not his wife? Didn't he want his wife to know what he was doing? Because if that is the case, why is his wife pursuing it now?'

'Mrs Carpenter came to us saying that she wanted to have closure on Tom's last wishes. Unfortunately, Tom isn't around to confirm or deny that she should be involved.'

Mouse felt Grace's eyes remain on her, and knew it was time to go. She stood and picked up her document case. 'Thank you for seeing us, Pam, and I'll look forward to your call.' She handed her card to Pam. 'Ring any time if you have questions. I'm sure there will be some, once we've gone. There always are.'

Pam shook both their hands and Mouse and Doris went to leave the room.

'I'll see them out, Pam,' Grace said. 'You stay and rest. I'll make us a fresh pot of tea in a minute.'

The three of them walked outside to Mouse's car. Doris got into the passenger seat, and Mouse turned to Grace. 'Is Pam okay?'

'She will be. It's time for her painkillers, and this has been an emotional morning for her. She hasn't asked any questions about the adoptive parents, and I know that will come once she's had time to put her thoughts in order.'

Mouse nodded. 'I didn't want to overburden her, but all these questions can be answered, obviously. Get her to make a list of any queries that occur to her. We will facilitate any meeting if she decides she wants to meet her daughter-in-law.'

Grace shook Mouse's hand. 'Thank you for coming today. There's one thing I do need to tell you, so that this is in the forefront of your mind when you are facilitating anything about this strange meeting – and I do believe it's strange. Pam Bird is worth much more than this.' She waved her hand to show the extent of the house and land. 'So much more. And I'm not talking thousands, or even hundreds of thousands. I won't disclose any figures, obviously, but I'll protect this woman and what is hers with every breath in my body. You understand?'

'I do indeed,' Mouse said. 'And so will Connection. You can be very sure of that.'

18

The three women sat around the kitchen table and listened to the recording of Bobby Outram's plea for help. They listened twice, not wanting to miss anything, making notes when they felt it was necessary.

Eventually they sat back, all temporarily quiet, while they digested what they had heard.

'She didn't come across as an evil cow who simply wanted to pay her sister back for some slight she had suffered at her hands?' Mouse asked Kat.

Kat grinned. 'Trust you to think up that scenario. No, she seemed almost apologetic as she talked to me. I believe every word she said. Judy thought her sister wouldn't blab about it, but Bobby seems to be a bit different to her sister. What do we do now? Do we give Judy her money back and tell her we can't work for her any longer? That's not really the answer though, is it. If we turn her down, she'll go somewhere else, if she's really hell bent on getting Pam's money. Ethically, we can't tell Pam about this while Judy is our client. We're going around in circles. And what would we say to Pam anyway? Your new daughter-in-law who isn't really your daughter-in-law because your son is dead, wants to take you for everything you have. So is the answer for us to go and talk to her? Tell her we've sussed her out, and we're going to be telling Pam?'

Mouse looked troubled. 'I think it's arrived at that point. We'll make up our invoice for the time we've spent on this, plus our disbursements, take that away from her advance, and give her a cheque for the difference. I don't want anything to do with this woman. She's bloody evil.'

'Don't swear, Mouse,' Doris said absently, working through the notes she had taken. 'We have a baby in the house.'

'She's up in her bedroom!'

'Kat doesn't swear. She's a deacon.'

Mouse frowned. 'Kat, do you swear?'

'Course I bloody don't.'

Mouse walked over to the fridge, took out the bottle of wine and topped up their glasses. 'I rest my case.'

Kat looked at the meagre amount of wine in her glass and sighed. It seemed that having a baby also turned you teetotal. 'So, where do we go from here? See Judy? And let's not forget the issue of little Henry. He's Pam's grandson; his actual DNA would prove or disprove that if it came to a court battle. And after having seen that photo of Tom, there's no doubt in my mind that he is Tom's son. Unfortunately, I bet Judy is able to see that too. All of this gives me an uncomfortable feeling, which I suspect is because of what we've been through with Leon. He would have solved it by taking people out.'

Mouse laughed. 'I think we all know Judy is a conwoman, but I don't see her as a murderer.'

'But money is involved, and after what Grace told you, it seems we're talking millions in the purse. People do stupid things for money.' Kat sounded troubled. 'I think we have to resolve this, but while we have Judy as a client we can do nothing. She may be planning to take Pam's millions one way or another, but a plan isn't a crime. She would actually have to do the deed, and we can stop that by dumping her, then telling Pam about her. We have confirmation of a kind on this recording, so let's do the right thing and go and see Judy.'

Doris had been quiet, but she nodded. 'I fully agree. If you two don't need me to be there, I'll watch the little one. Take my advice on this; wear something smart… a suit or something, it will intimidate her. And it will also show her we mean business. Make sure the invoice for her charges is accurate to the last penny and the cheque is countersigned by both of you. Let's show her she can't mess with Connection, not now and not ever again.'

'Okay,' Kat said. 'No ponytails tomorrow, the woman won't know what's hit her.'

***

Power dressing was the order of the day; Kat and Mouse looked at each other and collapsed into gales of laughter.

'You two scrub up well,' Doris said with a grin. 'I can't remember the last time I saw either of you dressed in anything other than jeans. Even when you had the huge bump you wore jeans, Kat, and you both look amazing.'

Kat groaned. 'Yes, but I've still got some baby belly left, and these trousers are a size twelve, so I hope we don't have to sit down when we get to Judy's. I can undo the button in the car, but it won't look very professional doing that in Judy's house when we've gone there to call her a con artist, will it.'

'Kat, you look stunning. Keep your button open, and walk behind me,' Mouse said, unable to hold in the laughter. 'Come on, the sooner we've done this, the sooner we can get back into our jeans. We need to call at the office first to raid the safe for the cheque book, and then we can go. Have we ever used the cheque book?'

Doris shook her head. 'No, it's really just for special one-off things like this. So let Kat write it, the bank will never understand your scrawl.'

'You'll be okay with Martha?' Kat asked. The baby responded by waving a hand from the depths of her crib.

'Kat Rowe, get on your way. I'm old, not senile. Besides I'm going to teach her a new nursery rhyme.'

'Oh dear,' Kat said, and headed for the front door, followed by Mouse. They paused before going out as they heard Doris start singing. *Roll me over, roll me over, roll me over, lay me down and do it again.*

'Is that really a nursery rhyme,' Kat whispered.

'Don't think so,' Mouse responded. 'That's going to be one open-minded baby when she grows up.'

***

Kat wrote the cheque while Mouse hunted out an envelope. She handed it to Kat, who grinned at the hieroglyphics on the front. 'Just pass me a blank one, Mouse, maybe I'll write her name.'

Mouse looked around the office while Kat secured the safe, and felt justifiably proud. The business had been successful from day one, and with the acquisition of contracts for investigative work from several large businesses in the Sheffield and Manchester areas, their turnover was increasing. Kat had already mentioned that maybe it was time to start thinking about paying rent for the shop as Mouse owned it, but Mouse didn't really want to go down that route. She owed Kat so much; she owed Kat her life. And what she owed to her nan was immeasurable, so no, she didn't want rent from the business, she wanted to ignore it.

They climbed back into the Range Rover and headed for Hope, a short ten-minute journey on a good day. On a bank holiday it could be half an hour, both places enjoying many tourists as visitors.

They turned off before reaching the centre of Hope, and pulled up outside Judy and Keeley's houses. Both cars were there; Kat and Mouse had decided against warning Judy they would be visiting, they wanted her to invite them in as if it was part of their routine, not suspect they were about to tell her to get lost, and keep them on the doorstep.

Keeley saw them arrive, and waved from her kitchen window. They both waved back, and headed down the path to Judy's front door. The air was still, the sun warm, a beautiful day, and they both felt hot in their suits. Kat quietly grumbling about high heels made Mouse smile.

Mouse rang the doorbell and waited patiently.

After a minute, she rang it again. There was still no response so she bent down to call through the letterbox. Silence.

'I'll nip next door and ask Keeley if she's seen her go out,' Mouse said.

***

Keeley saw Mouse open her garden gate, so dried her hands on her jeans and went to meet her at the door.

'Hi, Beth. Good to see you. Can I help?'

'Yes, Have you seen Mrs Carpenter leave? It's just that her car's here, and she's not answering. If she's asleep I'm happy to wait till she eventually hears us, but if she's out…'

'I've not seen her leave, and I've never seen her go anywhere without going in the car. We're not exactly near any shops in this little area, and it's quite a walk. I heard her about sevenish this morning in the garden, shouting at something that I assumed was a dog or cat because she was saying, "Get away from here" or something along those lines, but to be honest she actually woke me up so I didn't get up to see what she was yelling at. I didn't really care anyway, she's not the first person I'd rescue in a fire, is she? Having said that, it would be odd if she was asleep, she was certainly up by seven.'

'Thanks, Keeley. I'll nip round to her back garden, make sure she's not fallen or anything. I would hate to think she was injured because she chased after a cat.'

Mouse returned down the path and walked towards Kat. Judy's house was the end terrace and therefore had side access to her back garden, so the two of them headed that way, fighting through pyracanthus plants meant to deter burglars, and out into the rear of the property. The front garden, with its layer of gravel used for parking Judy's car, had been plain and boring with just a couple of planters to brighten up the uniform white layer, but the one that met their eyes as they emerged from the jungle of the side area was stunningly beautiful. So many flowers already in bloom, a pretty, small pond, paths leading around the garden to statuary that must have cost a fortune, a pergola shrouded in clematis and a climbing rose – Judy was obviously a talented garden designer. No wonder she had been shouting at a cat.

Mouse shielded her eyes and peered into the patio doors of the lounge, but could see no evidence of Judy. Kat was walking around the garden, checking that Judy hadn't fallen, so Mouse went to the back door and knocked. It swung open.

'Kat!'

Kat hurried back towards her, and they peered into what was a small dining room.

'Judy!' Kat called her name loudly but there was no response. She moved further into the house, checked the lounge, turned to Mouse and shook her head. They moved onwards into the kitchen, with still no sign of Judy.

'Should we go upstairs?' Mouse asked. It was almost as if she needed the reassurance of an older person, and Kat gave her a squeeze. 'I think we have to. That back door was ajar, which says something's wrong. If she's not there, we camp out in our car until she returns, and we tell her we've been in because the back door was open. Okay?'

Judy was in the first bedroom they checked out.

Kat rang DI Marsden and described the scene of horror they had walked into, and she told them to get out immediately provided they were sure she was dead.

'She's definitely dead,' Kat said. 'There can't be any blood left in her, it's on the walls, on the floor, it's everywhere. We've not gone beyond the doorway but my fingerprints will be on the handle. I'm not wiping them off in case there are other prints on there.'

'Okay, go outside now,' Tessa said. 'Don't touch anything you haven't already touched. There'll be police there within a couple of minutes. I'll be there in half an hour and talk to you then, so don't go anywhere. Are you both okay?'

'We are. Don't worry about us. We can handle most things, it was just a bit of a shock because she's a client of ours, and we came to give her a report.' Kat crossed her fingers at the tiny lie.

***

They let themselves out of the front door, using a tissue to turn the Yale lock. They waited and watched from the front garden as three police cars arrived, explaining to them that they had come out of the front door and left it open for police to access the property easily. They added that it was definitely locked prior to that but the back door leading out of the dining room was slightly ajar. The PC taking notes looked suitably impressed.

***

The arrival of the police cars had caused Keeley to come out onto her own path, but then returned to her kitchen to make Kat and Mouse a cup of tea. Kat, in particular, looked grey, and Keeley asked if there was anything further she could do.

'I don't think so, thanks, Keeley, but we certainly needed this cup of tea.'

'You're sure she's dead?' The worried expression on Keeley's face showed concern.

'Yes, there's nothing we could have done.'

'But why the hell didn't I hear something? It can't have been quiet; she would surely have been screaming, wouldn't she?'

'Not if her throat was the first part of her to be cut. It would all have been over very quickly if that was the case. Cutting the throat prevents any sound.'

Keeley looked at the two women drinking out of her mugs. 'My God, I wouldn't have your jobs for the world. Fancy having to know things like that.'

19

Kat and Mouse sat in the back of Tessa Marsden's vehicle, describing in detail exactly what they had done. Mouse admitted to feeling uneasy when Judy didn't respond to their knock on the front door. Her Astra was still parked on the drive, and it was, according to her neighbour, unusual for Mrs Carpenter to go out without her car. Mouse hastened to add that they didn't expect to find her dead, they thought she might be ill and in need of help.

They explained that they knew Keeley Roy and her little boy Henry because they had helped her with a small matter, and she had come outside to them as they had arrived.

Kat told Marsden about the seven o'clock shouting from Judy Carpenter, which was presumed by Keeley to have been at a cat or a dog in the immaculate garden belonging to Judy, but with hindsight that could have been a verbal warning towards her attacker.

'Okay,' Marsden said with a sigh. 'I thought I told you two I wanted no more dead bodies… Now go home to Mrs Lester, put your feet up and forget this until tomorrow. I'll need a statement from both of you, and I warn you now, I'll be wanting to know why Judith Carpenter was your client. It may have a bearing on her death, so no holding back. If you have documentation I want to see it. In fact, I don't want you coming to Chesterfield to do this, I'm coming to your office. If there's anything I pick up on that you "forget" to tell me, we can find it in your files, can't we?'

'We'll be there from nine,' Mouse said. 'Can we go now? It's only just over a week since Kat gave birth, and she's looking a bit unwell.'

'Of course. I'll see you in the morning.' She grinned at them. 'And make sure the coffee's on or I'll arrest the pair of you.'

They climbed out of the back seat and walked towards the Range Rover, not speaking. Mouse drove away and travelled back along the main road in the direction of Eyam.

After a couple of miles she pulled up, leaned her head against the steering wheel and said, 'Shit.'

'Couldn't agree more,' said Kat, staring out of the side window. 'Is it just us that attracts all this trouble?'

'I think it's you.'

'Huh. I *know* it's you.'

They turned to look at each other.

'That's a first, anyway,' Mouse said. 'We've lost a client. But who the hell hated her enough to kill her? I know she's obnoxious, but murder? Bit extreme, isn't it.'

'You think.'

'I think.'

'Come on, let's get back to Nan,' Kat said. 'She'll be full of questions.' They'd filled Doris in with the briefest of details – *Judy's dead, and it's murder* – but knew she would be worrying about them.

Mouse drove the final part of their journey almost on automatic pilot. Seeing all that blood had been a massive shock, and her head was pounding. She pulled the big car onto their drive, and they both climbed out, feeling as though every problem in the universe was sitting on their shoulders.

Nan opened the door to them, and held them both tightly. 'You have to go out again today?'

They shook their heads. 'No, our first journey out wasn't too successful, so we're going nowhere.'

'Then it's time for a brandy. You'll feel better after that.'

'A bottle?' Mouse asked.

***

They changed into their jeans and sat in the lounge, filling Doris in on their morning, explaining that Marsden wanted every last little detail about Judy Carpenter the next morning. 'You do know you can't keep anything back, don't you?' Doris warned them. 'And she has to listen to that recording with Bobby Outram.'

Mouse sighed. 'I know. But what does that say about us? We can't keep anything confidential? We really need to speak to Pam Bird about this as well, after all it is her daughter-in-law, and we're the only ones who know that. Nobody else is going to tell her, are they.'

'No, they're not at the moment, but after tomorrow Tessa Marsden will know because we'll have told her. Do we take the initiative and tell her today, or leave it to Marsden to approach her? I think we should tell her today,' Kat said. 'I feel quite responsible. We've built her up to meeting her son's wife, and now she's dead the day after we tell her. That's not going to go down well, is it.'

'You're going to tell her over the phone?' Doris asked.

'No, I think we have to go and see her.' Mouse sounded thoughtful.

'You've both had rather a large brandy.'

'Bugger.'

'Don't swear, please, Mouse,' her nan said. 'Of course, for a box of Ferrero Rocher I could be persuaded to drive.'

Kat looked at Mouse. 'Is this bribery or blackmail?'

'Corruption.' Mouse turned to her nan. 'How big a box?'

'Twenty-four. Non-negotiable.'

'And you'll bring us back as well?'

'Maybe.'

'Okay, agreed.'

'Shall we see if Enid can have Martha for a couple of hours, or shall we take her with us?' Doris asked, a huge smile on her face. Ferrero Rocher! She had originally thought a Mars bar might swing it; she was chancing her arm when she mentioned her favourites.

'We'll ask Mum, I think,' Kat said. 'In case we dump our driver in a lake and we have to walk back.'

***

Enid was waiting at the door, delighted to have her granddaughter to herself for a couple of hours. 'Don't rush back!' she called as they drove off.

***

Kat sat on the rear seat, feeling quite contemplative. It seemed to be working out fine; Martha had so many babysitters in their tightly knit circle, and so far there had been no problems continuing with her work. The biggest concern had been the constant *you're on maternity leave* from Mouse and Doris.

Pam Bird had been more than happy to see them; she said she had made decisions, and would talk to them when they arrived. They confirmed there would be three of them in the car, and she said to take care, and not to rush to get there, she wasn't going out. Grace would serve cake, coffee and tea when they arrived.

It all seemed very grown-up and relaxed. Pam had no idea what was coming to face her. They had brought the recording along for her to hear, and Kat knew it was bound to upset her.

***

Pam met them at the door, greeted them warmly and led them through to the lounge. Within seconds, Grace appeared, carrying a tray with their refreshments.

They waited until she had poured the drinks, and after Kat had been introduced to Grace, Kat asked her to stay. 'We may need you,' she added.

'Will I need a cup of tea?' Grace asked.

'Possibly,' Kat responded, and Grace left to get an extra cup.

She returned to find Doris and her employer deep in conversation about a painting on the wall by a Sheffield artist, Pete McKee, a painter greatly admired by Doris and obviously by Pam.

'I'm still looking for a house in the Eyam area,' Doris was saying, 'so my art works are still all boxed away. I miss seeing them.'

'I have this one in here,' Pam said, 'and two more upstairs. His style is fascinating, and everyone who comes here talks about them.'

Grace poured out her drink and sat down, leaving Mouse to open the conversation.

'Okay, we have several things to tell you, most of which have happened since we spoke to you yesterday. This morning we went to visit Judith Carpenter at her home, primarily because information had come to light that caused us to rethink taking on her case.'

Both Pam and Grace sat immobile, their cup and saucers held rigidly in front of them. Neither spoke, waiting for Mouse to continue.

'Initially we thought she wasn't in because she didn't answer to our knock, but her neighbour told us she never went out without the car and the car was right by us, in her front parking area. We walked around to the back garden, and the door into the dining room was slightly ajar so we went in. We called her name, checked all the downstairs rooms, and headed upstairs.'

Mouse paused for a moment. She was feeling overwhelmed by revisiting the morning's events.

'We entered a bedroom and found Mrs Carpenter. She was dead.'

There was a gasp, and the cup rattled in Grace's saucer. Pam leaned forward and placed her drink on the coffee table.

'Dead? But…'

'I'm sorry to have to be brutal about this,' Mouse continued, swallowing to moisten her mouth, 'but she had been murdered. It wasn't natural causes. There was blood everywhere and she was face down on the bed.'

'Oh, that poor woman,' Pam said, shock etched onto her face. Grace said nothing, but raised her cup to her lips. All colour had drained from her features.

'We don't know anything more about it because we left the room immediately and rang the police. We're meeting with them tomorrow morning to give our statements. This, of course, will impinge on you, Pam, because DI Marsden has made it very clear that she will want to know why Judy Carpenter came to us, just in case it has some bearing on who killed her. Judy was our client, not you, and as she is dead we have no moral right to withhold information about our case. The police would simply get a warrant forcing us to reveal it anyway, so we might as well get it all over with tomorrow. However, we do have other information that Kat acquired while we were with you yesterday. I'd like you to listen to a recording that Kat made of a conversation, with the person's full approval I should add. This is going to be passed on to the police.'

She reached into her bag and took out the small recorder.

***

Grace moved closer to her employer, slid an arm around her shoulders and gave her a gentle squeeze. 'Whatever this is, Pam, we'll deal with it.'

Pam nodded, but couldn't raise a smile.

20

Mouse switched on the recorder and almost immediately Bobby Outram spoke.

Doris's eyes were fixed firmly on Grace, who seemed to be struggling more than Pam with what was unfolding. She suspected that Grace was concerned about the effect the recording would have on Pam; her illness meant that it took very little stress to increase her pain levels and her movements.

They all listened carefully. Doris, Kat and Mouse knew it word for word, but the other two listened with increasing dismay.

It finished and Mouse switched off the small machine. 'Thoughts?'

There was an initial silence and then Pam clasped her hands together as if seeking comfort. 'Is this true? Did you believe her?'

Kat spoke gently. 'I met Bobby, and she came across as a very genuine person who was seeking help from Connection because she didn't know what else to do. She definitely didn't want to go to the police because when all's said and done, Judy was her sister, but she recognised that Judy needed stopping. I must stress that we know nothing of Pam's financial affairs, and don't want to, but we had reason to believe that Judy had seen your house, Pam, and our reticence in telling you more of Judy was due to feeling uncomfortable about her motives for tracking you down.'

Pam was listening with her eyes huge in her pale face, as if wondering what could possibly come next.

'When Doris and Mouse returned home from visiting you, we all sat together and listened to that recording. Any decisions made in our company are joint decisions. We all agreed that we had to give you this information, but couldn't while Judy Carpenter was our client. That was why we were at Judy's this morning, to return her advance minus what we had used already, and to tell her we could no longer act for her. We would not have passed on anything concerning you, but she did have considerable information anyway. We believe she came to us to make it look more official and she could pretend to be surprised at your wealth and lovely home when we facilitated the meeting between you both. I'm sorry, Pam, we took it so far in accordance with Judy's instructions, but it would have gone no further.'

'There is something else we can tell you,' Mouse said. 'Your lovely son,' she glanced at the picture on the fireplace that had already been placed in a frame, 'would have divorced her. His diagnosis and prognosis made him realise he had very little time left, and so he stayed with her.'

Kat froze, willing Mouse not to take that conversation any further. She breathed a sigh of relief when Pam picked up the picture, and said, 'What a lovely man. How I would have loved to have known him. Does my son have a grave?'

'I don't know,' Mouse said, 'but we will find out.'

Grace stood. 'I'm going to make fresh drinks, I think we need them. Pam, do you need anything? You're okay?'

Pam nodded. 'I'm fine, Grace. I'll sleep for a couple of hours later.'

Grace gathered up the used cups and carried the tray from the room.

'This will bring on a relapse?' Doris was concerned.

'Hopefully not. If my mind will shut down as well as my body this afternoon, I can probably avoid it, but this damn disease is so unpredictable. But Grace is so good to me, she watches everything I do in an attempt at minimising everything so it doesn't trigger a reaction. It's why she put her arm around me, it was the only thing she could do as she didn't know what was coming.'

Kat nodded. 'Would you rather we had no further contact, now that you know of Judy's deceit in all of this? If there is a grave for Tom, I can let you know by email, but I can't guarantee the police won't want to speak to you. We'll be giving them that recording.'

'You've all been admirable, Kat, and if you need to contact me then please do so. I'll cope with the fallout from it. I can't actually tell the police very much, can I. I didn't know her, I didn't know the lady on the recording; in fact most of the time I don't even know what day it is. My medication keeps me pretty free of pain, but one of the symptoms of this illness is something called brain fog, and that seems to be a permanent symptom these days.'

They chatted quietly for a couple of minutes then Grace returned with fresh drinks, pouring for everyone before she sat down. She handed a small dish to Pam with two tablets in it, and a glass of water.

'I've had them today, haven't I?' Pam said frowning.

'No, not these. If you have these now, you'll sleep better later.'

Pam smiled at her visitors. 'This is what I mean about brain fog. Without Grace I'd be lost. She keeps me on the right track by dispensing my medication at the right time.'

They finished their drinks and then stood to leave. Grace escorted them outside once again, and thanked them for their trouble.

'I'll either email or ring Pam when I find out about a gravesite for Tom,' Kat said. 'Take care of her, this has to have been a shock, but we had no choice but to tell her. It would have been a bigger shock if the police had turned up and she hadn't known anything.'

Grace smiled. 'She'll be asleep shortly. The pain can hit with no warning, and I try my hardest to prevent it. Those tablets were her Gabapentin, which normally keeps her reasonably pain free. Fingers crossed they will today.'

***

They drove down the short drive to the main road, and headed for home, each lost in their own thoughts until Doris said, 'I don't like her.'

'Pam?' There was surprise in Kat's voice.

'No, Grace. She's very protective of Pam, but it smacks of control. Still, it's nothing to do with us, and Pam seems happy to have her there.'

'Is it control,' Mouse asked, 'or is it that she's seen Pam in dreadful pain and just wants to try to prevent it? I must admit to not knowing about ME, but I certainly hope I never get it. I've seen Pam twice now, and she's seemed half asleep both times.'

'I had a friend with it, she died a couple of years ago,' Doris said. 'To look at her you wouldn't have known anything was wrong, but it's one of these invisible illnesses, like fibromyalgia. Even GPs don't understand it, yet there are consultants in all hospitals for it. It took years for them to diagnose Sandra, then one day she went for a hospital appointment to discuss the massive amount of pain she was in, and she took along a long list of symptoms she had experienced over the previous six months. The consultant took one look at the list and said you have ME.'

'How awful,' Kat said. 'Never knowing if you're going to wake up in pain, or if it's going to be an okay day. Poor Pam.'

Mouse put on the Range Rover's indicator, and headed through the Derbyshire hills and vales to collect Martha. The three of them spoke very little for the rest of the journey. It had been a bad day, and they were individually digesting what they had seen and heard. Meeting with DI Marsden wasn't going to be easy, but on one thing all three were united; Henry Roy would not be brought into any conversation.

* * *

The message on their answering machine, left by DI Marsden, was brief and to the point. 'Nine tomorrow morning, all three of you, please. Don't be late.'

The phone call to Enid and Victor was also brief and to the point. 'Is it okay if we drop Martha off with you tomorrow morning at half past eight, please?'

21

'No biscuits?' Marsden pulled her coffee towards her, and Doris smiled.

'We didn't want to be accused of bribery and corruption.'

She stood and took down the biscuit tin. She put a few on a plate and pushed it to the middle of Kat's desk. 'Help yourself,' Doris said.

'Thank you, I didn't have time for breakfast, and I'm staying in Eyam for Mr McLoughlin's funeral later. Will you be going?'

Kat answered for them all. 'No. Danny was a really good friend, but my husband killed him. It would be tantamount to rubbing salt into the wound for his family if we went, so we're going to close the office for the day and go home. We wouldn't even have opened up if you hadn't yelled at us on the answerphone.'

Tessa smiled. 'I was stressed. Just how many more murders are we going to have in this area? Deaths around here are usually road traffic accidents with crazy tourists not understanding the width and the twistiness of Derbyshire roads, to say nothing of dry-stone walling that doesn't move when you hit it at eighty miles an hour. The ferocity of the method of murder yesterday threw me. And I think you hold answers to things I need clarifying.'

'Judy Carpenter was our client, it's why we were there to see her.'

'You didn't have an appointment?'

'No, we went early to catch her before her day began, really. We didn't want to prewarn her. We had gone to give this to her.'

Kat pushed the envelope with the final account and the cheque towards Marsden. She picked it up, opened it and inspected the contents.

'What had she done to upset you?' she asked.

Mouse sighed. This was the part she had been dreading. 'We have a recording we would like you to hear.' Mouse took the little machine from her bag and placed it on the desk.

Once again the Connection team listened to it; Marsden's face showed nothing. The words stopped.

'I went to see Roberta yesterday, and she said nothing about this,' Marsden said.

'Would you?' Doris countered.

Tessa shook her head. 'I don't know. She did appear to be shocked, but I didn't feel she was holding back. I'll go and talk to her again, in light of this. You believed her?'

Kat gave a rueful smile. 'Unfortunately, yes. She came in here while Mouse and Doris were visiting Mrs Bird for the first time. Mrs Bird is Judy's late husband's birth mother, just to fix that in your mind. Judy wanted to track her down to fulfil Tom's last wish. Supposedly.'

'You didn't believe Judy?'

'Initially yes, but then we found out she had lied to us on a couple of matters, and we decided, after Bobby Outram had talked to me, that Judy had some knowledge of the birth mother's wealth, and that was the reason for her wanting to find her. We're sure she had found her and seen her home on Google Earth, and believe me, it's impressive, but it would have looked as though Judy knew nothing if we facilitated their first meeting. She was using us, we realised that, hence our visit of yesterday morning in high heels.'

'Power dressing, intimidating,' Marsden smiled. 'It was wasted. You did look smart though.'

'Certainly did. We're back to jeans today. Have you found anything out from the bedroom?' Kat slipped the question in seamlessly.

Marsden laughed. 'Nothing I'm going to tell you two Sherlocks.'

'But we found her!' Mouse looked a picture of innocence.

'I know. I'll have you in officially if I feel there's any more to be gleaned from that little statement.'

'That's not what I meant...'

'It's what I meant. It was no ordinary crime scene, believe me, and I'll pull in whoever I want to get to the bottom of it. One thing I will tell you. Because of the over the top way our victim was murdered, we expedited the post-mortem. The first few stab wounds were meant to incapacitate and create the splatter, leaving Judy weakened and unable to fight back, but only one hit the mark. It went straight to the heart, and it went deep, then the knife was twisted. She wasn't going to survive that. In all there were nineteen wounds, but only one killed her.'

All three women stared at Marsden. 'A crime of passion? In Hope?' Kat's eyes were huge, disbelief reflected in them. Then she realised how stupid she sounded, and let her head rest on her hands.

Marsden smiled. 'I know what you mean, Kat. It was kinda my reaction. Going for the heart does indicate passion, but it also indicates it's the quickest way of killing someone. Maybe Judy was trying to fight back.'

'You think it's a man or a woman?' Mouse knew she was pushing her luck; she didn't expect Marsden to come up with an answer.

'Gut feeling says a woman because I think a man would have subdued her. But there's no proof either way. We'll keep digging. After Mr McLoughlin's funeral I'm going out to see Mrs Bird. Tell me about her.'

'We don't really know anything,' Kat said.

Tessa stood. 'Okay, get in the car. I'm taking you to the station. Maybe you'll realise you do know something once we're there. And Kat, make sure you're covered for childcare overnight.'

Doris grinned. 'Sit down, DI Marsden. Kat was being an idiot. Pam Bird isn't even our client, so we can't claim client privilege on that one. We'll tell you what you want to know.'

Tessa took her seat at the desk. 'Okay, start talking. Mouse?'

Mouse, desperately trying to remember if everything had been legal that she had done, began by telling Tessa about the documents Tom Carpenter had ordered prior to his death, and how they had copies of them. She stood and walked to the filing cabinet, taking out one of the files. She handed it to Tessa.

'Everything's in that. Tom had always had his adoption certificate, which is in there, by the way, but when he applied for his adoption pack he then acquired his birth certificate, along with a letter from his birth mother. He then applied for her birth certificate. She was then Pam Farrar, and lived at ten Haddon Row in Grindleford. At sixteen she gave birth to Thomas Edward but her parents forced her to give him up for adoption. She asked that his new parents keep his given names, but had little hope of that happening. She was over the moon when we told her they had done as she asked.'

She paused for a moment to gather her thoughts. 'In 1998 Tom married Judy. They couldn't have children, and Tom didn't want to go down the adoption route. Reading between the lines, it was that fact that caused the rift in the marriage.'

'How do you know there was a rift?'

This time the pause was because she needed to come up with an answer that didn't involve Keeley Roy.

'I went to see Tom's aunt in Bradwell. She told me that Tom had taken all the documents to her, plus giving her the precious cross and chain given to him by his birth mother before he was taken from her, and when I asked why he didn't just leave them with his wife, she said because they were on the verge of separating when he was diagnosed with terminal cancer. He simply let her inherit the house and whatever monies he had. He hadn't the strength to fight. He died eighteen weeks later.'

'Thank you for that. Now, the birth mother. She lives in Buxton?'

'Indeed she does. A massive house that she shared with her husband until a year or so ago, when he was taken ill. I understand he died soon after, but don't quote me on that. She has help managing her affairs, and I understand she is a very rich woman, and the lady who helps her is called Grace. Grace also monitors Pam's medication because Pam herself isn't well, she has Myalgic Encephalomyelitis, ME to the laymen amongst us.'

'Is she bad with it?' Tessa asked.

'I think so. After we told her of Judy's death, she looked quite ill. I think her trigger must be stress.'

'So you told her.'

'We did.' Mouse sounded defiant. 'I didn't want you lot going in with your size tens and putting her in bed for a month. We told her gently, and without going into massive details about blood on the ceiling, dripping from the lampshade, pooling on the floor.'

Tessa laughed. 'Stop jumping, Beth. I just wanted to know how much she knew, and how careful I needed to be. Is there anything else I need to know?' She glanced at her watch. 'I'm going over to the church, but I'll call back here before I go to Buxton, and pick up this file. Thank you for being so helpful finally, and make a note if you think of anything else while I'm away.'

22

'I'm a bit scared.' Keeley Roy's voice was tremulous. 'They're taking all sorts of stuff out of Judy's house, and I've been questioned twice by officers.'

'Don't worry,' Mouse said into the receiver. 'They'll be gone soon if they're at the stage of taking stuff out, and everything will go back to normal.' Mouse had no idea if she was spouting rubbish or not, but she sensed she needed to calm Keeley down by whatever means possible. 'DI Marsden is calling in at the office in about half an hour. If I get any more information from her, I'll give you a ring this afternoon. It might be a good idea to take you and Henry out for the afternoon, and then you won't be constantly reminded by all the activity. Padley Gorge might be good, it's a lovely warm day.'

'You're right,' Keeley said with a sigh. 'I'm being paranoid. I'll make us a picnic, and we'll get away for a few hours. Thank you for listening to me. Maybe we'll talk later.'

***

'Problems?' Doris asked.

Mouse shook her head. 'Not really, it's Keeley having a bit of a meltdown. All this activity in what was Tom's house hasn't been good for her. I think she's panicking that it's going to come out about her and Tom, and that's going to affect Henry. They're taking lots of stuff from inside the house, and she's definitely not happy with the situation.'

The shop bell jingled and Marsden returned. 'That was an interesting hour.'

'Interesting,' she reconfirmed thoughtfully. 'First of all it was a cracking good funeral, as funerals go. It really was a celebration of Danny's life, lots of lovely loud music, bright clothes, brilliant. And then came a phone call as we got outside. It seems we've been authorised to send Leon's body to Canada. Did you know about this, Kat?'

Kat nodded. 'I did, but not when. I had to sign an authorisation form. He's going to his parents. They asked me and I said yes. It'll be a clean break for Martha and me. I'll tell her the full story when she's old enough to understand, and she can make up her own mind whether to visit his grave or not.'

'You haven't been pressured into this?' Marsden was concerned.

'Not at all. It's a relief, if I'm honest. I just want him out of my life for good. When I go to register Martha's birth, it won't be in the name of Rowe, I'll be Kat Silvers by then. I'm reverting to my maiden name. I'm getting rid of all of that life.'

Doris and Mouse looked at Kat, surprise on both their faces. This was the first time her original surname had been mentioned.

'He'll probably be gone within about four days, so I understand. You can change your mind until that plane takes off. Then you can't. But that's not all that phone call was about. My team have found a will in the Carpenter house, hidden under the mattress in the spare bedroom. It's countersigned by two people, neighbours from the little road where the Carpenter house is. It's Tom Carpenter's will, not Judy's, and it definitely hasn't been acted upon. I don't want to say anything further about it until I've had chance to study it, but this could open up a whole can of worms that would possibly be better eaten by the birds. And I am requesting that the three of you don't say a word about this to anyone until it is more public knowledge. I don't know yet what is in it. But I'm asking all three of you if you knew anything about this will prior to my having told you?'

Kat spoke for all of them. 'Not a thing, I promise you.'

Marsden walked to the door. 'I'll need to talk more with you, I'm sure, find out if there's anything you haven't told me, but until then, take care.'

***

'Shit…' Mouse said the word slowly, drawn out.

'Bad language, dear,' Doris said, her mind on anything but Mouse's expletive. 'A will. Let's have a guess what it will say.'

'He will have left something to either Keeley or Henry, or possibly both.' Kat's face screwed up in concentration. 'Never mind telling Keeley to take him to Padley Gorge, it might be easier for her if she takes him out of the country!'

'Should I ring her and warn her?' Mouse was worried.

'I think not. They don't know of our relationship to her, it will probably be better if it stays like that. If Marsden thinks we know her well, Keeley will clam up and we'll find nothing out. She won't be able to fake it if she knows before Marsden tells her about the will.' Doris had obviously thought it through.

'Why has life suddenly become complicated?' Kat grumbled. 'Everybody in our circle is becoming intertwined, aren't they. I need to go and have a few minutes in church, and I can't even do that because it's the funeral of the man my husband killed, and it would be insensitive to be there at this time.' She turned to face the other two. 'And I saw your faces when I spoke of changing my name. I've already taken the decision, it's going to happen, and that's an end to it.'

'Hey, don't snap at us. You know we'll back you, no matter what,' Doris said. She waved her hands around at the certificates on the walls. 'I'll just get the name changed on all of these, shall I?'

Kat stared around her. She sat down on her office chair, dropped her head onto her arms and burst into tears.

'How many times did you have to get up during the night, Kat?' Doris put her arm around Kat's heaving shoulders.

'Three.'

'Come on,' Doris said. 'Let's have you home. You go to bed and you sleep. We'll collect Martha and see to her needs, and you stay there as long as you want. You're still on maternity leave, you know, and this is exactly what it's for.'

The tears rolled down Kat's cheeks as she looked at Doris and Mouse. 'Bloody maternity leave.'

'Don't swear, please, Kat, it's unbecoming,' Doris said, trying to hide her smile. 'Go and get in the car with Mouse, I'll make sure everything's secure.'

***

Mouse and Doris were relaxing in the lounge; the television had been turned off for some time, neither of them feeling inclined to follow anything on screen. They were reading, both occasionally looking up from their books and staring into space as their thoughts drifted into their work life.

They heard Kat's bedroom door open, then the flush of the toilet. She came downstairs rubbing her hands through her hair.

'You're going for the scarecrow look then,' Mouse smiled.

'I am. It's not far off midnight. Have I slept all this time?'

'You have. Martha's in my room, and is staying there all night. I suggest you have something light to eat, and a milky drink, then get off back to bed.'

Kat sank onto the sofa and laid her head back. 'I didn't expect to feel like this. I thought I would simply give birth, and then get on with life with a sweet little baby in tow. The reality has been nothing like that.'

Doris grinned at her inherited granddaughter and stood. 'Hot chocolate and some toast?'

'Oh, Nan, that would be wonderful,' Kat said without opening her eyes.

'It would…' Mouse leaned back, mimicking Kat, and closed her eyes.

'Toast and hot chocolate for three it is then.' Doris headed for the kitchen.

'Who do you think's killed Judy?' Kat said, her eyes still closed.

'No idea yet,' Mouse said, as unmoving as her friend. 'But we will make it our place to find out, if we can. Surely…'

'…it can't be Keeley,' Kat finished off the sentence.

Mouse opened her eyes. 'We're thinking along the same lines.'

'We are. I just don't see her doing it. She's not come across as being particularly bolshie or brave; in fact, she's quite the opposite. And I don't think she'd do anything to jeopardise being with Henry. He's her reason for living, and she would lose him if she ended up in prison for life.'

'Quite apart from that, would she have thought to leave that back door ajar? She doesn't need to use conventional methods for getting into any of those six terraced houses, she can go up into the loft, and down into any of the homes there.'

Kat sat forward, her eyes now fully open. 'I'm assuming the police have been up into the loft at Judy's house. Surely it will have occurred to them there's a major security flaw in those houses.'

'I would hope so. I happen to think a major fire risk as well. Should we mention our concerns to Marsden?'

'No, she was quite stroppy with us, just because we found her a body.' Kat yawned. 'Let her realise it for herself. We didn't go out of our way to find her a body, did we? It was accidental. Neither of us think Keeley did it, and we'd only be piling trouble onto her head. Quite apart from that, we've no idea what this will says. Maybe Keeley's troubles are already sitting right on top of her head.'

23

The team gathered around Marsden, waiting expectantly. They seemed to have been working in the Eyam area for ever, one crime melding seamlessly into another. Leon Rowe was out of the picture, but it appeared he wouldn't just stay in his coffin and die. His wife had taken up the cudgel for the good guys, and subsequently they had another body.

Marsden walked over to the whiteboard and pointed to the picture of Judy Carpenter. 'Judith Carpenter,' she said. 'Died from a stab wound directly into the heart, but had eighteen other wounds as well. Some pre-mortem, some post mortem. Thoughts?'

'Were the pre-mortem ones enough to subdue her?' A voice from the back of the room carried above the hubbub of so many bodies.

'Not on their own,' Marsden responded. 'Good question, whoever that was. There was blunt force trauma to her head. We think that subdued her enough for the butchery to take place. But let's be clear on this, the pre-death stuff would not have killed her. The stab wound to the heart, pre-planned we believe, was the kill wound. She would have died within seconds. The killer then continued, just for the hell of it. Further thoughts?'

'It was a woman.'

'Who said that?'

'Me, boss.' Dave Irwin held up his hand.

'I'm inclined to agree, Dave, but let's not rule out the possibility it could be a man. I simply think that a man would have used more force when she was hit on the head, and I think there wouldn't have been quite so many repeated stabbings before and after death if it had been a man. This person actually took their time, almost as if it didn't matter whether they were caught or not. It was all about the act, not getting away with it.'

Marsden looked around the room. 'We need to clear this up fast. I want the neighbours interviewing, and I want every second of their time accounting for. That row of six cottages is interlinked by one huge attic space. It seems they work on a trust system, and they don't venture into each other's loft area, but is it possible somebody did? Did Judy upset somebody on that little road? Her next door neighbour thought she heard Judy shouting at what she presumed was a cat or a dog, telling it to go away, and that was at approximately seven o'clock. She was found around three hours later, so what happened in that period? Did anybody see anything? Any stranger? Anybody who wasn't a stranger? I'm going to interview the next door neighbour, but I'm bringing her in here. Dave is in charge, he'll allocate your jobs. Go – bring me back a murderer, team.'

They all smiled and headed back towards their desks. Tessa returned to the tiny office she sometimes felt she lived in, and pulled the copy of the will towards her. She'd glanced through it very quickly before the briefing, recognising its importance; was it important to the investigation or important to Keeley Roy?

Marsden studied it carefully, letting every word register. The writer, Thomas Edward Carpenter, had known he hadn't long to live. He stated in the will that he did not wish his wife, Judith Carpenter, to have sight of the will prior to his death. He left the house he shared with his wife, and wholly owned by him, for her use until her death. After that it would revert to his only child, his son, Henry Roy. In addition, the house in which Keeley and Henry Roy lived, and which was wholly owned by him, was to be transferred to Keeley Roy. All rents paid by her since the start date of her tenancy were to be refunded in total.

He left a sum of £10,000 to his aunt, Alice Small, along with ownership of one of the remaining two houses which he owned outright, and £50,000 to Keeley Roy. A substantial trust fund had been put on one side for when Henry reached twenty-one, plus shared ownership with Keeley Roy of house number four, and all rental income for the foreseeable future.

Tessa read through the details twice. Tom Carpenter had been a very wealthy man, and yet Judy had tried to work a con to get more. Wasn't she aware of his wealth? Did she know he owned four houses? The will was dated five days before Tom's death. Had the neighbours called in to see him at his request, and then been asked to sign the will?

There were clearly many more answers to be found, and Marsden made a list of the questions, so that nothing was missed.

***

Marsden took Hannah Granger with her to talk to the neighbours. Keeley Roy didn't appear to be in, but this didn't concern Tessa. She wanted to bring her into the station.

Philip Jones, the first of the signatories of the will, was at home at number five. He led them through to the back garden, where his wife was hanging out washing. She obligingly went in and made glasses of lemonade for everyone. Philip explained that he had received a text from Tom Carpenter, asking if he could call into see him. He obliged, knowing that Tom didn't have much longer left.

Tom had asked him to sign the will, but Philip said he had no idea what was in it. He said they chatted for a short while, but then Tom began to fall asleep, so Philip came home. He never saw Tom alive again.

Marsden and Hannah finished their drinks, thanked husband and wife for their hospitality, then went to number three to speak to Eric Davies, the man who had been second to sign his name on the document.

His story was marginally different. He too had responded to a text from Tom, and he too had signed the will form, noticing that Philip had already signed it.

But then Tom had explained he didn't want his wife having anything to do with it, and he had asked Eric to hide it under the mattress on the small double bed in the second bedroom.

'He said he was leaving instructions for it to be found after his funeral, and neither Philip nor I were to worry about it, the form needed our dated signatures on it. I thought no more about it until you turned up,' Eric finished.

'Was he of sound mind?' Marsden asked.

'Definitely,' Eric said. 'He was in some pain, and Judy brought him some pain relief in while I was there. He was a good man, one everybody got on with, always supported anything that was happening in the area. He owned four of these six houses, you know. Not mine, and not Philip's; we bought them from him some years ago, but he owns the rest. I suppose that will is going to clarify who owns them now. I never spoke to him again. He was asleep almost before I was out of his room. I did wonder how strong the tablets were that Judith had given to him, they worked very quickly.'

'Thank you for your help,' Marsden said, and she and Hannah left to head back to the station. Tessa had a lot of thinking to do, all of it centring around the will. It seemed he had fathered a child with his neighbour, and no one had known. He had hidden the will, but obviously had expected it to surface pretty quickly. He would not have left his lover and son without funds, but why had the will never been found?

It was a valid will, and it could be brought into force. Keeley Roy would be a very wealthy woman... unless she had been the one to kill Judy Carpenter.

Marsden's headache, initially just a niggle, was escalating into migraine proportions, and she swallowed a couple of painkillers. She knew something had gone seriously wrong with Tom's plans; he had meant that will to be found. She needed to know when Tom had slipped into a coma-state, making it impossible for him to tell anyone about its location. She thought about Philip and Eric's words; both of them had said that Tom was drifting into sleep. Had he never woken up fully again? Maybe Keeley Roy would be able to shed some light on that little query.

Roy needed to be brought into the station, and very soon.

24

Keeley had only been home two minutes after dropping Henry off at school, when the police car arrived. She was in the middle of loading the washing machine. The bang on the door startled her into dropping the little plastic top full of laundry detergent. She grabbed a tea towel, threw it on top of the spreading puddle, and headed down the hall.

Five minutes later, she was in the back of the patrol car wondering what was going on, and if she would be back for three to reclaim her son. Shell-shocked, scared, she sat trembling, not knowing what was happening to her.

***

'Is it okay if I call you Keeley?' Marsden spoke softly. She could introduce harshness as and when it was necessary.

***

Keeley nodded miserably. She couldn't believe loving someone could get her in this mess, and if this woman wanted to call her Genghis Khan she could, as long as she could go home to Henry afterwards.

***

'Right, Keeley. I need to ask you some questions, so please speak clearly for the tape, won't you.'

'Yes,' muttered Keeley, then more clearly, 'yes!'

'Let's begin with you getting to know Mr Carpenter.'

'I met him almost as soon as I moved in next door. He helped me carry some boxes in that I had taken down in my car from my old flat, a couple of days before the removal men came to move my furniture. He was really nice. I didn't meet his wife Judy until about a month later. She never introduced herself to me, not like he had. Tom.'

There was a bleakness about Keeley's expression and Marsden tried to dismiss it from her thoughts.

'About six months after I moved in. Nobody knew, nobody ever saw us as a couple. We could pass between the two houses via the loft, and we just waited for Judy to go out so we could be together. Tom worked from home, so was always there, and I worked nights in a care home. At least I did until I found out I was pregnant.'

***

Keeley paused. This was so much more difficult than she could ever have imagined. She had kept this love bottled inside her for so long, and now she was being forced to talk about it as though it was nothing.

'Please go on, Keeley.'

'I told Tom I was pregnant and he was over the moon. I had made up my mind to have an abortion; we had so much to lose by keeping the baby. Tom wouldn't hear of it. He said it would be the child he had always wanted, but thought he would never have. We agree not to rock the boat by moving in together because he feared for Judy's state of mind; her control over Tom, the household, everything, was well-known on our little road. He said he could live with being next door to his child, if I could handle the situation as well.'

Again she paused, but Marsden said nothing.

'I don't think for one minute that Judy suspected anything, not the affair, not the unplanned pregnancy, nothing. She was away for two weeks staying with her sister… Roberta?… when I went into labour, and Tom was able to take me into hospital and be there for the birth. It cemented everything between us, and he promised we would be together properly one day.'

'Did you believe him?'

Keeley smiled, deep into her thoughts. 'No. I knew he would never leave her, but it was lovely to talk about the time when he would, even if it would never happen. He began to be ill with niggling little things when Henry was about two, and at first the doctor said it was stress. Then he said Tom needed more exercise, so he got out and walked more, but nothing improved his general health. He took co-codamols because they helped the pain better than paracetamols, then finally the doctor sent him for tests.'

Keeley looked up at Marsden. 'Could I have some water, please? This is very hard.'

'Would you like a break?'

She shook her head. 'No thanks. I want to go home.'

Hannah went to get a drink, bringing both a coffee and a water back for Keeley.

Marsden waited until Keeley had helped herself to the water, and then said, 'The diagnosis was cancer?'

Keeley swallowed. 'It was. By the time they had completed the tests and all the consultations it was too late. It had spread into his bones, his liver – everywhere it could go, it had gone. They initially tried to say he would have about six months, but it was obvious it was too advanced for that. Our last three or four weeks we communicated by text. I saw Judy go out one day and was going to risk going through the loft to see him, but the Macmillan nurse arrived, so I couldn't.'

'Have you saved his texts?'

'Of course. I've screenshot them as well, just in case I lose the phone, or it breaks. My photos are all stored separately.'

'May I see?'

Keeley hesitated, then dipped into her bag and took out her Samsung. 'The screen has a crack on it, but the phone still works. Funds don't run to new phones now.'

Marsden looked at her, wondering if she was being genuine, or… no, she was genuine, she felt.

She scrolled to messages, and clicked on Tom. It actually said Tom xxx. She read through the texts, aware that Keeley felt uncomfortable having them scrutinised. The last two or three were very short on Tom's part. It was obvious from the half words that he was struggling to concentrate. The final one simply said **will**.

***

Marsden stared at it with her mouth open. 'There's no response to the last one, Keeley?' It suddenly became clear why the will had never been found. He'd not managed to tell anyone about it.

'No, it didn't make sense. I thought he must have been going to ask me something, and then either couldn't remember what it was, or he physically wasn't capable of writing the rest of the message. He was very ill, and very near the end. Judy, when she came around to tell me he was gone, said he'd been in a coma for the last three days.'

'And Judy hadn't seen any of these texts?'

'He was careful to delete everything, but maybe just that last one would have still been on the phone. It wasn't much of a message, and she couldn't have read anything into it, but she was really quite nasty when she came to tell me he'd gone. I would give anything to know what he wanted me to do for him, but that's not going to happen is it? In my moments when I'm really down, I like to think he was going to say, "Will you come around and sit with me?", but of course it wouldn't have been that.'

Keeley's head dropped and she sat quietly for a moment, before picking up the coffee cup.

'Sorry,' she said, 'I don't seem to be able to get over it, and talking to you about it certainly hasn't helped. But, you know, Judy means nothing to me. I neither like her nor dislike her. If I had ever been tempted to bump her off, it would have been long before this. She's obviously managed to upset somebody, and that doesn't surprise me, but I have very little interaction with her now. I loved her husband, not her.'

Marsden stood, feeling subdued and chastened. In all her years of interviewing suspects, she had never felt emotionally involved. It was a job. Today that job felt shitty.

'Thank you for being honest, Keeley. If you can bear our coffee, please finish your drink and PC Granger will take you home. I'll be coming out to see you in a couple of days, but I'll ring first to check you will be in.'

Marsden guessed that news of a will would filter through via Eric Davies and Philip Jones, but they needed to process the information at the station before she could officially inform the beneficiaries. And it wasn't only Keeley who was benefitting from this extraordinary man, a man who Marsden believed had tried to tell Keeley where his will had been hidden. **Will.**

***

Hannah Granger sat opposite her boss and waited for instructions.

'Keeley didn't speak on the journey?'

'No, she didn't say anything, other than thank you when she got out of the car. No protestation of innocence, nothing. It was almost as if she didn't care. I think we've well and truly drained her today.'

Marsden nodded. 'Know what you mean. It's how I felt when I came out of that room. I didn't have to ask her anything really. She was so open, just told her story in a take it or leave it fashion, and I believed her. Still do, after thinking about it for an hour. It must be awful to find your soulmate and then lose them. And he was only forty.'

'So what happens next?'

'We go to see his birth mother and his Aunt Alice. Those interviews are probably going to be a bit emotional as well. Still, it all beats gunning down Leon Rowe, I suppose.'

Hannah stood. 'Maybe.' She grinned as she left the tiny office.

25

Kat fastened Martha into the car and walked over to Mouse's Range Rover. 'Right, I'll see you in a bit. Thank you for giving me time out. I'm looking forward to seeing Alice, I wanted her to see Martha in the little jacket before she grows out of it.'

'Enjoy your day off,' Mouse said. She was relieved that Kat was looking so much better, and definitely not so tired. 'We'll be in the office all day if you need anything.'

***

Driving along Derbyshire's winding roads, Kat eventually arrived at the pretty cottage belonging to Alice Small. Bradwell wasn't a large village, but managed to be well known for the famous Bradwell's ice cream. She vowed to pick some up before she headed back home.

She felt a little disappointed and disgruntled when she realised there was no response to her knock on the door. She placed Martha on the floor in her car seat, and sat on the doorstep, wondering what to do next. Should she wait in the hope that Alice turned up, or head back to the office and see what the real workers in the company were doing?

She heard pounding footsteps and Alice appeared around the corner, dressed in jogging bottoms and a strappy top.

'Alice!' Kat jumped up and stared in amazement at the wiry pensioner. 'Should you be doing that?'

Alice laughed. 'Of course. I have to keep myself fit, I'm not ready to go to meet my maker just yet, you know.'

Kat's surprise was written all over her face. 'Do you do this a lot?'

'Every day. It's also a way of checking that friends dotted around the village are okay. They all give me a shout out as I pass. One or two occasionally join me, but not today, I was on my own. Have you come to show me this beautiful baby?'

'I have indeed.'

Alice bent and picked up the car seat, to have a closer look. 'You really are a little corker,' she said, and Martha obliged with a wave of her hand.

A key hanging around Alice's neck was used to enter the cottage, and Alice carried the car seat and baby through to her lounge. Kat was amazed by the fitness of the woman; she normally only saw her at church, and wearing either a skirt or a dress. It took twenty years off her to see her in fitness clothes.

Alice did a couple of stretches to unwind her muscles, then headed for the kitchen to make them a drink.

'Cold drinks okay?' she called. 'Or do you want tea?'

'Water will be fine,' Kat said, looking around the room at all the pretty antiques Alice had collected. She turned as the older woman entered carrying a tray.

'You have some beautiful things in here,' Kat said. 'My home just seems too... modern to fill it with antiques. And yet it isn't, it's a couple of centuries old. I think when we sorted out the interior it lost its old appeal. I love it in this room.'

'So do I, and so did Tom. I think he came here to escape from that woman. Now, can I see this baby properly, please?'

Kat grinned and unsnapped the restraints holding her daughter into the car seat. She lifted her out and passed her to the seated Alice. 'And she has my little jacket on,' she said. 'She really looks so beautiful, Katerina. You must be so proud.'

'Oh, I am,' Kat laughed. 'And I have three expert babysitters, she's spoilt rotten. I wanted to bring her to show you, so the other two have headed for the office, and I'm taking a day off. We've had a bad couple of days...' She paused.

'You have heard the news about Judy, haven't you?'

'News? She's found Tom's birth mother?'

'No, no… she's dead.'

'Really?' It almost seemed to Kat as if Alice didn't believe her, but then she said, 'How? Car accident?'

It all seemed too cold, clinical, and Kat didn't know how to respond. She thought the police would have notified Alice, but it was obvious that hadn't happened.

'I'm sorry, Alice, I really shouldn't be saying anything. It was partly my reason for coming here, because I thought the police would have told you. We did give them your name…'

'What? She's nothing to do with me. If, as you say, she's dead, then so be it. I can't grieve for her, she never cared for Tom, she just wanted his money. Maybe now it will go to the right people.'

'Tom had money?'

'Oh yes, but it's pretty much tied up. Judy gets an allowance, and I know he supported several charities. He said he was leaving a new will when I saw him about two weeks before he died, so I assume she's copped for the lot. I really hope… oh, never mind.'

Kat felt as if she was floundering in deep water. She couldn't say anything about a will only just having surfaced; Marsden had asked them not to speak of it. And now she'd opened the conversation, she had to tell Alice how Judy had died.

'Alice,' she said slowly, 'Judy was murdered. Stabbed in her bedroom. Mouse and I went to see her, and we found her.'

'Really?' There was still a coldness in Alice that was stopping Kat from saying anything further. For a Christian, Alice was being particularly uncaring.

Kat picked up her glass of water, and watched as Martha and Alice played with each other's fingers. 'Can I take a picture?' Kat asked.

She took out her phone and snapped several of the two of them, then went and stood by Alice's chair in order to get all three of them in the picture. 'Thank you,' Kat said. 'I'm making a memory book for Martha, so that she remembers everything from birth to her eighteenth birthday. It will be part of her celebrations, having this given to her.'

'What a lovely idea! Oh, it seems I have more visitors…'

Marsden's car pulled up outside.

'Then I'll leave you,' Kat said. She took Martha from Alice's arms and placed her back in the car seat. Alice went to the door to let the DI in, and Kat nodded at Marsden as she went by.

'Thank you, Alice,' Kat said. 'I'll bring her again soon.'

'Kat, I'm calling around to see you after I've spoken to Mrs Small. Office or home?'

'We're all at the office, even Martha,' she said with a laugh.

***

Marsden headed out of Bradwell in a troubled frame of mind. Alice Small had showed no emotion concerning Judy Carpenter's death, had wanted no details. When asked her whereabouts between 6am and mid-morning of the day of Judy's death, she said she had been running, as she did every day, and gave names of several friends who routinely looked out for her as she ran around the village.

'I'll put Hannah on to checking that out,' she mused aloud, but admitted to herself that it was just a tad unlikely that an eighty-year-old Christian lady would be able to overcome a much younger Judy Carpenter, killing her with a knife.

Marsden pulled up outside the shop in Eyam, locked her car and headed towards the door. The bell clanged as she entered; it was so old-fashioned, and yet everybody loved it.

Doris was in her usual place on reception, her laptop open, her fingers flying across the keys. 'DI Marsden, can I help you?'

'Kat didn't tell you I was calling in?'

'Kat flew in with a screaming baby. She went straight through to her office and all is once again peaceful, so I assume Martha needed feeding. Do you need all of us?'

'I do. I've come to realise over the time that I've known you, that we know different things. I want to pick brains.'

'Intriguing,' Doris said. 'Let me see what Kat and Mouse are up to, and we'll decide where to sit.'

She carefully opened the door to Kat's office, where Martha was being placed in her car seat, obviously fast asleep. Kat put a finger to her lips, and came out to reception.

'We all need to talk. Mouse's office?' Doris said.

Mouse was playing card games on her laptop, so they decided as she clearly had nothing better to do they would all squeeze into there.

'You have something for us?' Mouse began.

'A little bit. Information about the will that the SOCOs uncovered. A lot of what I'm saying is guesswork, but I feel it's accurate. We pulled in Keeley Roy yesterday and had an interesting chat with her. In a couple of days we're going to talk to her again, but it's going to be about the will.'

'Is it valid?' Mouse looked puzzled. 'Does Keeley benefit?'

'Why would Keeley benefit, Mouse?' Marsden said with a grin. 'You know, if you're going to withhold information from me, don't drop yourself in it when we have a general conversation.'

'Keeley is a client,' Mouse said, crossing her fingers as she told the minor white lie. 'I am assuming she has now told you certain facts about her relationship with Tom Carpenter.'

'She has, she was very open and forthcoming. It was almost as though it was a relief to have it out in the open. Would that have been a good enough motive to murder Judy Carpenter? I'm inclined to think not. But somebody did, and it was a particularly brutal assault. So, to go back to the will.'

She took a notepad out of her bag, and glanced quickly down the page. 'Tom Carpenter was very stable, financially. He inherited vast amounts of money when his adoptive parents died, but they had invested in him anyway. Over the years, nearly twenty I understand, he bought all of the houses on that little side road where he lived with Judy. When he married Judy he was already living in that corner house, and we don't think he ever told her about his finances. He rented all of them out, but about ten years ago two of the tenants approached the estate agent who acted as rent-collector to ask if they could buy their homes. He agreed, on condition they didn't reveal who the current owner was, and those two ex-tenants were the men he approached when he needed this will witnessing.'

She paused to once again check her facts. 'About seven years ago the house adjoining his own house became empty, and Keeley Roy became his tenant. It was all done through the estate agent; they look after the houses, see to maintenance, collect rents, re-let when necessary, and Tom Carpenter had nothing to do with any of it. Reading between the lines, I think it was to stop Judy finding out just how much money he had because his intention was to divorce her.'

'Sneaky,' Mouse responded.

'Don't forget most of this is supposition, but I sent one of the team to the estate agent's office yesterday, and they confirmed the secrecy Tom Carpenter insisted on being in place. Even Keeley didn't know he owned her house; she paid her rent every month for seven years or so, and didn't know she was paying it to her Tom. He has put things right, I might add. The will says that Judy is to have use of the house they have always lived in until her death, and then it goes to little Henry. That's the first major point.'

'Good grief, he's a bit little to be a landlord,' Doris said.

'That's not all Henry gets. He has a considerable trust fund set aside for him when he reaches... I think it's twenty-one. I hope it's thirty,' Tessa added. 'His mother, who still doesn't know Tom was her landlord, receives her house, fifty-thousand pounds, and all the rent she has ever paid is to be returned to her. Plus, she shares ownership of the fourth house and all rental income with Henry until one of them dies. Then it all reverts to the remaining one. Tom's left the final house to Alice Small, along with £10,000. As I said, he was a very wealthy man.'

There was silence for a moment as Kat, Mouse and Doris digested the information. Finally Mouse spoke. 'I'm not buying that this murder is about money though. It doesn't feel like it. The will was found after Judy's death. So nobody knew about his huge wealth until SOCOs found the document.'

Marsden sat back and waited.

'You're right,' Kat joined in. 'I don't see this as being about any financial gain. Yes there's going to be a lot, especially for Keeley, but there's an itch I can't scratch at the moment; I'm working on it. He didn't leave any actual cash to Judy? That seems a bit... strange. No wonder she saw potential in linking up with Pam Bird.'

***

Doris looked at her girls. Deep thinkers, both of them, and she knew they needed time to work this one through. Her own IT skills wouldn't help push this conundrum to any sort of conclusion. This was about life as much as about death.

'So... motive.' Kat frowned as she said the word. 'Why would anybody want to kill Judy? She hadn't done anything wrong. Yes she had a plan, but at that particular moment of her death, she had done nothing illegal or immoral. She hadn't even met Pam Bird, she was hanging fire so that it all looked innocent when we introduced the two of them.'

'You think the Pam Bird connection is somewhere hidden in this?' Marsden asked. 'I was going to see her today, but that nurse woman told me not to bother, she was out of it because she had woken up in so much pain. She sounded almost accusatory, as though it was all my fault she'd had to have extra painkillers.'

'Grace isn't a nurse as such,' Mouse explained. 'She was employed to help out with the business when Pam's husband was taken ill. When he died, Pam continued to employ Grace because Pam's own illness is so debilitating. She never knows from one day to the next if she's going to have manageable pain levels, so if it's any consolation, Tessa, I don't think she was bullshitting you, it would have been a genuine reason for you not being able to see Pam today.'

'Let's hope by tomorrow she's feeling much better because I'm going to see her,' Marsden said.

26

Marsden stayed for another half hour, batting thoughts backwards and forwards with the three women. She agreed to call in to the shop after she had spoken to Pam Bird, and fill them in on any developments, or even simply ideas her team had cast around the office.

Finally it felt as though they hadn't held anything back, although she did realise it was entirely down to the death of their client; their mouths would have been as if sewn tightly shut if Judy Carpenter had still been alive.

***

Pam Bird was lying on the sofa, a fleece cover placed over her. She had a book by her side, and a carafe of water with a glass over the neck of it on a small coffee table within easy reach. She looked comfortable, if a little drowsy.

'DI Marsden,' she said. 'Good to meet you. Kat and Beth have spoken of you and I know they think highly of you. I'm not sure how I can help, but if I can, I will.'

The door opened and Grace appeared with the obligatory tray of tea and coffee. Marsden smiled her thanks, and knew she would have to use the bathroom before driving away. Her bladder was already feeling slightly overwhelmed.

'Do you need me, Pam? Grace asked.

Marsden jumped in. 'No, Mrs Bird will be fine. I'm only here for a chat. I may need to speak to you separately, but I'll come and find you.'

Grace gave a reluctant smile, nodded and left the room saying she would be in the office.

'Do you mind if we record this conversation, Mrs Bird? It saves me making notes.'

'Not at all.' Pam said.

'Well I rather think Grace might raise objections, but it's not her I'm speaking with. She didn't appreciate me asking her to leave.'

'She's very good to me,' Pam said. 'But she can be a bit possessive. I honestly don't know where I would be without her. She gave me my pain medication just before you arrived instead of after lunch, in case I became stressed. I wouldn't have thought of doing that.'

No and neither would anybody else, Marsden's suspicious mind screamed out. 'What pain medication do you take, Mrs Bird?'

'I take Gabapentin three times a day, and Imipramine at night. I can top up if it's particularly severe with co-codamol and ibuprofen.'

'Powerful stuff,' Marsden said. 'So you've had your afternoon dose of Gabapentin a couple of hours early?'

'I have, but the pain is pretty bad today. Not as bad as yesterday but when I get a flare-up as awful as that one was, it takes me a few days to recover. I'm sorry if I sound a bit dozy, this drug has that effect on me. I think it's when I mix it with Imipramine... Makes me sleepy.'

'You've had that as well? Your bedtime medication?'

Pam nodded, and shuffled her body a little higher. 'Would you mind pouring me a coffee, please, DI Marsden, and help yourself to either tea or coffee. And we have scones! Grace makes beautiful scones and cakes. Please, help yourself.'

Marsden did as instructed but said no to the scone. She didn't want to take the risk of a sleeping tablet having been ground up and used in the scone mixture...

You're a cow, Marsden, she told herself. *She's probably a really nice caring person. Who dispenses evening sleeping tablets in the middle of the day.*

'Okay,' Marsden finally said, 'let's talk about your son. You had him, I understand, when you were only sixteen?'

'That's right, and forced into giving him away. It wasn't because I didn't love him, it was because I did love him. He would have had no life with me, a sixteen-year-old who knew nothing. I was still dependent on my parents, and there was no way they would let me keep him.'

Marsden nodded sympathetically.

'And now I'll never know him.' Pam glanced briefly at the picture standing proudly in the middle of the mantelpiece. 'He was a handsome man, wasn't he?'

'He certainly was. A man you can be proud of producing, and from what I've been told, he had a happy childhood.'

'But he didn't have a happy marriage, did he?' A frown briefly crossed Pam's face. 'I could have been taken in completely by this woman who was supposed to be coming to see me. I could so easily have believed that she wanted to fulfil Tom's last wishes that he find me, because that's what I wanted to believe. And she would have made it her business to become part of my life, wouldn't she?'

'Everything is pointing to that, I'm afraid,' Tessa said gently. She sipped at her coffee, enjoying the taste, the expensive taste. No instant in this house, she guessed.

'I would like to go to his grave, if he has one. Beth Walters said she would find out for me.'

'If Beth Walters said that, then she will. Judy Carpenter was her client, and under normal circumstances she would have simply asked her, but now Judy isn't there to ask. I'm seeing them later, so I'll remind her.'

It was clear that Pam was tiring, so Marsden put their cups back on the tray and stood. 'Have a nap, Mrs Bird. I don't think I'll need to trouble you again, but I would like to speak with Grace, just to tidy everything up here. And I'll remind Beth about the grave of your son. I do hope seeing it, if there is one, gives you some sort of closure.'

Pam smiled. 'Thank you. Grace is at the end of the hall, last door on the left. She's dealing with accounts and stuff in there, all the work my husband used to do. She keeps his assorted businesses ticking over nicely, attends all the meetings for me. I'd be lost without her.'

Pam's eyes were already closed by the time Tessa left the room, and she headed down the corridor, initially looking for the downstairs toilet. It was a relief when she found it.

***

Grace was sitting behind an imposing desk, the laptop open in front of her. She was on the telephone, and waved to the chair at the other side of the desk. Tessa sat and waited. It seemed Grace was on with one of the businesses she was looking after, and Tessa felt uneasy. Grace's tone was quite imperious; the words were meant to convey that what she said was gospel, and whoever was on the other end would obey.

Replacing the receiver, Grace turned her head and looked at Tessa. 'Can I help?'

'I'm not sure. It's just a general chat really, to get my thoughts in order. What do you do?'

'What do I do? I suppose I do most things. I was employed here when William Bird became ill, but that was coincidence really. He hired me to be a help to Pam. It was clear she couldn't do much, chronic pain illnesses can be horrific. However, almost from the start it was clear he wasn't on this earth for long, and I took on the role of looking after both of them. I began to handle almost all of William's affairs under his guidance, and continued to do so after his death. Pam isn't capable of dealing with anything really, and what's more she doesn't want to.'

Marsden nodded. 'How many businesses are we talking about here? I realise Mrs Bird is extremely wealthy, and I merely wondered why.'

'I look after ten, although really for most of them it's more a monitoring brief. He had excellent people in place, did William, and they've simply carried on. The businesses are varied. He used to buy into ailing developments, and make them whole again. He had a knack for recognising what was good and what was irrecoverable.'

'Thank you, Grace.' Tessa stood. 'I'll leave it all for now, but we may need to come back. It's officially a murder case, and that usually means a couple of visits to anyone who has the slightest connection with the victim. There is one thing I'm going to do though. I'm going to pop in and see Mrs Bird's doctor. I'm concerned that she is overdosing on her medication, and we don't want anything bad happening to her as a result of that, do we? And I have her words recorded where she told me she doesn't self-medicate, you see to every one of her tablets. I'll see you soon, Grace.'

27

arsden filled Kat and Mouse in on her activities in Buxton, then left for the drive back to Chesterfield.

Doris, returning to the shop in Mouse's Range Rover, gave her a wave as they passed.

'Anything new to report,' she asked as she re-joined her girls, still in Mouse's office.

'Not much, although Marsden is unhappy about Grace,' Mouse said. 'She's kind of put the gypsy's warning on her, letting her know that she is aware that Pam Bird is being overdosed and that Grace is doing it.'

'I told you I didn't like her,' Doris said. 'There's just something... and I have this niggling feeling that I know her. I don't know how, or where from, but there's something about her...'

'Let's run a check on her.'

Kat put her hands over her ears. 'I don't want to hear this.'

Mouse grinned at Doris. 'We'd better be quick then; our Kat is having palpitations.'

Doris smiled at Kat. 'Kat, what we're about to do, anybody could do. It's perfectly legal to track somebody. If it's available on the Internet, then you can legally find it. Sort of. The problem might come if we find anything we need to dig a bit deeper for, but we won't mention that to you, okay?'

Mouse chuckled. 'Nan, I think you've just made it worse. Kat, Martha is stirring, I can hear her. And can you ring Keeley for me and ask where Tom's grave is, please? If she knows, and I'm sure she will, will you ring Pam and tell her.'

Kat frowned at the two women and went into her own office. Martha had slept for ages, and wanted feeding again. She took the bottle out of the fridge, warmed it and fed it to Martha. It was quickly emptied, and Kat thought she had better prepare slightly bigger feeds from now onwards. Already she could see a plumper Martha, and she felt blessed that her child was proving to be fairly easy to bring up.

She rang Keeley, and felt instantly saddened when Keeley spoke with a sob in her voice. 'I'm sorry, Kat,' she said. 'It's brought everything back to me, because with Judy dying the house next door will have new tenants, and I'll have lost Tom for ever then. New tenants will change everything. It suddenly washed over me.'

'Oh, Keeley,' Kat responded, 'I'm so sorry. And now I'm likely to upset you even more because I have a query about Tom. His birth mother would like to visit his grave, but we don't know where it is, or even if he has one.'

There was silence for a moment, and Kat was starting to wonder if Keeley had gone, when she spoke. 'It's in Hope churchyard. He was cremated, but Judy had his ashes buried. I go a lot, but I can never take flowers. I mean… I could never take flowers. I suppose there's nothing stopping me now.'

'Thank you. If I pop down to see you tomorrow, will you be in or are you working?'

'I've taken this week off. I'll be in unless the police come for me again. We can walk across and I'll show you where he is.'

'That would be really helpful. Now go and give Henry a cuddle, I'm sure it will help. I'll see you tomorrow morning.'

***

The rising of the sun heralded a day that would prove to be a busy and productive one in several ways. Following a request from Enid to have a practise run at having her granddaughter for the full day, Kat dropped her off just before eight. She returned home to discuss with Mouse and Doris their actions for the next few hours, then left to go to Keeley's home.

Keeley opened the door with a smile. 'I've bought some flowers,' were her words as she greeted Kat. 'For the first time I've bought Tom some flowers.'

'Then let's go and give them to him,' Kat said.

Keeley went back inside, picked up the bouquet of roses and returned to Kat, who was waiting in the tiny front garden.

'I'm glad you're nice and early,' Keeley said. 'There's apparently a legal chap coming to see me at twelve, along with DI Marsden. I'm a tad concerned, but not too much. I haven't done anything wrong, and despite what they might think, I didn't kill Judy, and while I might have wanted her dead when Tom was alive, I certainly don't now, I would gain nothing from that.' The long speech showed her unease at the forthcoming interview. Inwardly, Kat smiled.

They walked down to the main road running through the village, and stood patiently as they waited for a gap in the traffic. It was part of life for Derbyshire villagers, learning to be tolerant while visitors drove into their world.

They reached the other side without breaking any bones, and strolled up towards the church of St Peter. Kat had made a point of learning about the beautiful churches in her area when she was studying to be a deacon, and she knew that St Peter's was said to be the oldest recorded Christian place of worship in the northern Peak District.

She would have loved to go inside for five minutes, just to offer up prayers for Keeley and the late Tom, but she knew it was closed during the week. She followed Keeley through the spacious churchyard until Keeley finally stopped and touched a new headstone.

'He's here,' she said softly. 'This is my Tom.' She bent and placed the bouquet of flowers at the base of the headstone, touched her fingers to her lips and transferred the kiss to the headstone.

CARPENTER

Thomas Edward

23-04-1976 to 05-05-2016

Aged 40

Dearly loved husband of Judith

Rest in Peace

Kat stared at the inscription – no mention of Tom's parents. It said more about Judy than Kat could ever have imagined. A mean woman, with a bitter and twisted mind.

She knelt down by the side of the grave and dipped her head in prayer. She felt Keeley's hand slide into hers as she too knelt, and Kat spoke aloud the words of the Lord's Prayer.

They remained in place for a minute, then stood. There were tears in Keeley's eyes as she turned to look at Kat. 'Thank you so much,' she whispered. 'That was so right, wasn't it?'

Kat nodded. 'It was. But in my world, Keeley, it's always right. And in my job I use those words, because sometimes my job isn't a nice job. If it's helped you to come to terms with anything, then that makes me happy.'

'I feel at peace finally,' Keeley responded. 'For so long it's felt as though there was a spring inside me, tightly wound and ready to bounce up and split me apart. Do you understand, Kat?'

'More than you could ever know,' Kat spoke softly. 'My husband was Leon Rowe, don't forget. That coiled spring was, and to some extent still is, inside me.'

They strolled back towards Keeley's house and stopped by Kat's car.

'Thank you, Kat, I feel so much better. I can face whatever's coming this afternoon, and I hope when Tom's birth mother visits the grave, she feels a sense of closure. Please make sure she understands what a lovely man he was, and how much I miss him.'

Kat nodded. 'I will, and if you need to talk after your visit this lunchtime, give me a ring.'

Keeley stared at her. 'You know, don't you? You know why they're coming to see me.'

'I do, but I can't tell you. All I will say is don't be worried, but you might want to talk things through.'

She drove away, leaving Keeley still standing on the pavement watching her.

***

At the same time as Kat and Keeley had been battling to cross the road, Hannah Granger had been picking up a hand-drawn map from Alice, showing the route she took every day on her run, with houses of her friends marked on it.

'If you had come a couple of hours ago, PC Granger, you could have done the run with me,' Alice said. It was clearly said as a joke but Hannah didn't feel as though Alice was laughing.

'No, you're fine running it on your own,' Hannah said, 'I'll be walking the route. It's just something we have to do, Mrs Small, we have to check everybody's alibi. I'm counting on losing a stone in weight checking yours,' she added.

Alice followed Hannah as she walked to her garden gate. 'You know, my friends are all as old as me. I run this route every day without fail, and I wave at them if they're in their windows. I don't actually knock on doors unless I know they're ill. There's seven of them, and they're not going to remember if I did the run on any given day. Strikes me as it's a bit of a pointless exercise.'

Hannah smiled. 'You may well be right, Mrs Small.' She began her walk and dropped the smile. *You may well be right, but I'm going to make sure every damn one of these friends is interviewed, and until I'm convinced they're remembering accurately, you stay on the suspect list.*

It was already hot, and Hannah began the initial steep climb towards the top of Bradwell. It seemed that it was quite a lengthy run, but Hannah had no intentions of missing any of it, albeit at walking pace.

The first house she stopped at was simply labelled "June" on the map. A fragile elderly lady answered the door and seemed surprised to be confronted by a young woman with a warrant card held out in front of her.

'Oh dear,' she said in a voice so quiet that Hannah struggled to hear it, 'am I in trouble?'

'Not at all.' Hannah smiled. 'I just have to check something with you.' She took her clipboard out of her bag and went through the questions she had put together the night before. By the time she had reached the end, it seemed June had seen Alice on that morning, although she did admit to feeling a little confused about days.

The second of Alice's friends, even higher into the village, said pretty much what June had said, and she too seemed surprised to be confronted by a policewoman. It appeared that Alice hadn't pre-warned them that they would be having a visit that morning.

Hannah stopped halfway around, sat on a bench and took her bottle of water out of her bag. The water was warm but it quenched her thirst. She had interviewed four of the seven on her list, all of them elderly and all of them admitting to not going out much, which was why Alice checked on them, just in case they needed anything. Praise for Alice had been high on their list when talking about their friend, and Hannah was starting to think it was all a waste of time.

She sat for ten minutes and checked through the notes on her clipboard. All of the four had stated that she was normally passing their house around half past eight; only one had said on that day it had been later. Alice had explained she had to wait for a parcel delivery.

Hannah rubbed her forehead. She knew she would have to check out the parcel delivery, Marsden didn't take kindly to things being presumed, she wanted clear-cut facts.

She continued her walk along the route, and it was only when she hit the last house that things changed. This was a much younger woman, listed on the map as Rosie, maybe in her fifties, and not at all confused by days. She went back inside and brought out her diary. 'I make a note of everything,' she explained. 'I like the physical action of writing, but I'm not clever enough to write a book. I keep a journal instead. It can be lonely living on your own, and this keeps me from constantly watching the television. I do little drawings and things in it, it keeps me amused.'

She opened the book to the right date and read aloud. 'Alice was late today, almost ten by the time she got here. She said she'd had to wait for a parcel delivery. I was starting to worry because she is usually here by nine at the latest, but she was okay. Her new trainers looked very smart.'

Hannah took out her mobile phone and photographed the page Rosie held out to show her. Had the new trainers been in the parcel she had said she waited in for? Further investigation was certainly needed, Hannah decided.

'Thank you, Rosie, you've been very helpful. We're only tying up loose ends so there's nothing to worry about.'

'I worry about very little, PC Granger,' Rosie said. 'If you want to arrest me, please go ahead. It will put a bit of a spark into my life.'

Hannah shook her hand, thinking what a nice visit that had turned out to be, and walked back towards Alice's house where she had left her car.

***

Mouse spent her morning hours looking into Grace Earle. Prior to her marriage, she had been Grace Dewhurst, and had lived her childhood years in Leeds before moving with her parents and siblings to Buxton. She had married, but the marriage had only lasted a year; there had been no children that Mouse could trace.

Checking out the parents first, Mouse could find nothing to raise any red flags; both of them were dead, nothing suspicious to cause any feelings of concern, so she moved on to the siblings. There were two younger sisters, Roberta and Judith.

28

Hannah called home and had a shower and change of clothing before heading back to the station. It had been something of a marathon, the route that Alice ran every day, and the heat had taken its toll.

She popped her head around Tessa's door, saw it was empty so headed for her own desk. She made a start on typing everything up, and loaded the picture from her phone that she had taken of Rosie's journal entry.

***

By the time Marsden returned from her visit to Keeley Roy, which had been emotional beyond belief, she felt bedraggled and exhausted. She could see Hannah at her desk, looking really refreshed, tidy, obviously typing her report from her morning's activities, and hoped something had come from it. She couldn't actually see Alice Small as a suspect, not at eighty years old, but this was a straw Marsden could clutch at, she reckoned, even if it was a bit of a paper straw.

She grabbed a can of Coke from her small fridge, along with a Mars bar, and sighed as she partook of both. She needed quarter of an hour to pull herself around from the tears that had erupted as Keeley began to realise what the father of her little boy had done to ensure their futures were worry free. And also what the murderer of her neighbour had done...

The phone rang and for a moment, Marsden didn't want to answer it. She needed peace. She picked up the receiver.

'DI Marsden.'

'Hi, it's Beth Walters. If I tell you something, I don't want you querying how I know it or anything. I've not done anything illegal, just taken shortcuts.'

Tessa sighed. 'Beth Walters, you'll be the death of me. Between you and Keeley Roy I am emotionally drained.'

'Was it bad?' Mouse asked sympathetically.

'Horrific. She loved that man so much, and now he's left her financially secure for the rest of her life. She had no idea he owned all those properties and had such vast amounts of money. Do you know what she said when we told her the contents of the will? She said, "Does this mean I can get Henry some Clark's shoes?" And she wasn't being clever, it was a genuine question. When I said yes, because I hadn't a clue how to handle her, she broke down, and it was a downwards spiral after that. Every time we said a new fact from the will, the tears came again. But enough about that. What have you found out that you shouldn't have?'

'I did a bit of checking on Grace Earle. It was triggered by something Nan said, about thinking that she knew her, and I felt the same. I tracked her parents, and found where they all lived. Her maiden name is Dewhurst. But the most important thing is she has two younger sisters. Roberta and Judith.'

There was silence for a moment and then the lights went on in Tessa's head. 'Bloody hell. Can you email me the stuff you've found, and I'll pretend it's all above board. I'm sending two officers out to bring her in. I knew there was something wrong, damn it. It was the overuse of medication, it didn't sit right with me. I'll stake my life on it being about money.'

'It's why we thought we knew her. She has the same characteristics as Judy, and you get occasional glimpses of it when she moves. I'm betting she looks like Bobby Outram as well, although I've not seen her so I can't confirm that. I'm emailing our report now, good luck with it.'

Tessa stood and moved out of her own office and into the main room. 'Hannah, Dave, can you get out to Mrs Bird's place at Buxton, and bring Grace Earle in, please.'

'Right boss,' both officers said, a little absently as they were wrapped up in typing reports of interviews.

***

Grace Earle? What was that all about? Hannah Granger felt puzzled; she would have bet her life that it would be Alice Small they would be bringing in next for a chat, or even Keeley Roy. For heaven's sake, didn't she have the most motive, if the will was anything to go by. And direct access via the loft to get into the murder house. She shrugged, picked up her bag and followed Dave Irwin out of the room and down to the car park.

'You want to drive?' Dave asked.

She shook her head. 'No, I'm good thanks. Wake me up when we get there. I've had a long bloody walk this morning.'

***

Dave banged loudly on the front door of the spectacular house in Buxton he was visiting for the first time. He knew a loud bang on the door intimidated whoever was inside, putting them straight into scared mode before they opened the door.

His first sight of Grace Earle told him he was wrong on all counts. She wasn't scared, in fact she was quite angry.

'Did you have to be so damned loud,' she hissed. 'Mrs Bird hasn't been well for a few days and is currently asleep. Or was. What do you want?'

'You, please, Ms Earle. You can tell Mrs Bird you'll be out for a while, but we need you to come now.'

'No. I can't leave her, and I'm expecting an important phone call.'

'Then you leave us with no choice but to arrest you. Grace Earle…'

'Whoa!' she said. 'Give me two minutes to see to Mrs Bird's needs, and I'll go with you. You're not bloody arresting me for anything, whatever you might think.'

They followed her into the house, and through to where Pam Bird was on the sofa. She was awake, but it was clear they had woken her. Hannah apologised immediately, then explained they were taking Grace Earle in for questioning.

'Do you need assistance, Mrs Bird? Is there someone we can call for you?'

Pam shook her head. 'I'll be fine. How long will Grace be gone?'

'We don't know.'

Grace intervened. 'I'll be back later this afternoon, Pam, so don't worry about your medication. I'll sort it when I get back.'

***

Pam stood and walked to the front window, watching as they held the top of Grace's head to put her in the back of the squad car.

She felt strangely liberated, unusually wide awake. The car drove away and she headed back to the sofa. She put her hand in between the seat cushions and removed the two small white tablets she had dropped down there earlier.

Imipramine. To be taken at night. So why was Grace giving them to her during the day as well? She walked into the kitchen and flushed them away, before filling a glass with water and taking a long drink.

It felt good to be able to walk around her house knowing she was there on her own, nobody to answer to, nobody asking if she was okay, nobody leading her back to that damn lounge that was starting to resemble a prison cell, and nobody to help her to bed at night.

She smiled as she briefly gave thought to ringing DI Marsden and asking her if she could keep Grace overnight.

She walked along the hallway to the office, determined to look up the side effects, the warnings, the instructions around stopping taking the drug Imipramine; she wanted to take control of her life. This had to be done while she was having a good day, and today she could feel very little pain. Bad pain days flattened her, but she had been given this opportunity by Grace being taken for interview…

It suddenly hit her. Grace being taken for interview by the police? What on earth could she possibly have done that would cause her to be taken to the station?

Pam sat down at the desk and looked around. She had always enjoyed her time in this office, sharing William's work, listening to him explaining things. Her awful illness had taken most of that away from her, but those times had been exciting as they had built his business. He had once tried to explain that it was spending to accumulate; he bought rundown businesses that were simply being mismanaged, turned them around while keeping as many of the same staff as practical, and phoenix-like, supervised their rising from the ashes. None of the businesses failed once William waved his magic wand.

She lifted the laptop lid; it was open at the last of the businesses he had bought. She could hear his words now, '*Pam, this could be a cracker of a business. This is the big one, and this is the last one. Our next adventure is to retire, and enjoy what we have.*'

The business had been a driver agency called BD Recruitment, the B and the D being the initials of the surnames of the two men who had started the business. William had slashed the massive salaries paid to the two original owners, increased the salaries of the administration workers who had been working for minimum wage, and increased the rates of pay for the drivers on the books. He then set about bringing other ventures to the business, specialising in wide loads, EU deliveries, and a variety of other sub-divisions.

He changed the name to BirD Recruiting, and turned it into a premier-level driver recruitment agency. Their reputation grew;

she knew how proud he had been of the fact that they had never let any customer down, not once.

Eight months later came the first stroke. She took up the reins, coped with the increasing pain, and they decided they needed somebody else to help out with everything.

Grace Earle.

Pam stared at the name on the screen, BirD Recruitment. She felt tears prickle her eyelids; of all the businesses, he had been most proud of this one. She clicked on the *Departments* tab, and saw the list had grown from the last time she had been on the website. She clicked through all the other tabs, and saw that everything seemed to be thriving. William would have been thrilled that his prediction about the business had so spectacularly been proved correct. The second stroke that took him from her had robbed him of knowing the details she could see on-screen.

She came out of the website, and logged into the business accounts at the bank.

***

Grace felt uncomfortable. She had been sitting in the godawful interview room for nearly an hour, gazing at the darkly depressive walls, waiting to see why they wanted to speak to her.

When the door opened admitting Tessa Marsden and Dave Irwin, Grace almost felt relieved. Marsden placed a file on the table, recorded the names for the tape, and initially sat and stared at her.

'It's true,' she said slowly. 'If you had your hair done in the same style as your sister, the sibling relationship would be obvious.'

Grace shifted uneasily on her chair. She didn't speak.

'When I came out to break the news of your sister's death to Mrs Bird, you didn't flinch. Why was that, Grace?'

'It's Mrs Earle. And why should it bother me? You came to tell Pam, didn't you?'

'But you must have known I was speaking about your sister, and you never said a word.'

Grace's mind was whirling. For the first time in many years, she didn't know how to handle something. She hadn't imagined for one minute that this was why she had been brought here, she had somewhat naively thought it was connected to Marsden's last sarcastic comment about the medication given to Pam.

'I did realise who Judith Carpenter was, yes. But it's a long time since I've had anything to do with her, and her connection to Mrs Bird had never been raised between Pam and myself. I'm sorry she's dead. As you say, she was my sister, but for all that, she wasn't a close acquaintance.'

'And you didn't think to mention this at the time?'

'No, it had nothing to do with the rather strange circumstances surrounding Judy's connection to Pam. You hadn't come to see me, you had come to see Pam.'

**

Marsden stared at Grace. *A cold fish indeed*, her brain said.

Tessa pulled the file towards her and opened it. She read through the transcript of the recording made with Bobby Outram's permission, and then looked up at Grace. 'So, Mrs Earle, you presumably don't want to talk about Roberta, your other sister, either?'

'No.'

'Well, I'm going to talk to you about her. She has given us quite a lot of information about Judy. She's told us about Judy deciding to track down Mrs Bird, knowing that she was Tom Carpenter's birth mother. Judy also knew Pam Bird had a lot of money, and that was her primary reason for getting involved with Pam. Roberta didn't like what was happening, knew it wasn't fair on Tom's birth mother, and decided to tell somebody about it before it escalated into a criminal act.'

Grace shrugged. 'It's nothing to do with me.'

'You've never met up with Judy, or spoken to her, or had any contact by email or letter, giving her information about the wealth of this rather poorly woman?'

'No. I haven't seen Judy for...' Grace paused to think. '...Around fifteen years, I guess. I left home to live with my then boyfriend, nobody approved of him, so I cut the whole family out of my life.'

Her reaction to Tessa's request for an alibi for the time Judy was killed was met with derision. 'I was, of course, at my employer's home in Buxton, keeping her alive and doing my work. You think I killed her?' She laughed. 'I didn't even know her, certainly didn't know where she lived. You seem to think I should be grieving, but I'm not. She was always a devious little cow when she was a child, so I've no reason to think she would have changed over the years. Now can I go home, please?'

'Not yet.' The door opened and Hannah Granger walked in. She handed a note to Marsden, who stood, notified the recording that she was leaving the room and switched it off.

'I have to take a phone call, Mrs Earle. I'll arrange to have a drink sent to you. PC Irwin will remain with you while I'm gone.'

29

Hannah filled her in on the conversation she had just finished with Pam Bird, and as soon as Marsden reached her office, she immediately rang Pam.

'Hi, Pam. You've spoken with Hannah, I understand. Can you start at the beginning and explain everything to me, please?'

***

It was a long conversation. Marsden listened carefully to everything Pam Bird said, taking notes, asking the occasional question so that it clarified everything in her mind before she went in to the interview room again.

'Approximately how much are we talking about?'

'I don't know,' Pam responded. 'I'm going into the bank tomorrow, along with our accountant. I think we're looking at hundreds of thousands of pounds. DI Marsden, I need to stop her coming here tonight. I'm alone…'

'Don't worry, she can be our guest for tonight. I'm going back to the interview room now, and we'll see what she has to say. On my team I have available to me a DS who has specialised in financial crime. I'd like to send him to you tomorrow morning to accompany you to the bank. Will you agree to that?'

'Oh, I definitely will.'

Marsden could hear the relief in Pam's voice. 'Good. I'll fill him in on everything you've told me, then he will be ringing you to arrange a time to come over. His name is DS Carl Heaton. He'll look after you.'

***

Marsden waited another hour before heading downstairs to the interview room. She guessed Earle would be getting close to chewing her nails, and she wanted to prolong the waiting.

She logged herself and Hannah into the room, and sat down once more, facing Grace Earle.

'Do I need a solicitor?'

'Do you want me to get you one, Mrs Earle?' Tessa checked her watch. 'It's getting pretty late but we can call one of your own choosing, or bring in a duty solicitor.'

'I want my own.'

'Fair enough.' She closed up the file she had opened seconds earlier, and stood. 'DI Marsden and PC Granger leaving the room, 18:05 hours. Somebody will be here shortly to facilitate your call to your solicitor. I'll see you later if you can get one to come to you now. If not, you'll be taken to a cell and detained until your solicitor arrives tomorrow morning.'

She gave Grace no chance to respond, and she and Hannah walked out once again, leaving a very young PC in the room with her.

***

DS Heaton was waiting for Marsden in her office. He eyed their cups of coffee. 'You get that from the machine?'

'We did, Carl. You want one? Hannah, pop back down and get one for Carl, will you? Milk, no sugar, if I remember correctly.'

'Good memory, boss. It must be nine months since we last worked together. The Leon Rowe case, wasn't it. His accounts needed a bit of checking, if I'm remembering correctly.'

She laughed. 'A bit of checking is about right. He goes off to Canada tomorrow, his parents have requested his body. His wife agreed, she just wants him out of her life for good.'

'Seems you've picked up another one that needs some financial checks put in place. I've had a chat with Mrs Bird, she seems quite knowledgeable.'

Tessa ran her hand through her hair. 'I need to tell you that she's quite ill. She has ME. It's one of these illnesses where to look at her you wouldn't think anything was wrong, but it's a chronic pain illness, and some days she can't even get out of bed. Be aware of that in all your dealings with her. Plus she has the added problem of having been overdosed on her pain medication, I think for some time, so she could be a bit non-functioning.'

'She sounded clear enough to me. It seems that the business her husband thought was the big one that would see them secure for the rest of their lives is on the failing/dead stop route now, and money has been siphoned from the accounts over a lengthy period of time, probably since Mr Bird died. I'm meeting her at her home in the morning, nine o'clock, and we're heading off to the bank. She seemed really grateful that I offered to drive, but in view of what you've told me about her health, that makes sense. She's spoken to their accountant, and he's said he raised concerns in an email to her about ten months ago, saying that BirD wasn't performing as well as it had been doing six months earlier. It seems that he received an email back from Mrs Bird, which she knows nothing about, saying that it was going to be sold on because of the poor performance. You have a devious suspect downstairs, DI Marsden.'

'I certainly do, Carl. I'll need a full report as soon as possible, after you've driven Mrs Bird back home.'

Hannah returned holding his coffee. 'There was a queue!' she said, sounding quite put about. 'Don't these people want to go home?'

'Do you?' Tessa smiled.

'Not on your life, not till we know where we stand with Grace Earle. Do you believe she's not seen her sisters for years?'

Marsden frowned. 'Not sure. She certainly didn't react in any way when I said Judy was dead, but it just seems too much of a coincidence that Judy is looking for Pam Bird, and Grace is working for the same woman. I'm really thinking that Judy told Grace about her plans, because let's not forget she knew who Tom's birth mother was before Tom died. Grace was already working for the Bird couple at that time, and I suspect Judy knew that. I think they were in cahoots from the beginning, and if that is the case, then I'm looking at Grace as a potential suspect for Judy's murder.'

'Sounds complicated.' Carl laughed. 'I think you need to write everything down, force your brain out of first gear and see what happens. Sometimes, when you're reading things on reports on the computer, you miss bits. If you've actually written it down, it might become clearer.'

Marsden reached around her computer to some paperwork on her desk, and waved it at him. 'Done,' she said, 'and in this instance, you're wrong. Nothing looked any clearer.'

***

It was quiet in the Rowe household. Doris was reading, Kat was working on her sermon, delighted to be back in the saddle at church, and Mouse was on the computer, putting in names and seeing what came up.

When her mobile rang she answered it quickly, not wanting it to wake Martha.

'Hi, Beth. Tessa Marsden. I just thought I'd fill you in, out of courtesy. It seems that your ferreting around really paid off. Grace Earle has admitted to being the sister of Judy and Bobby, but insists she hasn't seen them for years. She says she walked away from the family when they disapproved of her boyfriend, and she hasn't seen any of them since. However, that's not all we're finding out. Quite apart from keeping Mrs Bird heavily sedated so that she has no clue what day it is, let alone how her businesses are performing, she's been cleverly siphoning off money from one of the companies and putting it somewhere else. We suspect that somewhere else is a healthy bank account with her name on it.'

'Oh no! That's awful for Pam. How is she?'

'Not too bad. She hid the sleeping tablets that Grace tried to give her this morning, and she's a bit groggy but not as bad as she usually is. She'll have to discuss things with her doctor though, I think, you can't just stop taking such strong medication, it has to be reduced gradually.'

'Were they working together, Judy and Grace? Playing the long game to get everything?' Mouse's thoughts were spiralling, and she rubbed her forehead. 'Grace siphons off from the companies, Judy becomes Pam's best friend who inherits the personal fortune because she's the daughter-in-law, and while they're waiting for all this to happen, they're slowly killing the woman who is going to provide all these riches.'

'That's my take on it. Anyway, we have Grace Earle in the cells certainly until tomorrow morning. She rang her solicitor, but luckily for us the woman couldn't come tonight, she was already with another client. Apparently Earle really showed off when they locked her in the cell. Tomorrow a DS from our fraud squad is taking Pam to the bank for discussions and to try to find out roughly how much has gone, and hopefully where it's landed, then he'll report back to me. I just wanted to thank you, or thank Connection anyway, for your help with this.'

'You think Grace is connected to Judy's death? With Pam permanently asleep, as she pretty much was, Grace could easily have done it and made it back to Buxton before she was missed.'

'That's the part I'm going to be concentrating on. The financial side I can safely leave to Carl. I want the collar for the murder.'

30

Saturday morning dawned with bright sunshine, and the three of them, along with Martha in her pushchair, decided to head down to the Village Green café for breakfast. They had a leisurely stroll down that turned into a bit of a gallop as the rain came down in torrents.

They were laughing as they pushed open the door, rain dripping off their noses, their clothes spectacularly wet.

Lisa handed them a towel to dry their faces and arms along with the menu, and they eventually sat themselves in a corner so that the sleeping baby in the pushchair was out of the way.

'Full breakfasts?' Lisa asked, and they all said yes, each one of them wanting their eggs done differently.

'Kat Silvers, you were always awkward,' Lisa laughed. 'One poached, one scrambled for you then.'

She finished taking the rest of their orders, and Doris looked over the top of her glasses at Kat. 'Kat Silvers?'

'Means nothing,' she smiled. 'I've known Lisa since we were in the infants together, back in the days when I was Kat Silvers. And let's face it, I was Kat Silvers for a much longer time than I've been Kat Rowe. However, as we've kind of brought this up, I've been thinking things through about the name change.'

Doris and Mouse leaned forward onto the table.

'If I call Martha anything but Rowe, it's denying her a true heritage. She is Leon's child, Leon Rowe. She has grandparents called Rowe, but, and here's the biggy, I don't want to be a different name to my daughter. Therefore I have decided my name will remain as Rowe, and Martha will grow up knowing who she is, who her mummy is, who all of her grandparents are, and who her daddy was. I'll obviously have to cushion things until she's old enough to know the truth, but I'm sticking with Rowe.'

'Good,' Doris said. 'Have you told your mum and dad?'

'I have. I told them when I collected Martha last night. I think they're pleased I've actually reached a final decision, and on Monday I'm going to make an appointment to register her birth, then we'll see about having a christening.'

'And a party?' Mouse asked, pouring cups of tea for them.

'And a party,' Kat said.

The breakfasts arrived, and they watched the rain getting heavier. 'Okay,' Mouse said, waving a piece of sausage around on a fork, 'we're not going to be going anywhere until this lot has slowed down a bit, so let's talk. Does anybody else share this feeling that Marsden seems to be pursuing, that Grace Earle is a murderer?'

Doris and Kat shook their heads, their mouths too full of food to speak. Mouse pushed the sausage into her mouth, chewed silently for a moment, and then said, 'Neither do I.'

'Why not?' Doris asked, putting down her knife and fork for a moment to look at her granddaughter. 'Are you basing that on facts or feelings?'

'Feelings, I suppose, I just don't see her like that. A fraudster, yes. I can well believe she's helped herself to a lot of the family fortune, but it's the wrong sort of murder. I can see her planning and succeeding in killing Pam, because it's a non-violent murder, and I genuinely feel that might have been on the cards, but stabbing somebody? That takes some strength, some bottle. She actually comes across as quite middle-class – and I'm not saying middle-class people don't commit murders – but to me it was almost as if she couldn't lower herself to stab somebody. Any murder she committed would be… middle-class.'

Kat almost choked on her scrambled egg. 'Mouse Walters, I love you,' she finally managed to say. 'You have a way of putting things into perspective that is quite unique.'

'Crazy, I call it,' Doris muttered, and returned to enjoying her breakfast.

But Mouse couldn't let it go. 'I know you both understand what I mean. And I genuinely think our local friendly DI has got it wrong.'

'Just as a matter of interest, Mouse,' her nan said, 'who do you think has killed Judy?'

'I don't know yet. But I will.' She picked up her cup of tea and sipped it. 'This is hot.'

'It's made with boiling water.'

'Kat Rowe, don't get clever with me. I'm going to stop talking and start thinking. And eat the rest of my sausage.'

Doris and Kat found it difficult to eat anything, as they tried to hold back the laughter. Mouse was still so easy to wind up, and yet they both knew they fully agreed with her.

***

The rain didn't stop, and by the time they arrived home they were once again soaked, but definitely no longer hungry.

All three of them sat around the kitchen table, laptops open. Kat was polishing her sermon, and she knew her excitement at recommencing her deacon work at the church had to be bouncing off her. She missed her quiet time, the time when she just sat on a pew and let the silence, the peace, the tranquillity surround and infiltrate her soul. It hadn't happened in a while, but the next day it would. She changed a couple of words, and then sent it to the printer.

'You finished?' Doris asked.

'I have. It's been quite difficult. I've felt as though I had to be careful of everything I put into it. Danny's wife will be there, I'm presuming, and I don't want to upset her any more than she already is.'

'You seriously think she will be there?' There was concern in Mouse's voice. 'You need the two of us to be there?'

Kat smiled. 'I'll be fine, honestly. And I do think Bibi will come to the service. She attends every week. If she doesn't, I'm not sure how I'll deal with it. And Mum and Dad will both be there. They're going to have Martha while I take the service. I'm going to introduce her to the congregation, that should diffuse any bad feelings, I hope.'

She went to the printer to collect her printouts. 'I'll be fine,' she repeated, but the other two recognised desperation when they heard it.

***

Carl Heaton escorted Pam Bird through her front door, then closed it gently behind him.

'Let me hang up your coat,' he said. 'It will soon dry.' It hadn't been raining when they went into the bank, but it was monsoon-like when they emerged some time later. It had been a fraught hour and a half, but the outcome had been that Grace Earle, the trusted personal assistant made signatory on the accounts by Pam herself, had defrauded Pam's business of at least quarter of a million pounds.

He made sure she was seated on the sofa, and then went to make her the cup of tea he had promised her while travelling back to her home.

'Do you need any medication with this drink?' he asked, placing the tray carefully on the coffee table.

She shook her head. 'No, thank you. I took some this morning, and my consultant is coming to see me this afternoon to discuss how we deal with regulating my tablets to get me on the right dose again. Apparently, I can't just go back to what it used to be before that woman began to overdose me because I will have severe withdrawal symptoms – and trust me, Carl, I don't need any extra pain.'

How the other half lives, he thought, *a consultant doing a house call to his patient on a Saturday afternoon. And a bank manager working on a Saturday morning for one highly prized customer.*

'Then I'll have a cuppa with you, and head back to the station. DI Marsden will be wanting to know the outcome of this morning's meeting before she interviews Grace Earle again.'

'She's not been interviewed? Is that normal?'

'Perfectly normal. DI Marsden doesn't have all the facts yet. She'll want them at her fingertips when she's interviewing this particular suspect. And I'll let you into a little secret, making a suspect wait for interview tips them over the edge, and they say all sorts of stuff through nerves. But I've not told you that, have I.'

'Definitely not, young man,' she smiled. She had a beautiful smile, now she was awake enough to perform the action.

He finished his drink, poured her a second one, and left her organising a locksmith to come and change every lock on the property... *Just in case*, she had said. He could see the fear in her eyes.

Carl spoke to Marsden at length on the drive back to the station, gave her all the information he currently had on the situation and promised a full written report by the time he left for home.

***

Marsden opened the questioning by asking where Grace was on the morning of Judy's murder, and Marsden carefully specified day, date and window of time.

Grace turned to Elena Taylor, her solicitor. 'I have to answer that?'

'Yes. Just answer the questions. No elaborating.'

Grace faced Marsden once again. 'I was at home with Pam. She will confirm that.'

'Then there we have our first problem, Mrs Earle,' Marsden said. She glanced down at her notes, but it was only for effect. 'You see, Mrs Bird was packed so full of drugs she hasn't a clue about your whereabouts at that time, so is there anyone else who can verify your presence in the house?'

'No, of course not. But why are you asking me? You think I killed Judy? My own sister?'

'A sister you walked away from a long time ago, and, according to you, you hadn't seen for many years. So please answer my question. Is there anybody at all who can say for definite that they saw you in that house at that time?'

Grace Earle visibly crumpled. 'No,' she whispered.

'Please speak louder for the tape, Mrs Earle.'

'No, damn you, no.'

'Then let's move on for the moment. We'll come back to those potential charges later.'

'Charges? Charges for what?'

Elena Taylor leaned across and touched her client's hand. 'Calm down, Grace, please. We'll sort this.'

'Oh good.' Grace Earle's voice was loaded with sarcasm.

'Let's move on to the next item, Mrs Earle,' Marsden interrupted, aware of the panic bubbling out of her suspect.

'Next item? I thought I was here because you accused me of giving Pam a couple of tablets too many! What next fucking item?' All pretence of the ladylike exterior was evaporating in front of Tessa and Hannah's eyes.

***

Hannah could hardly believe what she was seeing. She was watching her boss, who she had the greatest of admiration for, demolish a suspect without faltering in any way.

She had seen lots of interviews in these rooms, and learned something new from each one. This one was a masterclass in how to crucify a person in three easy stages.

Grace Earle was collapsing, it was obvious. And yet Grace didn't appear to know it was happening; she thought Elena Taylor was going to point a magic wand at Marsden, whisper 'Alarte Ascendare', and Marsden would become a projectile disappearing at speed through the roof.

Hannah waited, hardly daring to breathe; she wanted to see where Marsden would take this next.

***

Marsden gave a slight cough, showing that she had heard the profanity and didn't like it. In reality, the same word left her own mouth several times a day, and, as a policewoman, it was simply a part of the job. She didn't want Grace Earle to realise that.

'Mrs Earle, there appears to be a large amount of money missing from the accounts of BirD. Perhaps you can shed some light on where it is?'

Saturday came to a close with several more, and different, words of profanity.

31

'It seems that when she'd managed to siphon off half a million she was going to disappear.' Marsden gave a short bark of laughter. 'It only took one night in the cells to convince her she had to confess. But that's only to the money, and she's not told us where it is yet. I still half like her for Judy Carpenter's murder, but unless it was just a simple falling out of thieves, I can't see a motive.'

'We had a talk about it yesterday,' Mouse said. 'It was something to do while we were being held prisoner in the Village Green. It was pouring with rain. None of us could see Grace as a killer, not as a violent killer anyway, and there had to be some power behind that vicious stabbing. I can see Grace doing what you seem to have stopped her doing, and that's slowly killing Pam Bird with her own medication, but I don't see her as an angry killer, and there was anger in that room when we walked in and found Judy.' Mouse gave a shudder as she had a momentary flashback.

'We're still holding on to her, there's a lot more investigating to do around Grace Earle. We'll obviously be charging her with fraud, but I'm hopeful we can pin attempted murder on her for Pam. We are still checking other alibis but if we can throw the whole lot at Grace Earle it would be helpful.' She laughed. 'That's really not going to happen is it? You know what, Beth, it's my day off and all I can do is sit around in the station, on my own, and try to stop my thoughts. I need an open mind really, I could be so wrong about Earle.'

'Come for a meal,' Mouse said. 'Come and talk your thoughts through with us, we're good listeners, and we've got our secret weapon: Kat. However, and more important than that, Nan is cooking. She's doing a massive beef joint that will probably feed us all week, roast potatoes, Yorkshire pu–'

'I'll be there in half an hour.'

***

After the totally and brilliantly perfect meal, Doris, Mouse and Tessa waddled through to the lounge, Tessa now claiming she was carrying a full term food baby.

'Do you eat like this all the time?'

'Nah.' Mouse laughed. 'Only when Nan gets fed up of pizza and Chinese takeaway.'

'It certainly beat my microwave spag bol,' Tessa said.

'You live on your own?' Mouse asked. It dawned on her she knew nothing about Tessa, other than that she was a DI.

'I do. What man would put up with the hours I work?'

'Another policeman, I suppose.'

'Tried that, didn't work. We lasted a year. He's still in London, I'm in Derbyshire, and now we're divorced we're good friends.'

Kat pushed the lounge door open with her bum, carefully carrying a tray of coffees to the coffee table. 'Okay, dishwasher loaded and running, coffees made, does anybody want anything else?'

'Not for another week,' Tessa said with a sigh.

They chatted about anything and everything for half an hour, but their talk inevitably led on to the case. 'I've brought some work home with me to go through again tonight. I have a sizeable report from Hannah Granger, and one from Dave Irwin. Hannah checked out Alice Small's alibi, and Dave checked out the alibis of the five people still left living in the row of six cottages. One of the houses, the last one in the row, is awaiting a new tenant, but the other four are occupied by Keeley Roy, Eric Davies, Philip and Emma Jones, and…' she searched her notes, 'Owen Ashton, who is still living with his parents in Bournemouth for another month, then moving up to Hope to start a new job. He will be renting the property, not buying it. We've confirmed he was in Bournemouth on the day of the murder.'

'You think the answer is locked somewhere in the alibis? Somebody is lying?'

'I'm the sort of old school copper that thinks the answer is nearly always in the alibis. Let's have a look at Hannah's report. I'll fill you in on what we knew before she set out to test Alice's alibi for truthfulness. Alice said she goes for a run every day, and she checks in with friends on the route who are all with limited mobility. She does a bit of shopping for them, that sort of thing. She's a lovely lady, but because of her relationship to Judy, we had to check her out. It turns out that this run is one she does at speed, she is over eighty and fitter than we are, and that day she did the run but a little later than usual because she had to wait in for a delivery. We have to check that part, to prove she is telling the truth. Take a look,' she said, and passed the report across to Mouse.

Mouse read through it at speed and then passed it to her nan. 'Rosie? The journal entry.'

Tessa nodded. 'Hannah's done a good report, missed nothing out. She said Rosie is very credible, and came across as honest. We're going to be ringing around all parcel delivery companies tomorrow, trying to track this delivery that Alice waited in for. If it's all above board, we can agree her alibi is good.'

'And if you can't find anyone who delivered to her, she moves to the top of the suspect list?' Doris asked. 'Maybe the new trainers were the delivery.'

***

'We still need to prove the delivery happened at the time she says. I hope she's telling the truth. I like Alice Small, feisty old lady.'

'And motive? Why would she want to kill Judy? She's lost Tom, but that wasn't Judy's fault, he had cancer. The will didn't leave her such a lot; £10,000 and the house where the Bournemouth chap is going to live. Keeley received a lot more, and quite rightly so.' Doris looked and sounded perplexed.

'I don't understand it any more than you do, Doris,' Tessa said. 'I just know it will become clear, and in the end, we'll find the right one. Maybe we're looking in the wrong direction completely.'

Kat picked up the report and skimmed through it. 'They love her, don't they? All these people, all vouching for her, all relying on her. Remarkable woman. And fit. I couldn't do that run, and definitely not every day.'

'Fit enough to overpower Judy, who is twenty-five years younger?' Tessa threw the question into the debate.

'I don't know. If you take anybody by surprise, you have the advantage.'

'But we believe Judy had already seen her attacker. Don't forget she was heard to shout out to somebody in her back garden around seven in the morning.' Tessa once again had a point to make.

'Somebody that could have been a cat. Nobody else saw anyone. Let me throw something in here. The untenanted house at the end of the row and the one that Aston... Ashton? ... is going to rent, have they been checked over? Could somebody have been in one of them, biding their time until they could drop down into Judy's house? Maybe hearing Judy out in the garden shouting at whatever, was the start they needed to go up through the loft space and down into Judy's house.' Kat shrugged. 'Just throwing that in as a possible scenario.'

'Somebody who was fit?' Tessa countered. 'And the one at the end has been checked, because that does have loft access, so we went down and had a look around. It's empty, no signs of anyone having been in there.'

'Which brings us back to Alice, if the criteria is that they would have to be fit.'

'We did check through the loft hatch of the Ashton house, but it didn't have a built in loft ladder like the other five, so we couldn't get down into the house itself. We also didn't have a key to get in by the normal route of the front door, but I'm betting the estate agents do.' Tessa took out her notebook and wrote a brief message to herself. 'That's on the list for tomorrow. See, I knew you three would spark something else.' She grinned. 'And I promise I'll let you know if we find anything.'

'And I promise I'll let you know when I find out if there really was a parcel delivery,' Mouse said.

'How the hell...? No, I won't ask. When you tell me, you say you rang up with a query about it. Okay?'

'Tessa, stop worrying.' Kat smiled. 'She'll probably blame me if it all goes pear-shaped anyway. I'm taking Pam Bird out tomorrow, just for the record, not going on any computer.'

'Anywhere nice?' Tessa asked.

'For her, yes. I'm taking her to Tom's grave. She has an appointment at the bank at twelve thirty, so I'm going to pick her up at ten, and bring her down into Hope. I'll take her for a coffee afterwards, I think she might need it, then return her to Buxton in time for your man to collect her. She liked him, by the way.'

'Who wouldn't? Everybody likes Carl except his ex-wife. She preferred the local butcher. Carl's a smart man though. A DS who will go higher. He's not on my team as such, but he's in my bank of experts I can call on when needed. Until we have all the proof we require for this Grace Earle case, he's seconded to me.'

'She still locked up?'

'Oh, yes. We need to know where the money is, and she has charges of attempted murder hanging over her for Pam's over-medication. She's not going anywhere in a hurry.'

Rustling noises came from the baby monitor and Kat stood. 'Peace over, the fourth Connection is awake and hungry.'

'Can I feed her, please?' Tessa asked.

Doris eased herself out of the chair. 'I'll get the bottle, you get the baby, Kat, and Tessa gets the honour. Let's hope she's not sick down that snazzy silk blouse, Tessa.' Doris laughed.

***

Tessa stared down at the baby cradled in her arms, and sighed. One miscarriage had been her only attempt at motherhood, and she knew her rising career would preclude any babies. But it took more than a career to squash maternal feelings;

this was the perfect ending to a perfect afternoon.

An hour later, she reluctantly handed a sleeping Martha back to be placed in her crib, and headed for the door. Kat walked with her.

'You're very welcome anytime you want a change from police stuff, Tessa. We've all really enjoyed today.'

Tessa pulled her into a hug. 'Thank you so much. It's eased me away from all the strain and the stress, and your daughter is so beautiful. I can't remember the last time I spent such a relaxed Sunday, even though we have talked death and crime.'

They walked out to the car, and Tessa wound down the window, reaching for Kat's hand. 'Leon went to Canada yesterday,' she said. 'Now start to live again.'

32

Kat laid the huge bouquet of flowers on the back seat, and helped Pam into the front. 'Have you already been out buying flowers?' Kat smiled at her passenger.

'No, I won't be doing any driving until I'm sure these drugs are out of my system and back to normal levels. I had Waitrose deliver them at seven this morning. I'd almost forgotten I could do things like that. That awful woman has taken over my life to such an extent, I did nothing for myself.'

'Today is just for you. We'll go visit Tom, then head for a coffee shop and have coffee and a big fat cream bun. I've booked us a table for two for eleven thirty, and we'll be back here in time for your date with Carl. How does that sound?'

'It sounds perfect. I've done nothing like this for years, not since William's first stroke.'

Kat drove carefully; despite Pam's brave and upbeat words, she could tell how frail she was. She parked the car as close as she could get to church, and then helped Pam out. 'Shall I carry the flowers for you?'

'Would you mind? In my head I'm getting stronger, but my legs don't always agree.' Pam smiled at her companion.

'Not at all.' They walked through the gate of the churchyard, and slowly headed towards Tom's final resting place. Pam reached out a hand, and tucked it into Kat's arm.

'You're okay to carry on?' Kat asked. 'It's about another twenty-five yards, that's all.'

'I'm fine. I can just feel… oh, I don't know what I can feel, Kat. This is my son, the baby boy I loved so much. And he died before me.'

They moved slowly onwards, and then Pam gave a huge sigh as she saw the name Carpenter.

'Oh, Tom,' and tears leaked from her eyes. 'Oh, my Tom.' She touched the headstone, and Kat stepped back, allowing her the moment to herself.

***

Keeley looked around the tidy kitchen, the one she had cleaned after Henry's temper tantrum surrounding cornflakes versus Coco Pops, and picked up the roses she had gathered in the garden. She wanted to take them to Tom, to say thank you for everything, and to simply have time with him.

It didn't take long to walk to the church, and as she walked up the central driveway leading to Tom's grave, she could see two people in close proximity to where she was heading. She hesitated; she didn't want to disturb their time with their loved ones. Her steps slowed but as she drew nearer she realised that one of the two people was familiar: Kat Rowe. Logical conclusion led her to realise the other person had to be Tom's birth mother, and she turned around to walk away.

At the same time Kat moved, and saw Keeley heading off in the opposite direction. She touched Pam on the arm, and said, 'I'll leave you for a minute. There's someone I'd like you to meet.'

She ran down towards Keeley, who spun around when she heard Kat's footsteps.

'Is that...?' Keeley said, glancing towards the lady standing by Tom's graveside.

'It is. Are you brave enough to meet her? I'll be with you. I can simply introduce you as Tom's friend and neighbour, you don't have to say anything beyond that. She knows nothing of Henry at the moment, but one day you will want her to meet him, I'm sure. What do you say?'

Keeley's brain spun. This almost seemed like fate and she nodded. 'Yes, if you think it's right to meet her, then let's do it.'

They walked back towards Tom's grave, where his mother was kneeling and placing the flowers she had brought, taking care not to squash the blooms that had been there before her and Kat had arrived.

Pam stood and watched as the two women walked towards her.

Kat put her arm around a hesitant Keeley. 'Pam Bird, this is a good friend and next door neighbour of Tom, Keeley Roy.'

'Keeley, I'm delighted to meet you.' Pam held out her hand and Keeley shook it. 'You knew Tom was adopted?'

'I did,' Keeley replied, 'and I knew how much he wanted to trace you. In the end he just didn't have the time. Pam, I have to say it's obvious he was your son. He had your eyes, your chin...' but she couldn't add 'and so does your grandson'. Not yet, it was too early.

'You don't know how much it pleases me to hear that, Keeley. I have a picture of him as an adult, but not as a child; I missed so much.'

Keeley smiled. 'I'm happy to tell you as much as I know. I only live across the road from here, so if you would like to come and have a cup of tea when you've finished here, you'd be very welcome.'

'Great minds think alike.' Kat smiled. 'We've booked a table for coffee and cake – please join us Keeley, we'd love it if you could.'

***

It didn't take long for Mouse to track down the delivery Alice had used for her excuse for being late doing her run; it was exactly at the time Alice had said, just a day earlier.

'Shit,' she said, under her breath.

Doris was engrossed in a document she was checking, red pen poised to make suggested amendments. 'What's wrong?'

'Everything, I think.'

'Alice? She lied?'

Mouse nodded. 'The delivery was timed at 9.32, except it was a day earlier, the day before Judy was murdered. In other words, she had no alibi for the day in question, and she certainly did her run later than normal. I have to tell Tessa.'

'Do you? Is it our job to keep her informed?'

'It is if we want to keep the channels open that are already open. It would be a shame to lose Tessa's trust, and to be honest, if Alice is connected to this murder, she'll have to pay for that. It doesn't matter how much we like her, I have to give this information to the police.'

'How are you going to explain having got the information? You can't tell Tessa you hacked into Yodel's or DPD's computer system, or, heaven forbid, the Royal Mail one, you just can't.'

'I know. I'm going to wait until this time tomorrow, and then ring Tessa and see if they've managed to trace the delivery. I'm hoping they find it on their own, then I don't need to say anything. But in the meantime, we've got the facts… how do we use them?'

'Pre-warn Alice?' Doris said.

'Should we?' Mouse frowned and looked at her nan.

'No we shouldn't! I was only joking. If Alice is connected to this murder, then… I'm struggling to see how she could be, she would have nothing to gain from Judy's death. I know she didn't like her, but I don't think she hated her enough to kill her. And the one thing we're ignoring here is that, like our Kat, she is a practising Christian. She's a person who doesn't just pay lip service to her God, she actually walks the walk. She cares enough for her friends that she checks in with them every day, gets shopping in for them, and that's just the bits we know she does. Something's out of kilter here, but I'm buggered if I know what it is.'

'Buggered?' Mouse covered her lips to hide the bubble of laughter that threatened to escape. 'I'm too young to listen to that sort of language.'

Doris threw her red pen at her granddaughter. 'Go and make us a coffee, and break out the biscuits, sassy one. And stop being cheeky to your elders.'

***

The coffee and cakes went down a treat, and Keeley told Pam of Tom's childhood, all the little bits he had mentioned to her as they lay satiated and drowsy after their lovemaking. She thought it expedient not to mention the circumstances leading up to her gaining the knowledge about him, but it was clear Pam was enthralled, listening to the stories.

'This is so much more than I expected from today. Thank you, you two, you've made an elderly lady very happy. I only ever had Tom. I didn't meet William until I was forty, so we decided not to have children, we reckoned we were both too old – he was a few years older than me. I know you have a tiny baby, Kat. Do you have children, Keeley?'

Keeley's eyes flashed to Kat, and Kat shrugged. The inference was it's your call, you decide whether to tell her about Henry now or in the future.

'I have a little boy, Henry, six years old. We're in the middle of a spat at the moment.' She hesitated. 'I asked what he wanted for breakfast and he said cornflakes. I placed the bowl in front of him and he'd changed his mind, he wanted Coco Pops. I argued about it, he slammed his hand down, catching the edge of the cornflakes dish and it catapulted into the air. Milk and cornflakes everywhere. We were running a bit late, so I threw some Coco Pops into a bowl, he ate them at top speed, knowing I wasn't happy, and we had to run to get to school on time. I came back to a kitchen that looked like a war zone.'

'Oops. He'll have recovered by the time he comes home from school?' Pam smiled.

'I'm sure he will, he's not the sort of kid who bears grudges. And he's normally very protective of me, doesn't like me to be upset. Recently he's seen me upset a couple of times, and when that happens he doesn't leave my side.'

'He sounds lovely. Do you have a picture?'

There was a deathly silence. Both Kat and Keeley knew if she saw a picture of Henry it would be so obvious to her who his father was. That fact had been the reason Kat had pushed Keeley into joining them for a drink, rather than going to Keeley's house – photographs were everywhere.

'Not with me, no,' Keeley said.

'Oh, that's a shame. Maybe I'll see him in the flesh one day. I'd like that.'

'Of course,' Keeley said. 'It would be a pleasure to introduce you to him.'

***

Kat and Pam left Keeley to walk around the corner to her home, and then drove back to Buxton where Pam had made arrangements to meet with Carl Heaton for her visit to the bank.

Kat went inside with Pam. The older woman was clearly buzzing from her morning's activities, and had relived every moment on the journey home. Keeley had handed over her phone number, pleased that the word phone hadn't triggered a request to look at a picture of Henry in her phone pictures.

Pam had every intention of ringing Keeley that evening and thanking her for her company, and for her knowledge of her son's life that she had chosen to share with her.

Deciding that a suit of some sort would be more in keeping for a trip to the bank, Pam disappeared upstairs to change, asking Kat if she wouldn't mind waiting to let in the DS, as he was due to arrive.

Kat opened the door just a minute later, to be faced with a tall craggy man with light brown hair and eyes that lit up in surprise.

'Well, Mrs Bird, you've changed,' he said with a laugh.

'Kat Rowe,' she said, 'I've been out with Pam all morning. We've been to Hope. To the churchyard. To a coffee shop.' She was aware she was babbling inanely.

'Kat Rowe of Connection?'

'Yes. Or Kat Rowe of Leon Rowe fame.'

Heaton smiled, laughter lines etched into the sides of his eyes. 'I prefer Kat Rowe of Connection. My current boss speaks very highly of you. She didn't say you're beautiful though. I call that not passing on enough information.'

She blushed, and felt a silly giggle begin to erupt; she changed it to a cough. 'Thank you, kind sir. A proper Prince Charming. Would you like to come in?'

'Indeed I would. Is Mrs Bird okay?'

'She's fine. We've had a lovely morning, and I don't doubt I'll be doing a return trip to the same place with her. She's very sensibly said that she doesn't want to drive until the drugs she has to take have stabilised.'

Kat led him into the lounge and a minute later heard the bedroom door close.

***

Pam joined them, and noticed the tinge of red in Kat's cheeks. Either she'd been out in the sun too long, or her handsome escort had clearly seen Kat's charms and flirted with her. Pam decided that was a result.

The journey to the bank didn't take long, but Pam noticed Carl managed to mention Kat three times on the journey. Maybe a little bit of matchmaking might be in order, she decided. A friend had done that for her and William and they'd had a lovely life as a result.

She didn't have to matchmake. It seemed Carl Heaton was perfectly capable of doing it himself.

'You have Kat's mobile number?' he asked, as he left her.

Pam handed him her mobile phone. 'It's under R for Rowe,' she said with a smile.

***

All three of them were sitting reading. No laptops were in sight, although Mouse was feeling a bit edgy that Tessa hadn't rung to say they'd tracked the parcel delivery. She might just have to confess to having located it herself.

There was a slight ping, and Kat put down her book. She leaned across to the coffee table and picked up her phone, expecting it to be from her mother, saying her usual goodnight and sending a kiss to Martha. It wasn't.

She didn't recognise the number but once again her cheeks turned red.

It was lovely to meet you earlier and I meant every word I said. You're a beautiful lady. Will you do me a massive favour and go for a coffee with me one day? Please don't say no! Carl x

There wasn't even a momentary hesitation.

Yes! Kat x

'Your mum?' Doris asked, lifting her head out of her book.

'Isn't it always,' Kat answered. 'She has to send her kiss for Martha every night.'

There was a second ping.

This Friday, 1pm, Village Green café in Eyam? x

The red that was fading in her cheeks came back in force.

Yes, don't be late! x

A third ping.

As if... x

'Nanny has sent three kisses tonight, then.' Doris spoke without even lifting her head from her book, and Kat's cheeks burnt like a forest fire.

33

'Hi, Beth. DI Marsden here.'

Beth recognised that Tessa was being professional and formal. She responded in kind, assuming someone was with her.

'DI Marsden. How can I help you?'

'Are you in the office?'

'We will be in ten minutes.'

'Good, I'm coming over. See you soon.'

Kat was strapping Martha into the baby seat, and looked up in query.

'Tessa's coming to the office. Let's wait and see if she's got the info she needs on the parcel delivery before we are forced into telling her we've got it,' Mouse said.

Kat shook her head, hiding her smile. One day Mouse would be in serious trouble for her hacking skills, she felt sure. 'Okay, I'm ready to roll. See you down there.'

Kat had decided to take her own car; a cancellation at the registry office had given her the chance to register Martha's birth at half past three. Having her own transport meant not troubling the two women who, she felt, constantly supported her.

The journey down into the centre of the village took very little time, and Kat placed Martha's car seat on the floor while she raised the shutters and unlocked the door. She grabbed her tiny daughter and moved swiftly inside to get to the alarm before it woke up the whole of Derbyshire. Martha watched her mummy for a minute or so, then closed her eyes.

'Sleepyhead,' Kat said, and bent down to kiss her. She carried her through to her own office, set up the baby monitor, then gently closed the door.

Seconds later her co-workers appeared, and she pointed to her room before they asked the question.

Coffee was switched on in Mouse's room, and Mouse placed her briefcase under her desk, with the printout showing the date and time of delivery of Alice's parcel safely secured inside it.

Kat was placing a plate of biscuits on the desk when Marsden arrived.

'Smells heavenly,' Tessa commented. 'Coffee at work always tastes burnt. It's why most of our prisoners confess to anything, rather than have to endure more coffee.'

They sat around the desk, and eventually the talk turned to Alice Small. 'We're bringing her in this afternoon for a little chat.'

'You've tracked the delivery?' Mouse held her breath.

'We have. It was delivered the day before Judy was killed, but you probably knew that.' She looked at Mouse, daring her to deny it. Mouse simply shrugged, but relief washed over her.

Kat jumped in, saving Mouse from having to respond. 'So Alice has no alibi for that morning?'

'Not unless she can come up with someone who can place her in Bradwell for that entire three-hour period. Let's not forget that by car she's only five minutes away from the Carpenter house, and she's an accomplished runner, so could probably head across the fields in pretty much the same time. As it stands, she started her daily run around ten. Judy was dead by then, she died sometime between Keeley hearing her shout around seven, and you finding the body around ten.'

Kat felt sick. She found it impossible to see Alice Small as a murderer, and although she was around five feet eight inches despite her surname, Kat wasn't convinced Alice would have the strength to stun Judy with a blow to the head, and then proceed to butcher her.

'Do you think Alice murdered her?' Doris asked the question knowing it would come from the girls if she didn't.

There was a long thoughtful silence, then Tessa spoke. 'Honestly? I have no idea. The evidence says yes; she has no alibi and she lied about the parcel delivery, but is that slip up attributable to her age? She's over eighty, and memory lapses are common in older people, no matter how fit they are.'

Mouse grinned at the woman who was morphing into a friend. 'So you've gone off the idea of a murderous Grace Earle?'

'Huh. Not likely. The more I interview her, the more I dislike her. She's obnoxious.'

'You've never once said it could be a man,' Kat said thoughtfully. 'Is there a reason for that? There are men in that row of houses, all of whom could have gone through that loft space and down into Judy's house. The two signatories were men. The chap who's in Bournemouth – does he have an alibi that will bear scrutiny? Surely stabbing is more a male method for murder?'

'Not really. I bet it's fifty–fifty. It's nearly always planned in advance though. The thought has to be there, so that the knife can be in the murderer's possession, and I'm pretty sure Judy's was planned. We haven't found either the knife or whatever was used to hit her on the head. And we also don't know how the killer got into the house.'

Mouse responded quickly. 'The back door was open when we arrived.'

'With the loft access, the back door could just be a diversion to make it look as though the approach was through the back garden. This open-plan attic is what's made this investigation so convoluted. Why would you leave six houses with shared loft space? It doesn't make sense. And I'm pretty sure it's a fire hazard. That untenanted one, the one that's going to be rented to the chap from Bournemouth, hasn't even got a fitted loft access. Whoever lived there would have used a ladder to store stuff up there. It's the only one we haven't checked out inside, partly because there's nobody in it, and partly because we haven't got a key for it yet. We're meeting the estate agent there tomorrow morning. I don't expect to get anything from going inside, but it's something else ticked off the to-do list.'

Mouse responded with a laugh. 'Think these houses are pretty old. They didn't have building regs and suchlike.'

The bell above the shop door pinged, and Doris stood to see who had arrived. 'Hannah! You here for your boss?'

'Yep. I'm going with her to take Mrs Small to the station. One of the lads has just dropped me off. It did occur to me that we spend more time investigating cases in your neck of the woods than we do in Chesterfield, so it would be a good idea to move our station here.'

Tessa walked out of Mouse's office, having heard Hannah's chatter, and five minutes later they had headed for Bradwell to collect Alice.

**

Kat felt sick. Could Alice possibly be the cold-blooded killer Tessa was leading them to believe? She moved to the large shop window and separated the blind slats, watching as Tessa's car disappeared up the hill heading in the general direction of the pretty village where Alice lived. Kat felt so tempted to ring Alice and warn her, but knew they would lose Tessa's trust immediately.

'This can't be right,' she murmured under her breath.

Doris stepped up behind her and put an arm around her shoulders. 'Keep the faith, Kat. If Alice is innocent, it will be proved.' There was a moment of hesitation. 'If she's innocent.'

**

Kat walked out of the registry office with a huge smile on her face and a birth certificate for Martha in her hand. She had taken her marriage certificate and Leon's death certificate, and in the end there had been no problem in registering the baby as Martha Rowe, whose daddy was Leon Rowe.

She walked back to the car, hugged her daughter as if she never wanted to let her go, and drove home to Eyam. The text sent to her mother had informed that Martha was now officially a legal member of the family, and she had sent a photo of the birth certificate.

Arriving home, she was surprised to see her dad's car on the drive, squeezed in the middle of Mouse's Range Rover, and Doris's much smaller Golf.

She opened the front door, and was greeted by cheers and clapping. Enid took Martha from her and removed her jacket. She handed a large box to Kat.

'This is your christening gown, Kat. We'd be honoured if you used it, but don't feel you have to if you've seen something else.'

Kat opened the box and gasped. Inside was a long lacy creation, with tiny matching shoes. 'It's perfect,' she whispered, and felt tears prickle her eyes. 'Perfect.'

***

Mouse received a text just before seven, and she too felt she could smile again.

Alice back home.

She breathed a sigh of relief, and passed the news on to Doris and Kat.

'Should I ring Tessa? I think she felt it was cut and dried, but if Alice is back home…'

'Leave it for tonight. It's been a long day, not only for us but also for her. She's probably gone home to her microwave meal,' Doris added.

***

Alice felt angry. She felt dirty. They had kept her in that pokey little room for hours, to no avail. They asked her for an alibi, she once again provided one, and they said the parcel had been delivered the day before.

She denied it, eventually admitting that her brain wasn't as active as it had once been, and she might have got the wrong day. If that was the case, then she was sorry for misleading them. When every day was the same, it was easy to make mistakes, and if that meant she didn't have an alibi, then so be it. She wasn't a murderer, her trust was in the Lord, and she could do no more to help them.

The result was a return to her home, but with instructions to not leave the area. They would probably want to speak with her again. Hannah went in with her, concerned that the ordeal had been considerable for someone of her age. She didn't want the elderly lady collapsing or something... She was quite surprised when Alice dismissed her immediately, saying she wanted to get the sounds and the smell of the station out of her system and she was going in the shower.

***

Alice stepped into the cascading stream of hot water and scrubbed at her skin until it felt raw. She dried herself, then wrapped her slender ageing body in the fluffy white towel. Running a comb through her thinning grey hair, she stared at the face reflected in the mirror. Lined, but still a healthy colour helped by her daily run in all weathers, she gave a small smile. 'Thank you, Lord,' she whispered. 'Thank you.'

***

And Kat received a text.

Three more sleeps x

She didn't respond, merely smiled. Happily.

34

Wednesday morning brought rain. The trees looked miserable, the army of visitors who descended on Eyam every day looked miserable, tables outside tearooms and cafés were unoccupied, and the whole village had an air of grumpiness.

Kat had disappeared to church to book in Martha's christening and to take a prayer meeting; she felt happy to be easing back into the role she had cherished and relished for so many years. Her prayer for Leon brought tears; she knew tears would have been shed in Canada too, and Martha's other grandparents got a special mention. She lit a candle for her husband, and one for his parents. One day she would tell them how much she had loved him.

***

An hour later she was back in Connection, ringing her mother to check that Martha was okay.

'Of course she is. Your dad is teaching her to count.'

'She's maybe a bit young.'

'Not according to your dad. Now get back to work and stop worrying. Just book Martha in on an accountancy course in case your dad gets one to ten wrong.'

Kat disconnected, a smile on her face. She was so lucky to have such amazing back-up for her daughter while she pursued her church and Connection careers.

Rain or no rain, life was good.

***

Hope didn't miss out on the rain either. Marsden and Hannah sat in the car, waiting for the estate agent to show up with a key. He arrived on a bike. Dripping water everywhere, he unlocked the front door and ushered them in.

'Maybe I should have brought the car this morning,' he said.

'Maybe you should.' Marsden smiled. She bent down and picked up the four letters lying on the floor. All appeared to be junk. Three were addressed to Mr John Cannon, all wanting him to buy insurance policies, and one was addressed to Mrs A Small. That one wanted Alice to have a credit card.

'Mr John Cannon?' Tessa asked the estate agent.

'The last tenant. He left about three months ago.'

'Mrs Small?'

'She was sort of the tenant before Mr Cannon. Peppercorn tenant. The owner was her nephew. She left a couple of years ago, bought a house in Bradwell, I believe. Oh…' his brain clicked into gear, 'but you'll probably know that, won't you, in view of what's gone on here.'

Marsden simply shook her head. Why hadn't she known this? She asked Hannah to check everywhere downstairs, told the red-faced man to wait in the hall, and she headed upstairs.

She stood below the loft hatch and carefully inspected it. Nothing looked… off. The smaller bedroom was empty, and the bigger double bedroom was almost empty; it did have a ladder in the large built-in wardrobe.

She took out her phone. 'Send a SOCO team. I need a ladder, a loft hatch and anything else necessary checking for fingerprints and blood traces.'

She headed downstairs. The estate agent was sitting on the bottom tread, waiting for them.

'We're going to be a while,' Marsden said, 'and I have to ask you now to go outside.'

'It's raining. How long will you be?'

'Depends how long it takes them to get a team together, then they have to get here from Chesterfield, then do the job…'

'I'll head back to the office,' he said. 'But we will need that key back for when Mr Ashton moves in.'

'I'll personally guarantee you will get it back.' Marsden smiled. 'Don't worry about it.'

She watched as he mounted his bike and rode off, turning right onto the main road leading into Castleton. She just hoped he didn't have to ride up Winnat's Pass to get to wherever he was going next.

Hannah joined her in the hallway. 'Shall we get out of the way and wait in the car, boss? There's nowhere to sit.'

'Good idea. And we can sit and think about why we didn't know Alice Small used to live here, and possibly still has a key to get in. She's proper giving us the run-around, isn't she?'

They left the door unlocked and made a dash for the car.

'Crap weather,' Hannah grumbled. 'I thought this was summer.'

'Have patience,' her boss said, 'the sun will come out again. It may take a couple of weeks...'

'So, you reckon that ladder is how access was gained to Judy Carpenter's place?'

'I do. I'm not convinced we're going to find Alice Small's fingerprints on it though. I think the ladder is part and parcel of the fixtures in this house, because there's no other access to the loft. And whatever else I think about Alice Small, I definitely don't think she's stupid enough to handle it without gloves. No, there'll be no fingerprints, but there may be a spot or two of blood. I don't think she would have risked going out the back door, which is what we were meant to think happened, I think she'll have gone back up into the attics, and out via here. I suspect she got changed in the bedroom after she killed Judy, transported the bloodied clothes in some sort of bag and disposed of them when she got home. Hence the new trainers. It's a bit pie in the sky, I know, but I'm crossing my fingers that a bit of the blood found its way onto those ladders.'

'Why?'

'Why what?'

'Why did she kill her?'

Marsden sighed. 'I don't know. I know she loved her nephew, but he'd been dead over a year when Judy was killed. It could be connected with Keeley Roy, and Henry of course.'

'So there's no motive?'

'Hannah, stop being so logical. My brain's hurting enough,' Tessa grumbled. 'Somewhere there is a motive.'

'Maybe, but I'm still leaning away from Alice, and towards Grace Earle. What if she decided she didn't want to share the money with Judy? Because I reckon they were in the fraud together, and I reckon it was initially set up by Grace, but then Judy realised Pam Bird, Tom's birth mother, was the woman her sister was fleecing of lots of money. We've seen just how greedy Grace is.'

Marsden leaned her head back against the headrest and closed her eyes. Her mind was going around and around in circles. Throw Keeley Roy into the mix, and there were simply too many suspects. Maybe they'd done a Julius Caesar on Judy, and all had a stab or two.

Would Judy be able to supply the answer? What was so wrong about the woman that anybody would want to murder her?

Suddenly Marsden couldn't wait to get back to the station, go through every minute detail about Judy Carpenter.

That was the point Tessa Marsden knew she desperately didn't want Alice Small to be the killer.

***

Marsden pushed everything to one side, all the paperwork, the file folders, the half-eaten Mars bar, and stared at her screen.

'Judy Carpenter, what am I not seeing?' she murmured.

Her phone rang and she got the information from SOCO that she had half expected. No blood, fingerprints clearly available on the ladder from two people on file, and one other person not on file.

'Who are the people on file?'

'John Cannon and Keeley Roy.'

'Thank you, that's really helpful.'

She replaced the receiver and typed John Cannon into her search box. He had, apparently, fenced some televisions in his youth, and received community service. Nothing since. Nothing that said he might have leanings towards murder. And his fingerprints would have been on the ladder anyway.

But Keeley Roy? Why on earth would her fingerprints be on the ladder, unless…

Time to find out.

***

Marsden and Hannah walked up Keeley's small front path and knocked on the door. She opened the door carefully, and then smiled when she saw who was standing there.

'Sorry, I'm still a bit paranoid. Suppose I will be until you catch Judy's killer.'

'You're quite right to be careful, Keeley,' Marsden countered. 'The most unlikely people can become murderers.'

She held the door open further. 'Come in. You need me for something?'

They followed her into the kitchen. Henry was home from school and sitting reading at the kitchen table. Keeley asked him to go into the lounge for a minute, and he disappeared, sneaking an apple out with him.

'Would you like a drink?'

'No, we're fine, thank you, Keeley. Something has come to light that I wanted to follow up with you. Did you notice we were here yesterday? At number four?'

'John's place? Yes, I saw the crime scene van, but I didn't see you.'

'We asked them to check for fingerprints and possibly blood contamination on a stepladder that was upstairs.'

'The one in the wardrobe? He put it in there out of the way, once he'd packed all his clothes.'

'You knew about it then?'

'Knew about it? I went up and down it at least half a dozen times back in January or February. Can't remember the exact date. It was a couple of days before he left.'

'Why?' Tessa gave a slight frown.

'It was me being a good Samaritan. John had a pretty bad fall on ice, and had a cast on his leg and ankle and his right arm in a sling. Something he'd damaged in his shoulder. He couldn't manage to get up and down the ladder and carry stuff, but he'd got the moving van booked and a new job to start, so he asked if he could go up via my loft ladder, which as you know is really like a set of stairs, work his way across to his and drop his boxes down through his loft hatch. Can you imagine the result of that?'

Tessa smiled. 'I can. So you went back with him, and got the boxes down the ladder for him?'

Keeley nodded. 'I did. There was only one heavy one and we kind of slid that one down the ladder, me holding it at the top, and him steering it down with his left hand. The rest I managed on my own, and then I got them downstairs and into the hall for him. I put the ladder back in the wardrobe because he said that's where it was when he moved in. That was really the first time I'd spoken at length to him, he always seemed to be at work. We'd say hello if we bumped into each other, but that was it. He left a couple of days after my removal job.'

Marsden felt peculiarly relieved. And sad. That effectively took Keeley out of the picture but it put Alice back in it. Marsden had no doubt that when she contacted John Cannon later, he would confirm everything Keeley had said.

She thanked Keeley for her cooperation, and they drove away.

**

Keeley watched them go, unease settling over her like a huge grey cloud. Damn Judy Carpenter to hell and back.

35

The rain had stopped by Thursday morning, although the sun hadn't put in any sort of appearance, not even a weak one. The pavements still looked dark grey, as though they had absorbed so much water they might never dry out again. Trees dripped occasional droplets as their branches moved in the slight breeze, and Kat watched as the girls at the Village Green café wiped down the outside furniture, knowing that the stalwart hikers preferred to eat and drink al fresco. Only torrential rain teeming down into their lattes sent them scurrying inside.

Kat felt nervous. Her late night text the previous evening had said, **Two more sleeps x**, and Carl's messages were now at the stage of making her giggle. She hoped he didn't want to sit outside the Village Green; it was a little too close to the office for comfort, and she didn't want to have to explain anything to Mouse and Doris, not yet. Inside the café, she could hide.

She was still looking out of the office window when Marsden pulled up. Hannah got out of the driving seat, and Marsden out of the passenger side. They walked into the reception, and one look at their faces convinced both Kat and Mouse that they needed to take the two police officers into one of the back rooms.

'We'll go in mine,' Mouse whispered and Kat nodded.

All four of them sat around Mouse's desk.

'Is your nan not here?' Tessa asked.

'She's gone for a hair-do,' Mouse said. 'She said she looked like a Dulux dog. She'll be in later when they've turned her back into a terrier.'

Marsden smiled, but the smile soon disappeared. 'I'm killing time, coming here,' she said. 'We're here to take Alice Small in for further questioning, and she won't be back from her run yet. I don't want her to have the embarrassment of a police car waiting outside for her, so we'll go about eleven.'

'You think she did it?' Kat was shocked.

'Yes, I do. I've had a long talk this morning with my boss, and he agrees with me. She's certainly fit and strong enough, and, although there are no fingerprints of hers on the ladder used for access to the loft above number four, I believe she's not so stupid as to do the deed without wearing gloves. Bear with me while I go through what I think happened.'

Kat and Mouse exchanged a glance. This wasn't sounding good. Kat pulled a notepad from her bag. 'Just in case anything occurs to me,' she explained.

'I think,' Marsden began, 'that Alice has, or had, something massive against Judy. I suspect she knew why Judy was searching for Mrs Bird, and I think she knew she had to do something about it, for the sake of her nephew. She certainly loved Tom. Before Alice bought that property at Bradwell, she lived in one of Tom's houses, the one where the chap from Bournemouth is going to live, number four. I believe she retained a key to that property, either deliberately or accidentally.'

Marsden paused to gather her thoughts. 'On the morning of Judy's death she was late setting off for her run and tried to say it was because she had to stay in for a delivery.'

Both Kat and Mouse nodded. 'We all now know that the delivery was the day before. She tried to explain the error away by saying her memory isn't what it used to be, and yet when she did do her run on that morning, at a later hour than normal, she told two of her friends, one being Rosie who writes everything down, that she'd had to wait for a delivery.'

There was a quick glance between Kat and Mouse. Marsden was making sense.

'So to the deed itself.' Again there was a pause, and Kat knew Marsden didn't want to accept the facts. 'I believe she reached the back gardens of that row of cottages, and that is who Judy saw when she called out. It wasn't to scare a cat or a dog off, it was to tell the woman she despised to bugger off, she wasn't wanted around there. I suspect Alice was surprised to be seen so early in a morning – it was around seven – and she did leave, but only as far as two doors down where she used her key to enter number four. I checked with the estate agents last night, and she handed in two front door keys but only one back door key when she left. She said Tom had the other one in case he needed to get in to her at any time.'

Kat felt sick. A lot of it was circumstantial, but powerful nevertheless.

Marsden was relentless. 'She used the loft ladder that she had used when she lived there to go up into the attics, walked along until she reached the end one, then waited until she heard Judy go into the bathroom and either the bath or the shower be activated. Alice lowered the loft ladder, came down and raised it again. The next part is guesswork but I believe she waited in the bedroom, possibly behind the door, and she attacked Judy with something heavy to lay her out cold. We haven't found the weapon that caused the massive wound on her head. Then she stabbed her.'

'You can't prove this theory.' Mouse's voice was flat, emotionless. The theory echoed her own thoughts, and she had dismissed them as fanciful rubbish, Alice wouldn't stab anybody. Alice was like Kat; a Christian who believed thou shalt not kill.

'No, you're right, I can't. And I'm gutted that I have to try. I like Alice, but it's my belief that she did it. And what's more, I think she will admit it. We have traced the most direct line she would run between the cottages at Hope and her cottage in Bradwell, and we have dozens of officers doing a fingertip search, looking for either bloody clothing, a knife or a bloodied weapon that she used to hit Judy on the back of her head. We will find something. It's a lot of ground for them to cover, but they'll cover every inch of it.'

All four sat in silence, taking in everything Marsden had spelled out, and then Hannah spoke. 'Shall I make us a cup of tea?' Her voice shook, an indication that there were four people in that room who didn't want Alice to have done it.

They all nodded, and Hannah stood. 'For what it's worth, and I know I shouldn't say this, boss, but I'm Team Alice.'

Marsden gave a rueful smile. 'So am I, Hannah, so am I.'

***

Alice didn't argue. She had been prepared for this, in a way. Hannah escorted her upstairs while she showered and changed out of the sweaty jogging clothes and into a skirt and top, then both of them returned to where Tessa was waiting in the lounge. She had inspected all of the photographs: there were several of Tom, a picture of a couple that she guessed would be Tom's adoptive parents, and, funnily enough, one of Keeley and Henry Roy. Not one single photograph showed Judy Carpenter.

Marsden turned as Hannah and Alice entered the lounge.

'There's medication I need to take regularly,' Alice said.

'If you get it for me, I'll take it to the station for you. Do you require a doctor in attendance?'

Alice gave a slow, gentle smile. 'No, I have enough tablets.' She cast a long lingering look around her lounge. 'I don't suppose I'll see this place again, but I've been happy here. Thank you for your consideration, DI Marsden. I do appreciate it.'

She crossed to her sideboard and picked up two boxes of tablets, along with two small tablet bottles. 'The rest are in the kitchen.'

'Would you like me to get them?' Hannah asked.

'Would you mind, dear? It's a yellow plastic basket on my fridge. Just bring the basket, I need them all.'

Hannah smiled but wanted to cry. She walked into the kitchen, took a carrier bag from a holder on the wall, and placed the tablet basket inside it. She took a deep breath and returned to the lounge, wanting the horrible day to be over.

***

Hannah was driving, the other two sharing the back seat. They were almost at the station before Alice spoke. 'What do I do about my hospital appointment tomorrow?'

Marsden felt uncomfortable. This was quite surreal. The elderly lady by her side seemed to have accepted she wouldn't be going home, and yet she had made no admission of guilt, in fact had hardly said anything. Marsden knew that unless they found one of the weapons involved, the rest was pretty circumstantial. She thought for a moment. 'Can it be postponed?'

There was a small laugh from Alice. 'Not really.'

'Then I'll make sure we get you there. Which hospital is it?'

'Weston Park.'

Hannah's head swivelled towards the back seat, and then just as quickly reverted to watching the road. The oncology hospital was known throughout Yorkshire and Derbyshire, and you didn't go there if you had anything other than cancer.

There was a deep sigh from Marsden. 'Where is it? The cancer…'

'Lungs, liver and I'm at the stage now where I will be having brain tumours. That's endstage. You'll not get your trial, DI Marsden.'

'Mrs Small, I'm so sorry.'

'Don't be. I'm ready to go. I've had a wonderful life, and although Tom was my sister's son, he spent a lot of time with me, and that brought me a great deal of happiness. When I was diagnosed a year ago, I decided I would carry on with my running, keep as fit as I possibly could, and if God was gracious he would let me simply collapse and die while running the fields around Bradwell and Hope. That's clearly not going to happen now, but I think once my running stops, the cancer will overwhelm.'

Hannah parked in the police station car park, trying to shut out the conversation she had just heard. She couldn't begin to imagine what would happen now. Surely they couldn't put this old lady in a cell until she died.

They walked into the station and Hannah booked Alice in while Marsden led her to an interview room. A constable followed them in, and she asked him to get a cup of tea for the prisoner. He disappeared, and Hannah joined them.

'Don't treat me like glass,' Alice smiled. 'I'm a tough old bird. But I will enjoy a cup of tea. Now, DI Marsden, I'm going to tell you everything when you've got yourself organised. I had hoped you wouldn't have been quite so smart and I would have had a bit longer, but it's not to be, so… Everything is written down at my home, and I know the envelope will be found when you search the place. You will be searching it, won't you.'

Tessa nodded, feeling out of control. 'Please don't say anything else, Alice, until the tape is running.' The door opened and the constable carried in her cup of tea, placing it on the table. Tessa started the recording and everyone logged themselves in. Alice took a sip of her tea, and waited patiently.

***

Doris felt angry. She listened to her two girls tell of everything that had happened while she was having her hair done. 'Do we believe Alice did it?' she demanded.

'Tessa does, but I'm not convinced Hannah Granger agrees with the boss.' Kat checked her watch. 'It's just after two, so they're bound to be interviewing her now.' She pulled the notebook towards her where she'd tried to write down every point Tessa had made, showing how guilty Alice was. She handed it to Doris. 'I think there's something missing from this.'

Doris looked at Kat. 'Something that will help Alice?'

'Strictly speaking, no. But I don't see anything that tells us why. What motive did she have? Nobody kills somebody just because they can. Do they? Surely there has to be some sort of reason for it. Alice didn't particularly like Judy, but that was because she was a rubbish wife to Tom. And Tom died some time ago, so why kill Judy now? I tell you, I'm floored by this.'

'Think Tessa will ring us?' Mouse asked. 'She used us as a sounding board this morning, so I'd like to know what's happening.'

'Why didn't Alice tell us she used to live at number four, do you think?' Kat mused. 'You know what, in my head it's starting to look as though she could have done it. She's fit, she's healthy – she runs miles, not just a few yards. But I still can't see why. We'll have to hope Tessa can work this one out so she can tell us.'

***

The group of police searching their way through fields between Hope and Bradwell were recalled. It seemed that the hammer used to hit and knock-out Judy Carpenter and the knife used to pierce her heart had been found. In a shed. In the back garden of a pretty cottage in Bradwell.

And that was almost the end of that Thursday.

36

With Alice charged, Tessa felt she could finally breathe again. The confession had been full and explicit, and it seemed that Judy had been bad-mouthing Tom for some considerable time, until Alice could take no more. It was Judy wanting the tiny silver cross and chain that had been the worst insult in Alice's eyes. No way would she allow that to happen, Tom had given it to her.

This was followed by Judy telling her she was planning to fleece Pam Bird of her wealth, and it was really the final straw when she discovered Judy's sister Grace was as involved as she was. Judy had to die.

The terminal diagnosis spurred her on to kill sooner rather than later, and the act itself had been exactly as calculated by Tessa Marsden.

The letter had been found in the drawer of the sideboard at the cottage, and addressed to DI Marsden. She hadn't read it yet; she felt exhausted and emotionally drained. This woman might be a cold and calculating merciless killer, but what the hell, she liked her. Included with the letter was a small blue jewellery box that held a tiny silver cross and chain. She guessed that when she read the letter it would explain where the child's necklace had to go.

Tessa had sent Hannah home. The young officer had held it together while they listened to the story told by Alice, but it was clear when they left the interview room that Hannah needed time out. Tessa stood at the one-way window looking into the room, and watched as Alice visibly slumped. Marsden saw a young policewoman enter the room, carrying a glass of water and two tablets for Alice, and cursed aloud. Why hadn't she thought to ask if Alice needed anything? She was probably in considerable pain and needed her medication.

She would make sure it was her who took Alice to hospital. For security reasons she would take Hannah along as well, but she doubted there would be any attempt at escape.

The officer handed her the two tablets, then the glass of water. She turned before leaving the room and asked a question of Alice, presumably wanting to know if she needed anything else. Alice smiled at her and shook her head.

Her hand went to her mouth and she took a sip of the water, then sank back in her chair and relaxed, obviously waiting for the medication to kick in and give her some relief from the pain.

Tessa walked up to her own office, and as she entered the briefing room, there was prolonged clapping and shouts of 'well done, boss'. She tried to smile, to acknowledge the congratulations. In her own tiny office she wiped away a tear.

What a fucking mess.

She picked up her phone and spoke to the custody sergeant. 'I want Alice Small in her cell with extra blankets and a proper pillow within the next five minutes. She is seriously ill, and she may need to sleep as she has just taken morphine. Is it already done?'

'It is, ma'am,' he said, and within two minutes it was.

***

Marsden didn't want to go home. The house held no comfort for her, and she needed solace that night. She considered ringing Kat, but knew she would have to go through everything again; the next day was soon enough for that.

She called in to the Star and Garter for a carvery meal, loaded up her plate, and ate only the carrots. Then she finally went home, played a Johnny Mathis CD and opened a bottle of very expensive malt.

She fell asleep before she'd taken one sip; it was almost as if her guardian angel was watching over her, preventing her getting blind drunk no matter whether she wanted to or not.

***

Alice stared at the four walls of the tiny cell. They had brought her a pillow, a second mattress to place on top of the existing one and two or three blankets. She somehow knew Tessa Marsden had organised these extras. She asked the young lady who had delivered the blankets if she could have a glass of water, and two minutes later a bottle and a plastic beaker arrived, along with two slices of toast.

Alice wondered how Tessa and young Hannah were feeling; they had clearly been disturbed as she had told her story, and she took a minute to offer up a prayer for them. God would help them.

She rested her head on the pillow, but couldn't sleep. The pain was bad because she hadn't taken the tablets brought to her earlier. The skirt she had chosen to wear had pockets, and she had dropped the two hefty painkillers in there. She offered up an extra prayer for God to help her get through the next couple of hours.

He did.

***

Eventually the little window in the door opened and two eyes peered in. 'Are you okay, Alice? Do you need any more medication?'

'Yes, please,' she said. 'I need two more of my morphine. They will see me through to tomorrow morning as long as you don't wake me. Is that okay?'

'I'll get them now, sweetheart,' PC Vincent said, and he disappeared. Two minutes later he returned with two tablets. Whatever she wants, she gets, DI Marsden had said, and he wasn't about to go against her. He opened the door and walked across to Alice. He handed her a couple of biscuits on a plastic plate. 'Don't take tablets like this on an empty stomach,' he said. 'It's lights out in fifteen minutes, and we've not put you near anybody else, so you try to sleep. Shout out if you need me during the night. My name's Stuart, Stuart Vincent.'

Alice smiled gratefully at him. 'Thank you so much. You've been very kind.'

He went out and locked the door, then stood for a moment. *Sweet old girl*, he thought, *pity she's done what she's done.*

Alice ate the biscuits, then placed the two tablets he had just brought her on the plate. She added the two from her pocket, then undid the back fastening on her bra. She slid the straps down her arms, and pulled the entire bra out down the front of her top.

On the inside of the bra she had made a tiny pocket. In it were ten tablets wrapped carefully in clingfilm so that they laid flat. The bra had been ready for a week, and she was grateful that she had been allowed the shower earlier, so that she could wear it. She pulled out the thread closing up the top of the pocket and took out the tablets, tipping them onto the plate to join the other four.

She slid the plate under her pillow; she didn't want anyone to have sight of them.

The next few minutes she gave to her God.

The lights went out, but darkness didn't descend. There was still a glow coming from the corridor that never had its lights switched off.

She topped up her glass with the rest of the water, and took the tablets. When all fourteen had gone, she laid her head back on the pillow, and waited. The pain went quickly. She knew no more.

***

Stuart did his rounds at just before four, thankful they didn't have any drunks in; it had proved to be a remarkably quiet night. His shift finished at five and he was ready for his own bed. He reached Alice's cell, and opened the small window in the door. She was still lying with her back to him, as she had been every time he had checked the cells.

In fact, he thought, *she hasn't moved at all.*

He felt a surge of panic wash over him. He unlocked the door and entered the room. The smell of faeces hit him, and he groaned. He crossed to her and shook her. Stuart felt for a pulse and then shouted for help. He had known as soon as the smell had hit him; bowels and bladder usually voided after death.

Help came quickly but it was several hours too late.

***

Tessa took the call around quarter past four. She slowly disconnected and sat on the edge of her bed, her head hanging down.

She pictured Alice as she had seen her coming home before they arrested her, jogging up the lane leading to her cottage. Alive, eyes bright, and in control. Too much in control? Or was the cancer more advanced than even Alice had known?

The answers would be there after the forensic examination, and as this was a death in custody, the post-mortem would be prioritised.

Marsden showered quickly, then headed downstairs to make a slice of toast. The carrots hadn't been very filling, and she needed something to get her through the day. She filled a travel cup with coffee, and headed for the station.

There was a strange air about the place, obvious from the second she walked through the double doors.

'Is Stuart Vincent still here?' she asked, and was told he was in the canteen, having a coffee. *Having a fucking coffee?* She fumed inwardly, but then saw him as she opened the canteen doors. He looked broken. His back was to her, and she watched him for a moment. His head was down and the coffee cup was pushed to the other side of the table, balanced precariously. Obviously, someone had told him to go get a coffee, it would make him feel better, and just as obviously it wasn't happening.

'Stuart,' she said quietly.

He turned himself around to look at her. 'Ma'am. I'm sorry...'

She held up a hand. 'Stop. Did you do your job? Did you check on her every two hours?'

'Yes, ma'am, I did. She said the tablets would make her sleep and that's what she needed. It was only when I did my last round for the night that I realised she hadn't moved at all, and then when I opened the cell door, the smell…'

'Has she been moved?'

'No, ma'am. They're taking photographs of everything, as you can imagine. Deaths in custody and all that.'

'So go through what happened from when she went into the cell.' Marsden opened her notebook.

'She was issued with a pillow, an extra mattress and three extra blankets. She asked for a glass of water and was provided with a litre of bottled water and a beaker. We also did her a couple of slices of toast, which she ate. I checked on her later and she was fine, but she said she needed two of her morphine tablets. I took her a couple of biscuits as well, because I didn't like her having such powerful drugs on an empty stomach. I told her lights out in fifteen minutes, and that was it until I did my checks. One at midnight, one at two-ish, and then my round at four when…'

'You found her. She was terminally ill, you know. Don't beat yourself up about it. She hadn't much longer left. I know there'll be an enquiry, but you've done nothing wrong. Is your shift over now?'

'Yes, ma'am.'

'Then get off home. People will want to talk to you when you come back on tonight, but try to sleep in the meantime.'

She headed for her own office, knowing Stuart Vincent would never forget this shift. She also knew she would never forget either. And now she had to ring Hannah.

37

Friday dawned sunny. After working through half her wardrobe, Kat decided to wear a dress. She had no intentions of revealing the truth about where she was going at lunchtime, and she knew that wearing a dress would be more in keeping when she told Doris and Mouse she had a meeting at church.

'You look stunning,' Mouse remarked. 'You seeing some dishy bishop or something?'

'Bishops don't usually come with the tag line dishy,' Kat laughed. 'No, the sun was out so I thought I'd put a dress on.'

Mouse obviously wasn't convinced but refrained from further comment.

***

Kat was fastening Martha into the car when they heard the phone ring. Doris was already in the passenger seat of the Range Rover, with Mouse walking towards the driving seat. Mouse waved her hand in a "shall I, shan't I" sort of movement, and then made a dash for the front door, to reach it before it stopped.

By the time she had unlocked the door and cancelled the alarm, it had gone to answerphone, and she heard Tessa's voice.

Snatching up the receiver, Mouse said, 'Hi, it's me. We were just heading out to the office.'

'I need to talk to you. We got Alice's full confession last night, but by the time I left the station it was getting late, so didn't bother you. We also found both weapons she used in her garden shed, and a full written confession in her sideboard.'

'Oh…' Mouse didn't want to speak, but felt something in acknowledgement was called for.

'That's not the end. We had to bring her medication with us – she is eighty, and I assumed it was stuff like statins that the doctors seem to feel everybody over the age of fifty should take, but as we were bringing her in, she asked about a hospital appointment, scheduled for this morning. I asked her if it could be postponed and she said no, so I said we would make sure she attended. When I asked which hospital it was, she said Weston Park.'

Mouse felt her breath catch in her throat. 'Shit...'

'I think that was our reaction too. I asked her where the cancer was, and she said lungs and liver, I think, then said it was at the stage when brain tumours form and that was the endstage. I tell you, the way we treated her then wasn't by the rule book.'

Doris appeared in the doorway and mouthed, 'Everything okay?' to her granddaughter, who shook her head and mouthed back, 'Tessa.'

'So are you taking her to hospital?'

'No, that's what I'm ringing to tell you. She died during the night. The whole station seems to be in meltdown, I feel like the big bad guy because I brought an eighty-year-old woman in to die, but honestly, Beth, I had no reason at all to suspect she was ill. When we went to pick her up, she wasn't there. She arrived a couple of minutes after us, and she jogged up that lane like a twenty-year-old.'

Mouse leaned against the wall and slid down. She felt tears prick her eyes, and Doris took the phone from her.

'Tessa? It's Doris. Beth's on the floor. What's happened?' She listened while Marsden explained it all again. Doris wanted to join Beth on the floor.

She sighed. 'If only she had died at home. One day, one goddamn day. And we had no idea she was even ill! What happens now?'

'There will be a post-mortem because it's a death in custody, even if it is natural causes, and then her relatives will be able to organise her funeral.'

'I'm not sure she has any apart from little Henry,' Doris said. 'I'll pass this news on to Kat, and I'm so sorry to hear it. I liked Alice, despite what she's done. Thank you for letting us know.'

She put down the receiver, and helped Mouse get up from the floor. She looked stunned. 'How can that have happened,' she said. 'When you die from cancer, you're in a hospice, or at home surrounded by nursing staff and your family, you're helped at the end. What happened with Alice? She dies in a cell, even though she was still able to continue her running. Something's wrong, I know it is.'

'Come on, sweetheart, let's go to work. I'm sure Tessa will tell us when there's something we might want to know.'

***

Kat was devastated. They dropped Martha off with Enid and Victor, then drove into the centre of the village and parked the car. Kat hardly spoke, her mind running riot with what ifs, and she disappeared into her own room. She needed to be on her own.

Slowly she allowed the quietness of her office to heal her, and deep down she recognised that if Alice was that close to dying, the cancer must have been sending radiating waves of pain out constantly.

Finally, Kat stood and went to look out of her window. The view wasn't spectacular but it was green: bushes, trees, grass. She asked for the peace of the Lord to be with Alice, and stood for a few moments longer.

In reception, Doris and Mouse were speaking in quiet voices. All three came together and hugged each other. It was enough.

***

Five minutes before the witching hour of one o'clock, Kat left the office for her "meeting" at the church. She walked towards the Village Green café and saw Carl, already there waiting for her.

'Thank you,' he said. 'I heard the news about Mrs Small, and wondered if you would still come. Marsden told me she was a friend of yours through church as well as this case. Are you okay?'

'Half and half,' Kat said. 'She had terminal cancer, and half of me says it's maybe better that she went peacefully even if it was in a prison cell, but the other half of me says I liked her a lot and I'll miss her. She made a beautiful baby jacket and hat for my little one, and I'll always treasure it.'

Carl reached out and grasped her hand. 'Do you want to go inside or stay out here?'

'Inside, please. My colleagues don't know I'm seeing you, they think I'm at a church meeting. I'd rather they didn't see me. I couldn't stand the jokes, not today.'

He nodded. 'Good. I've asked them to keep the table for two in the far corner. If necessary we can get underneath it and hide.' His eyes crinkled as he smiled down at her.

***

She couldn't remember having such an enjoyable time for many months. Carl was a fascinating, informative man, who made her laugh. She needed to laugh.

He told her about his job, the intricacies of proving fraud, and he spoke of Pam, saying what a lovely lady she was. She was slowly recovering from the overdose situation and Grace Earle had been charged with fraud. That in itself had caused Pam to feel much happier; with Grace locked up until her trial following her refusal to say where she had stashed the money, Pam no longer felt threatened. Charges for attempted murder were bound to follow.

They had a simple quiche and salad for lunch, and afterwards both felt reluctant to say goodbye.

'Can I see you again, Kat?'

'I'd like that.'

'Sunday? Maybe we can go for a drive to Monsaldale or somewhere equally nice, and have some lunch. Does Martha drink pints?'

Kat laughed. 'Not yet. Give her six months before she moves on to that. You want me to bring Martha?'

'Kat,' he said, and took both of her hands in his, 'we both come with baggage. You've not met my mother yet. Of course I want to meet Martha. Do I need to buy a car seat?'

She smiled. 'No, she comes complete with one. It's part of the pushchair, so the seat holds her securely in the car, and the wheels go in the boot. Are you sure about this?'

'Kat Rowe, I've never been more sure.' He reached forward and kissed her cheek. 'Thank you for today. I can't tell you how much I've looked forward to it.'

'I kind of got the message,' she laughed. 'Three more sleeps, two more sleeps... It told me you'd definitely turn up. And I'd like you to meet Martha, because we're an item, Martha and I.'

'You have church Sunday morning?'

'Always,' she said. 'I'm finished by around twelve, so I can meet you by the church gate if you like. Martha goes to church with me, but Mum and Dad have her when I'm taking the service. You'll have to meet them because they'll be with me.'

'Then I'll have a shower and a shave,' he said with a laugh. 'Kat, I won't let you down. I'm fairly quiet when I'm not giddy with taking a remarkable woman out. I know what you've been through for the last eighteen months or so, and I have to admire you, you're a strong person.'

She smiled, suddenly shy. 'I have to go now, I've an appointment at two thirty, but I'll see you Sunday.'

***

He watched her walk away, and she turned and waved from the bottom of the hill before disappearing towards her office. He punched the air. 'Bloody fantastic,' he said, 'bloody fantastic.

***

She walked into Connection unable to stop the smile that was suddenly a permanent part of her face.

Doris glanced up as the shop bell pinged. 'Hi, Kat. Good meeting?' Then she looked again. 'Why are you smiling?'

'It was a good meeting.'

'Usually you stomp around like an angry rhino when you've been to a church meeting because there's always somebody who puts forward some stupid idea. I'm not daft, Katerina Rowe. Did he turn out to be a dishy bishop then?'

Kat could feel laughter bubbling up inside her, and she mentally cursed Carl for making her feel like this. 'I know several bishops, Nan, and none of them are remotely dishy.'

'Something's cheered you up. You went from here really miserable, and now you've got rosy cheeks and a smile. I'm going to see Mouse about this. She might know what's going on.'

Kat shook her head, walked towards her own office and said, 'Has anybody made the coffee?'

***

Tessa Marsden arrived just before they were ready to lock up and go home, so Kat rang her mum and said they would be late.

'Is everything okay?' Mouse asked.

'No, far from it,' Tessa answered. 'We've now cleaned out the cell where Alice spent her last night, and we've found things that have led us to believe that it was suicide, and not an escalation of her cancer problems.'

'What?'

'She removed her bra. On the inside she'd sewed a little pocket, hardly noticeable really. We also found a small piece of clingfilm that had tablet powder on it. We think this was planned for when we eventually worked out who had killed Judy. We've tested the size of the tablets we took to the station to see how many would fit in this little pocket, and we reckon there must have been about ten. She also had the two that our officer took to her before she went to sleep, and we've now looked at CCTV of the interview room and it looks as though she didn't take the tablets in the afternoon, but pocketed them. She knew exactly what she was doing. She must have been in considerable pain by the time she took that lot.'

'Oh no!' Kat held her hand to her mouth. Why had Alice's time on earth descended to the darkest of levels, when she should have been living out her final years in comfort? Kat couldn't bear it. 'Are you able to prove it?'

'As soon as we have toxicology results from the post-mortem. The results from that are showing that she would have had maybe another six weeks before her organs gave up on her, so we're pretty sure that the toxicology will show she overdosed on her morphine.'

'Has anyone told Keeley?'

Marsden nodded. 'She doesn't know we suspect suicide, but she is aware that Alice is dead. She was very upset, but Emma Jones from number five came and sat with her. She was in good hands. I think her tears were more for Henry because he now has no relatives at all on his father's side.'

'I can't take much more today,' Mouse said. 'Can we go and collect Martha and go home, and pretend to be normal, please?'

Marsden gave her a hug. 'That's a good idea, Beth. And have an early night. If you're asleep, you're not thinking.'

38

The coldness and the brightness of the morning meant that Alan and Sue Rowe had to dress warmly. Sue helped Alan into the wheelchair, pulled his scarf a little tighter around his neck and covered him with a tartan fleece to keep his legs warm.

They had told no one of their plans for today other than the funeral home who had collected Leon from the airport and Jeff, their vicar, who was taking the somewhat shortened service; the church where Leon was to be laid to rest was only five hundred yards away and they had decided to walk. Or, in Alan's case, be pushed.

Sue locked the door behind her, and they set off down the bungalow's ramp. It was on a slight incline, but nothing that Sue couldn't handle. It was far harder for Alan to handle the fact that he needed to be pushed down it. He waved a hand towards her, telling her he needed her to come close to hear his words. She bent her head.

'Love you,' he whispered.

'Love you too, my darling,' she said back, and wiped the sudden tear from her eye.

Their neighbour, Colin, came out of his front door as they reached the bottom of the ramp, and called across to see if Sue needed any help getting Alan into the car.

'I'm fine, thanks,' she responded. 'We're going out for a little walk, it's such a lovely day.'

A lovely day to be burying your only son.

They turned right at the bottom of the ramp and headed towards the distant church. She walked this route two or three times a week, sometimes with Alan, sometimes on her own; she often felt God was the only person listening to her.

Alan said nothing further for the entire journey. It grieved her deeply that he understood everything still and yet found it so hard to communicate. It was almost a silent life for both of them.

At first, following the stroke, she had kept up a constant stream of chatter, but now there was nothing. There was only so much conversation you could have without getting a reply.

Her mind flew back to the evening when Kat had rung and told them the news about Leon. Deep in her heart, she had known it was coming. His crimes had been so bad there was never any chance of a good outcome, and reading between the lines of Kat's tearful conversation with them, Leon had chosen his own way of dying.

That night she had had to speak with Alan. His communication with her was mainly by nods. He simply agreed with everything she said. And then her man cried.

She had told Jeff the full story, and he had reassured her that it was of no interest to the staff who would be dealing with lowering Leon into the ground who the deceased was. He would simply be Leon Rowe. And then they had prayed together.

Alan and Sue would be the only mourners, and the entire service would be a graveside one. She wished she could have seen Leon's beautiful face for one last time, but she doubted there was much left of it. She was thankful for her memories, her photographs; he had been so handsome.

She felt her footsteps dragging as they neared the church and a quick glance at her watch showed they were almost half an hour early.

'We'll have some time in church,' she said to Alan, and he nodded.

She wheeled him down to the front and placed the wheelchair at the side of the end front seat. She sat by his side and they held hands. She bowed her head in prayer.

***

Alan couldn't pray. His mind told him he should be thanking God for giving Leon to them in the first place, but all he wanted to do was berate Him for taking Leon from this world, for allowing Leon to take the path he had taken.

Alan whimpered slightly. He was reliving how he had learned of Leon's criminal life; the lowlife who had turned up at his door and told him exactly what his son was involved with: the drugs, the money laundering, everything.

It had been Alan who had suggested they move to Canada. He had half-hoped Leon would say he wanted to emigrate with them, but he didn't, and they had turned their back on England and all the pain that he knew was there, for a life in Canada. With so many miles between them, he hoped it would be a case of out of sight, out of mind, concerning his knowledge of his son's life of crime.

And they thought he had swung his life around with his marriage to Katerina Silvers. Alan could feel his tears returning.

***

Sue heard footsteps behind them and turned.

'Leon's here, Sue, Alan.'

'Oh.' Sue felt flustered for a second. 'Right, thank you, Jeff.'

'Would you like me to wheel Alan out?'

'No, thank you. I'll see to him. We're in this together,' she said.

She turned the wheelchair around and followed the vicar out of the church.

Her moan of 'N-o-o-o' was audible to everyone, following her first sight of the coffin inside the hearse, as the driver waited to drive the fifty yards or so down the path to where the grave had been dug.

Jeff signalled to the driver to move, and the hearse travelled slowly enough for Alan and Sue to be following closely for the final part of Leon's journey. Four men were waiting at the graveside for the lowering of the coffin and once that was done, they melted away into the background.

Sue heard nothing of the service. She had moved close to the edge of the grave, and her eyes remained fixed on the coffin, mentally communicating with its occupant.

The service was quick, and they moved away.

'Would you like to go back into church, Sue?' Jeff asked.

'No, thank you, Jeff.' She gave half a smile. 'I'm going to get Alan home out of this cold and do some lunch. Thank you for this. At least we are near to him now.'

***

Jeff smiled. He loved this gentle couple, hated to see what they were going through. 'If you want anything, Sue, anything at all, you ring me.'

'Thank you, Jeff, I will,' she said, and wheeled Alan on the return journey.

***

As they neared their front gate, Sue could see that Colin was standing by their gate.

'Please, Sue, Alan, come in will you?'

'I was just going to get Alan settled out of the cold...'

'I know. Diane and I have done a warm lunch for you, to say how sorry we are.'

'But...'

'Sue, we have relatives in England. Remember Jack and Amanda? We all had a meal together one night when they came to visit? You spoke of Leon and Kat. They told us of Leon's death. I kind of guessed you were having a private service or something for him this morning, so we wanted to show we care. Please, come in out of the cold.'

It was only when they got inside and were eating the delicious soup Diane had made, that Sue opened up and told them it had actually been the burial of their son, not simply a memorial service for him.

'Sue,' Diane said. 'We know how much you loved him, even if you couldn't get to England to see him. Between us we'll make sure his grave always has flowers on it. Now, some cheese and biscuits?'

***

Alan felt strange. Things were going in and out of focus with him, and his tiredness was starting to overwhelm him. His head drooped onto his chest, and he felt Sue touch his arm.

'Come on, sweetheart, let's get you back in bed for an hour.' She turned to their hosts. 'Thank you so much for this today. It means a lot. But we have to go. I think my man is falling asleep in his chair.'

Alan lifted his head and smiled.

Colin insisted on wheeling the wheelchair for Sue, and took Alan straight to the bedroom. Sue walked back to the front door with Colin and thanked him once again.

'Sue, it's no problem. What's happened to you and Alan could happen to anybody. We aren't our children's keepers, you know. They make their own way in this world, and we have to accept that. But even so, I know how much you loved Leon, and I am truly sorry for your loss. You need anything, anything at all, you come get us.'

***

Five minutes later, Sue was helping Alan into bed, and almost immediately his eyes closed.

'See you in an hour or so,' she said, and kissed the top of his head. He murmured a response, and she left, closing the door quietly behind her.

Sue was crocheting a new throw for the sofa, ready for the cold winter months, and she took it out of her basket and began to work. She allowed her thoughts to roam, remembering Leon as a child, a teenager who was already showing signs of the man he would become, and then the husband he ultimately became. She had thought Kat had rescued him, and she was certain that the birth of his daughter would have been his saving grace if only he had lived long enough to see her.

Martha. A smile came to Sue's face and she placed her work and her crochet hook on her lap, and let her head fall back. How she longed to see her grandchild, to hold something that was such an essential part of Leon. Her eyes closed, and she drifted to sleep.

***

When she woke, she woke slowly, stared around her feeling a little puzzled, and then, as the crochet work fell to the floor, she remembered what she had been doing. 'Sue Rowe, it's not like you to sleep during the day,' she muttered to herself, and then realised it was after four. If she left Alan much longer he'd not sleep that night.

She headed down the corridor to the bedroom and opened the door. She could still only see the top of his head she had kissed earlier. 'Hey, sleepyhead, time to wake up,' she said, and kissed him again. He didn't move.

'Alan?' She shook him slightly. 'Alan!' This time it was louder. And she knew.

She stood for a moment looking at the man who had been her rock all her life, then sat on the edge of the bed, and pulled his arm out from under the covers. She held his hand for a moment, then walked to the hallstand.

She picked up the receiver. 'Jeff, it's Sue. I need you.'

Epilogue

Six weeks later

Keeley sat by Tom's grave, nursing the urn containing Alice's ashes. She hadn't expected to feel quite so bereft, so heartbroken. Her mind was going over and over the actions, consequences, whatever, of the last few weeks, and she felt stunned to actually be in the position she now found herself – free, unfettered.

When she and Alice had first discussed getting rid of Judy, it had almost been said as a joke. Somehow Judy had worked out that Henry was Tom's son; it hadn't taken rocket science, he was Tom's double.

Storming around to Keeley's, Judy had told her she had to leave the house, and Keeley's first instinct had been to go and talk to Alice. Judy had been scary and insistent that she had proof that Henry was Tom's bastard; Keeley's denial had carried no weight at all. Alice had been wonderful, calming her down and saying not to worry, they would take time to think about everything.

They had to sort something out – somewhere hidden in that house was the will Tom had got his aunt to type for him, leaving virtually everything to Keeley and Henry, hidden by Tom who died before he could tell anybody where it was.

Keeley's faced creased into a smile when she thought about DI Marsden checking her phone and seeing the one word "will" in her text messages. Keeley had known the meaning but been unable to do anything about it, and so had played dumb; Marsden had realised it was a final attempt at saying where it was on Tom's part.

Keeley stroked the headstone. If she could, she would visit her love every day, tell him her news, but she still had to be careful. She wanted nobody knowing her business. After all, she was a killer.

Alice had explained that the house would be turned upside down following a murder, and the police would find the will for them. But it had to be done before Judy herself found it; she would destroy it.

A brief smile flashed across Keeley's face as she remembered the day following Judy's verbal attack. Alice had run across the fields from Bradwell to Hope, and waved at Judy standing in her kitchen. She ran up Keeley's garden path, making it very clear whose side she was on.

Keeley hugged the urn tighter, seeking to let Alice know how much she had loved her. Alice had given her hope that she wouldn't lose everything that made her happy. She needed to be next door to where Tom had lived, she needed to be close to his grave.

And Alice had talked to her for most of that day. She had explained about the cancer, about the time limits she was having to build into what remained of her life. 'We can kill her,' she had said. 'It's the only way you will stop her ruining your life and making you as miserable as she made Tom.'

The plan had been perfected over the next week. Alice had admitted that although she was keeping up her fitness levels, she didn't think she was strong enough to do the deed. But she was strong enough to take the blame.

Keeley shivered. It had all seemed so plausible when they had been discussing it, but Alice actually dying because of it had been hard to bear.

Keeley flinched as she remembered that awful morning; Alice appeared and she let her in. It was unfortunate that Judy had seen her, but they used the shouting to add to the story, in case anyone else had been awake and seen Alice in the back gardens.

Taking Henry to school had been an effort; Keeley had felt sick with nerves. By the time she had got home, Alice had lowered the loft ladder and they were ready to go.

She knew she would never forget waiting in the attics for the sound of the shower, and even now, after all this time, the memory of creeping down those stairs with a hammer in her hand and a knife down her jeans was overwhelming.

It had been hard to lift the ladder back up quietly; they had agreed this would be difficult, but they knew that if Judy came out of the bathroom and saw the loft ladder in the downwards position, it would get very nasty, very quickly.

Keeley tried to brush away her memories of waiting behind the bedroom door, wearing blue rubbery gloves on her hands, watching Judy walk in with a towel wrapped around her; the hammer hitting Judy's head. It had made a loud thud, and Judy collapsed onto the bed, face down.

'Alice,' she whispered, gripping the urn, 'it was so hard stabbing her with that knife. Even when you appeared to help me turn her over, it didn't make it any easier. I remember you saying one stab to the heart and it will be over, but it isn't, Alice, is it? It's so unreal living with that memory, all that blood. I killed her, Alice, I killed her.'

And all the acting, the pretence that she knew nothing of the will. All orchestrated by Alice. Try not to speak, Alice had advised, then you can't slip up. They'll understand you're upset, you loved Tom.

Keeley placed the urn on the grave and stood. There was no one around, and she took off the lid. She scattered some of the contents around the grave, then replaced the lid.

'I'm taking the rest of you home with me, Alice,' she said, keeping her voice low. 'When I move into Tom's house, I'm going to put the rest of your ashes into the back garden, so that you'll always be with me. I'll always have you to talk to, won't I.'

She took a carrier bag out of her handbag and eased the urn into it. She didn't want Pam to know she had brought the ashes; it was her secret.

'I'll be grateful for the rest of my life, Alice, for what you did. You gave everything; your good name, your Christian beliefs, your life.' She continued to whisper to the woman who had helped set her free from Judy, clutching the urn to her heart.

***

Keeley looked up and saw Pam walking towards her, holding Henry's hand. He had, for the first time, stayed over at his nanna's house, and they were clearly becoming the best of friends. Henry ran towards his mother.

'Nanna says we can go for an ice cream when we've finished at Daddy's grave. Can we, Mummy? Please?'

Keeley smiled at her son and looked up at Pam. 'Oh, I think we can manage that, don't you, Nanna?'

Keeley picked up the carrier bag, and they walked across the road to the café, Nanna and Mummy holding on to Henry's hands. His Clark's shoes gleamed brightly following the polish Nanna had applied before they had left her house that morning.

***

Martha smiled and everyone's heart melted. She had proved to be a good baby, and was recognising faces and voices now.

'Who's a good girl then,' Kat whispered, and Mouse said, 'Me.'

'You sure?' was Kat's response.

'Certain. Are you?'

'Am I what?'

Doris interrupted. 'A good girl?'

'I am.'

'You got something to tell us?' Doris again.

'No, I don't think so.'

'Carl Heaton?'

Kat's face instantly glowed with a pinkish hue. 'Er...' She looked at both of them and realised they were choking on their laughter.

'How long have you known?'

'Ever since your mum and dad met him when he picked you and Martha up to take you to Monsaldale.' Doris was enjoying this.

'What? Mum told you?'

Doris nodded, and Mouse couldn't stop the huge grin. 'That afternoon,' Doris confirmed.

'And you've let me creep around and make up excuse after excuse for all this time?'

'Yep.'

Kat sank down on a kitchen chair, placed her arms on the table and dropped her head. She pretended to cry, and the other two women instantly stopped their laughter.

'Aw, Kat, come on, we didn't mean to upset you. Honestly, we think it's great,' Mouse said.

'It'll cost you,' was the muffled reply from Kat.

'Cost us what?' Mouse sounded perplexed.

Kat lifted her head. 'A twenty-four box of Ferrero Rocher, you… you…'

'Is she mad?' asked Doris.

'She's mad,' said Mouse.

THE END

Follow Kat and Mouse's next venture in part three of the trilogy, Murder Unearthed.

Acknowledgements

There are many people to thank for seeing me through part two of the Kat and Mouse trilogy, starting with my Advance Reading Copy group who have valiantly downloaded book one, Murder Undeniable, read it, and reviewed it. Hopefully they will manage to download this one as well! It is no easy feat, and yet every one persevered until they had the ARC. You're all stars. There are too many names to list, but you know who you are.

Three people kindly volunteered to allow me to use their names in this book; Danny McLoughlin who wanted to be dismembered into tiny pieces (sorry, Danny, I only managed to blow off your head), Keeley Roy, my next-door-neighbour who stalks me to ask me questions about what happens next in my books because she can't wait to find out, and Pam Bird, someone who never fails to buy my books and who I have known for over fifty years. A massive thank you to all three of you for your support.

And then we come to little Henry. I ran a competition in my ARC group for a child's name for Keeley's son. Gillian Lillford suggested Henry because she has a grandson with that name. I wrote down every name suggested on a great long list, passed them over the fence to Keeley to choose one, and she said she loved Henry.

So thank you, Henry, you've played a cracking part in this book!

And special thanks go to the Village Green café in Eyam. This is a real place, serves fantastic scones, and they didn't mind me using their name!

As always, my thanks go to Fred Freeman and Betsy Reavley of Bloodhound Books and all their staff members, Alexina Golding,

Sumaira Wilson, Heather Fitt and Emma Welton. They're not just publishers, they're amazing people.

Morgen Bailey, my editor par excellence, as always you inspire me to remove excess words, pay a bit more attention to loose plot holes, and this year we shared the NaNoWriMo journey. Fifty thousand words in thirty days… I did it, did you?

Book three in this trilogy is already started, and will be called Murder Unearthed. See you at the end of that one!

Anita Waller
Sheffield, November 2018

Lightning Source UK Ltd.
Milton Keynes UK
UKHW021603020219
336624UK00001B/60/P